# THE
# LIGHTED
# SWORD

# THE LIGHTED SWORD

## CHIP SIMMONS

*To Grace*
*Best Wishes*
*Chip Simmons*

Deeds Publishing | Atlanta

Published by Deeds Publishing in Athens, GA
www.deedspublishing.com

Printed in The United States of America

Cover design by Matt King & Mark Babcock. Text layout by Matt King. Map Design by Matt King.

Library of Congress Cataloging-in-Publications data is available upon request.

ISBN 978-1-944193-96-6

Books are available in quantity for promotional or premium use. For information, email info@deedspublishing.com.

First Edition, 2017

10 9 8 7 6 5 4 3 2 1

*To my loving wife, Mary Sue, and son, Neil, who encouraged me to share this tale of adventure with others*

# TABLE OF CONTENTS

# Map of Anzenar

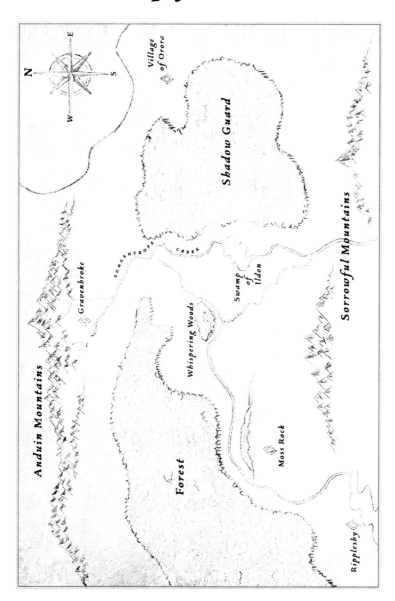

# 1. THE MISSING

ONE SINGLE DROP OF DEW SLIPPED OFF A LEAF, SPLATTERING THE already irritated Tenara on the head. And if that was not enough, her friend Joen shifted her weight at the same time, causing the floating island to sway and sending both into the water.

"Joen!" yelled Tenara, her long legs clawing at the water as she broke the surface. She turned around and saw her friend jump to the bank. "You could have waited in the water for me, you know," said the larger frog.

"Sorry," she admitted, half smiling, although she was not feeling at all contrite about what happened. Somewhere along the line she had come to think herself as very special, sometimes at the expense of her friends. They had known each other all their lives.

Tenara squinted at the many homes that lined their village in the distance. "Why don't we swim back to Rippleshy and see if Whiskers is around?"

"You really want to see that ole long-eared busy body?" Joen frowned.

Whiskers was a catfish that everyone regarded as the community news machine. On any given day, you could pretty much count on her for the local gossip. Everyone wondered how she got around and who was working for her.

"Last time we listened to that mud mouth," Joen continued, "she said the local turtles were learning how to float upside down."

Tenara looked around and, in a serious tone, asked, "Where is everyone?"

"What do you mean?"

"I mean no one's come by since morning."

"So?"

"You don't think that's strange?" Tenara glanced at her friend, remembering the day Joen was adopted by her parents. She had been five years old at the time, and Tenara was six. Joen's parents had been attacked by a fearsome skink during an outing in the woods. Ever since, Tenara had protected her so she would never have to face another terrifying moment. But now that Joen was fifteen, she had become more defiant and independent. Often, Tenara became frustrated when she had to compromise on her own desires for what Joen wanted. She looked around again. "Tealick isn't nearby either.

"You like him, don't you?" Joen asked, grinning.

Tenara ignored the comment and began brushing the water off her suit of twisted green and yellow vines. She shook the small black sash that hung from her waist, still dripping. Joen stared at its dismal color with disdain. It certainly matched Tenara's present mood: always worrying about something. On the other hand, Joen saw herself as more upbeat, which was reflected in her choice of a red sash made from the sunset plants that grew near her window: her mother's favorite color.

"So you coming or not?" Tenara asked abruptly.

Joen twisted her mouth in a wry grin. "Yeah. It might be less boring than sitting here."

Soon, they arrived at an immense log, which they hid behind. With care, they looked over the top and saw Whiskers delivering the news.

"…some have not been seen for days and others an entire week. Take Prince for instance. He's always sitting next to the beaver hole, then *poof*, nowhere to be seen. And then there's Puddy." Whiskers pointed to the shore. "He usually hangs out near the grassy log over there, but now?" Tenara knew both personally.

***

Further away, a giant bullfrog sat staring across the fast stream that spilled into the pond. Zacker's eyes flickered toward a ripple in the water moving lazily across the surface. He knew it at once as Butiss the snake. At first he thought to ignore him but suddenly changed his mind and croaked, "Where are you going so early on such a fine day?"

"Something takes themsssss," he hissed.

"What in mud holes does that mean?"

The snake stopped and turned its head toward Zacker.

"Zakersss must help if we're to livessss."

"I don't understand. Speak some sense," said Zacker, frowning; he didn't like riddles.

"Come to the place of the Hot Feet."

With that, the snake turned its head and whipped its tail into a frenzy, pushing itself up the creek and out of sight. Zacker was watching it disappear when Millard Dew, the matriarch of Rippleshy, paddled up.

"Zacker, I saw Butiss go round the corner up there. Did he talk to you?"

"Yup, but it was a bunch of slimy nonsense, not that I expected more. Said I needed to come up to Hot Feet."

"That's way up the water!" she said in her typical gruff voice, narrowing her forever blinking eyes. "Word's come down from Whiskers that there's something strange going on. Some of us are missin'! You best be listening for clues now!"

"Missin'?" But Millard Dew had already left.

A short time later, Butiss was curled up waiting for everyone at the place known as Hot Feet: a large rock at the headwaters of the pond where he would lie in the warm sun occasionally. After several more minutes, everyone had arrived, Millard Dew being last.

Butiss then rose his head and hissed, "They takes them, the giants."

Tenara sucked in her breath.

The snake droned on, "Butiss cannot help."

One of the villagers beside Joen spoke up. "You make no sense," he said, warily watching the snake, who was much larger than him.

Butiss looked upstream. "You must find help among the tall ones, where the bottoms of the trees are green." And with that, Butiss uncoiled and dropped into the water.

"Someone needs to go up there," said Millard Dew in a loud voice.

Tenara looked over at her and nodded.

"No!" Joen said emphatically, looking up at her friend with fear.

Tenara turned around. "Joen?"

"No. You can't go! That's what my parents did. They left one day and never came back. The same thing will happen to us!" Abruptly, she turned and sped back to Rippleshy.

Tenara looked back at Millard Dew, who replied, "No one's asking either of you to go."

"Have you seen my parents?" Tenara asked fearfully.

"Yes, I know where they are, missy." 'Missy' was any woman younger than her. "Go to Joen now."

Tenara reentered the water and raced back to Rippleshy. As she came closer, she noticed how quiet the village seemed. But she dismissed it, knowing that most all her neighbors were still at the gathering. Within a few minutes of climbing out, she caught sight of her house and the plants crushed underneath one of the windows …and a door, which had been ripped away. She stood there, astonished, and yelled, "Joen?!!"

There was no response.

She carefully entered her home to find it empty. Everywhere she looked, she saw claw marks that covered the floor and walls. The shock of it sent multiple daggers of fear into her heart, freezing her feet in place. "No! Not her too," she breathed out loud.

Then, a single scream was heard.

Within a moment, she recovered and ran out of the house, yelling Joen's name repeatedly. She searched frantically while running from house to house. When she came to the third one, she saw her childhood friend being dragged into the forest by a large skink.

"Joen!" she yelled.

The skink turned around slowly and grinned. "You'll be next!"

Tenara bolted toward the creature and pounced on its back. With all her strength, she began beating it senselessly. But it was a short fight. Stunned at the brazen attack, the skink threw her on the ground with ease.

A voice yelled from deep in the forest, "Forget it. We have enough."

The skink walked over to Tenara and lifted its foot, but before it could slam it down on Tenara's chest, Joen smashed into its side, sending it tumbling to the ground.

It quickly recovered however, and was reaching for her when the voice came again, calling the skink. It looked down at her with its teeth showing. "Hope we never meet again," it said menancingly, and then it disappeared in the woods, leaving Joen and Tenara shaking violently on the ground.

# 2. THE DECISION

TENARA STARED OVER AT JOEN IN ASTONISHMENT AND THEN jumped up to hug her friend. "I thought I lost you. You ok?!"

Joen shook her head, at the point of tears. "I was so scared!"

Tenara released her. "I know. I was too."

"I'm sorry. Back at Hot Rock, I thought you were going to leave me and look for the ones missing yourself."

Tenara smiled, shaking her head. "I promised long ago that I wouldn't ever leave you."

"I don't want that to happen to anyone else."

Tenara stood up and then pulled Joen to her feet. "Neither do I. But we can't stop it if we stay here, and we can't do it alone. We need help. Perhaps we can find it in the place that Butiss suggested."

Joen nodded.

Tenara lowered her voice. "I cannot promise that we will be safe or even if we will survive. Neither of us knows anything of the forest, only the stories we've been told. All I know is that somewhere out there, our friends are scared and need our help. Am I to go alone?

Joen gazed into the forest nearby and said quietly, "No." Then she asked, "Did you tell Millard Dew you were leaving to look for the ones missing?"

"We'll leave a note. Whiskers will find it, I'm sure."

Later that morning, they left Rippleshy and soon found themselves paddling slowly upstream against a strong current. The exercise was grueling and neither had the energy to speak. Joen noticed the canyon sides begin to narrow and the current of the river increase. She groaned out loud, "I don't think I can do this! Where is this green tree bottom place anyway?"

"It can't be far, I'm sure. Please don't stop," huffed Tenara.

Actually, she was not sure, but she thought a positive word the best reply. Since they had left, the land and river had both changed, along with the fish that occasionally swam beneath the surface.

They were both exhausted and ready to swim to shore when the stream suddenly turned to the right. In the distance, was a large turtle sitting quietly on the ground.

"Hello there!" yelled Tenara, panting as she swam against the current. "Do you…" she asked, breathing hard "…know of a place… where the bottoms of the trees are green?"

The turtle, disturbed by the intrusion, withdrew its head from its shell and looked disdainfully at the two creatures in the water.

"I know of it," he replied indifferently.

"Yes, well, my good friend….do you know how far it is?" Tenara was struggling to hold herself up now.

"Why do you want to know?" the turtle asked indifferently.

Tenara grimaced at Joen and then back at the turtle. "We

are looking for those like us…and were told…by Butiss that we could find someone…there…that might help us." She noticed Joen falling behind and immediately grabbed her hand. But their fatigue was so great they were now losing ground against the water.

"Butiss! I know that snake. You shouldn't listen to snakes. They aren't to be trusted," he replied, slowly working each word out.

"We trust him," interrupted Joen weakly.

The turtle narrowed his eyes at the impertinent creature, but then thought about how he had first met that snake. It had slithered by, and then, for some mysterious reason, told him of a particularly good patch of flowers nearby. Then it just kept going, didn't even stop. It had no reason to say that; it wasn't like a snake to do so. But it was right. The flowers were real tasty. And he had not forgotten it. But still, he didn't trust snakes. In fact, he trusted no one. Then again, there was something about these two that piqued his interest. And he was obliged to the snake. So he lifted his head.

"The place you seek is called Moss Rock. It is a gathering place of many kinds and very close. I suggest you watch yourself. It's a day's walk for me, perhaps less for you." The turtle then lowered its head to the grass and hoped that it wouldn't be disturbed again.

"Thank you. Uh, do you have a name?" But there was only silence.

Joen's energy returned at knowing they were not as far away as she had feared. Both paddled faster and soon found the current more agreeable. It wasn't long before the afternoon was nearly gone and both were exhausted.

Just as the sun was setting, a huge willow tree overlooking a carpet of velvety green came into view. Its limbs hung to the ground like some morbid beast with tentacles that protected its lair. Seeing nothing and no one, they both moved to the protection of the tall grass that hugged the side of the stream. Tenara looked up and saw in the distance two oddly dressed creatures much like themselves perched on top of a large cliff, both staring intently their way. They had weapons and neither was smiling.

# 3. TEALICK

IT HAD BEEN THREE DAYS SINCE TEALICK AND HIS FRIENDS WERE captured. Some were plucked from the pond by terrible skinks and forced into the trees beyond their village where they were immediately prodded into the forest by two monstrous lizards. Others were pulled directly from their homes during the night and driven into the woods by the same skinks that tied their hands. All of this was apparently spread out over several days, causing the village to slowly miss the disappearances for some time.

One of the lizards ordered the skinks to cover the prisoners' eyes before forcing them up the hills and into the valley beyond.

"Bind their hands as well," growled the other.

"Already being done," said the other, slurring his speech like it was chewing something. It just smiled at the prisoners' misery as the knots were pulled tighter.

Tealick watched one of the skinks approach with a rope hanging from its hand. As soon as it was within reach, he blew its legs out from under it and then jumped on its back, sending both to the ground. The other guards looked on in shock when they saw the malice in the prisoner's eyes. But the larger lizard was indifferent and simply smiled.

It watched closely as Tealick placed his hands on the skink's neck and began to squeeze. But his success was short lived. The monstrous dragon walked over and slammed its claw directly into the skink's head, sending it flying into the side of a tree and Tealick into a large bush. It then bounded over and faced the skink, rows of teeth bared, and with a single claw, tossed it several feet further into a prickly bush.

"You are no guard. Leave!" it growled menacingly. In rigid fear, the skink pulled itself off and skulked away while the others of its kind watched in horror.

Just as it did that, one of the other prisoners took advantage of the moment. He dropped to the ground quickly and forced his blindfold off by pushing his face across the dirt. He then ran to Tealick and whispered, "Why antagonize them?"

Tealick ignored the comment and watched the lizard carefully. "Parsnippy, did you see that? The skinks fear him," he murmured in a raspy voice.

But before another word could be said, one of the other guards pounced on them both and began beating them to the ground.

The second lizard snarled, "Enough! Release their eyes now. We cross the river!"

The nights were cold, but at least their blindfolds were gone. Each prisoner pulled their clothes of woven grass and vines tighter, as if they could be a defense against the darkness that surrounded them. Tealick remained quiet. He just stared at the immense lizards, watching them closely.

On the afternoon of the fourth day, they were driven into a valley where a loud stream disappeared into an immense beaver pond. Before their eyes was a stark place where the trees had been torn away, leaving only mangled stumps drying in the hot sun. Just on the other side of the dam, where the stream disappeared into the forest, stood a huge lizard, larger and more terrifying than the ones that led them there. It watched them carefully as they were herded along the side of the water and into a desolate cave under a hill. As they entered it, the guards counted them to ensure that none were missing.

The next morning, the skinks pushed away the stone entrance and shoved them out viciously. Then, they were each given a shovel and ordered to dig.

None of this made sense to Tealick, but he remained quiet for the moment. However, after several days of the same routine, he abruptly threw his shovel on the ground. A guard noticed it instantly.

"You there! Pick it up!" he demanded, pointing to the tool. "And you," he walked up to Parsnippy, who was nearby, "push that dirt higher and get those stones on top."

Tealick ignored him and looked around at his friends as they shaped the walls that surrounded the clearing. Each day they labored on the fortifications, but were never told the reason. He glanced downstream and saw a beaver busily felling another tree. And nearby, perched on a huge boulder, rested the giant lizard that glared at them day after day.

Parsnippy motioned to Tealick. "P-Pick it up."

"Why do they keep us here?"

"I don't know." He grimaced. "Tealick, please. You-you risk all of us! Don't aggravate them!"

Seeing that neither of the two was following his orders, the skink walked up to Tealick. It strained its face, almost as if it were begging.

"Go on. Move it," he ordered, looking straight at the two prisoners.

"Why?" asked Tealick indifferently.

Parsnippy just winced at the remark.

"What do ye mean, why?" asked the guard, shocked at the defiance. It glanced at the great lizard. "Do ye know whose bidding it is that we do?" he asked nervously.

"You fear him, don't you?"

The skink glowered and immediately yelled out. Two chameleons scurried to his side, one accidently stepping on his tail. "Watch it! I already lost a piece of it this week! This one talks too much. Take him to Scalar!"

Tealick faced the skink. "Why are we here anyway? And why do we build this?"

"It's not important for you to know why," said the other skink, driving a stick into his back.

Tealick lost his breath at the pain. "You don't know why either, do you?" he croaked. Another jab nearly made him fall to the ground.

Parsnippy watched in horror at his friend's foolishness.

After repeatedly being jabbed in the back, Tealick was pushed over to the huge lizard, who sat languidly on the large rock in the sun. It was a monstrous thing, hideous and menacing in every way.

Tealick's escorts kicked his back one last time and abruptly backed away, hoping to shield themselves from the lizards' eyes. "This one does not dig, sire."

The dangerous lizard lowered its head, glowered at the insignificant creature, and then swept its eyes across the fortifications and rising walls being built in the distance, noting their progress.

It smiled at the creature before it and rumbled, "You and your kind have yet to complete the walls. Shall I consider that you have failed me?"

"No," replied Tealick, trying to keep his composure, "but we are tired and need rest."

Ignoring him, the monster flexed his claws "Why do you test me with your insolence? One of my aides saw the same in you on your way here." His eyes narrowed further and the smile dropped. He then leaned his head down within inches of Tealick's ear. "I want you to know that it was I that ordered all of you to be taken from your land and brought here. You have ten days to complete the work."

Tealick was visibly shaken, shocked that something as hideous as this existed. With what remaining courage he had left, he moved his eyes down to the rock. "Do you fear us so much that you cannot tell us what we build?" Scalar had started to extend his claw downward when, suddenly, a small green skink approached from the forest.

"What do you want?" he growled, pulling his huge claw back.

But before the answer came, Scalar whipped around and swatted Tealick into the rushing stream below the dam. "Do I look like I fear you?" he sneered.

Tealick flailed against the water, trying to keep his head up, and saw the dragon lizard turn his attention back to the skink. He heard him loudly say, "You have something more?!" And then, "Tell them to find and kill this creature."

"Yes sir." It stepped backwards and quickly left. Scalar looked down at the skinks that had brought Tealick before him. "You have something to add?"

The skinks shook their heads and scampered over to Tealick. "You will not be so lucky in the future." They both leaned down, grabbed Tealick by the neck, and slowly dragged him up the bank beside Parsnippy, then threw him on the ground.

At the same time, secluded within the shadow of the dam, a large beaver witnessed what had occurred, taking particular note of the one who challenged the dragon lizard. A smile spread across the beaver's face before he slipped under the water.

"You ok?" Parsnippy asked breathlessly, holding his shovel.

Tealick looked at the beast in the distance as he stood up. "Did you know that it was he who ordered us here?"

Parsnippy shook his head nervously. "D-did it give a reason?"

"No." Tealick turned around. "But it appeared quite upset when that skink told it something. I think it worried the scaly one. And that may be of use to us."

Suddenly, Tealick was thrown face down on the ground. "I said get to work!" cried the skink guard. Tealick started to leap at the guard but Parsnippy pulled him back.

"Sorry," Parsnippy said dolefully to the skink while passing a shovel over to Tealick. "It-it won't happen again."

Biting his lip, Tealick glared back at the guard. "I guess I should thank you for that."

Parsnippy ignored the remark. "Did you learn anything else?"

"I fear they have no interest in returning us when this work is done."

"What do we do?"

"Watch them and look for weakness. These guards fear the lizard as well and that may help us."

## 4. THE LIZARD'S ANGER – SCALAR CREATES A COUP

At the same time, far to the north, clouds boiled up the side of the Anduin Mountain. The condensation sent rivulets of dew sliding over the rocks forming tiny cascades that fell into the crevasses below. There, the water pooled before escaping over the roots of craggy trees and mossy covered stones, growing until it emerged as a formidable stream that noisily made its way into one great waterfall.

From there, it carefully rushed across a desolate clearing carved out long ago in a titanic avalanche that crashed down the mountain. This was the land known as Gravenbroke, a place of scattered boulders that was the home of the Saurians, huge reptiles with jagged ridges and long claws.

They ruled the hills and the edge of the northern forest of Anzenar that bordered the slopes of the snowy mountain above them. All creatures here paid homage to them for fear of losing their lives and especially to the one who commanded them all.

Keltar, resting high up on a boulder, stared intently as a short-tailed lizard walked slowly into the clearing.

19

The smaller one bowed. "My king. I am your trustworthy servant who has searched for the scent of Scalar for many suns."

The huge lizard narrowed its eyes and with a deep voice that echoed among the rocks, asked, "What news do you have of my treacherous brother?"

"Not enough for a campaign, sire, but enough to know that he still lurks within the forest and has not escaped beyond the mountain where I stand now."

"Is that all!" thundered Keltar.

The other lizard stood still, fearfully maintaining eye contact with the king. "No. We have ordered the crows to search for him as well. They have no allegiance and can, for the most part, be relied upon for information."

"What about the snakes and beavers?" Keltar growled.

"For different reasons, neither are friends. We have threatened the beavers but have learned nothing of your brother or his traitorous companions. As for the snakes, they scurry away and hide in their cowardly fashion. I would have pressed them further but thought it may be dangerous, as they have allies in deep places."

Keltar leaned down. "Dangerous? You fear them?"

The messenger stepped back. "Of course not!" he said quickly. "Perhaps the beaver that lives among the old trees that border our water to the south will know something. He is called Darmok. I will find him and see if he knows of Scalar."

"No. You will look in other places. Send the Dither twins to this beaver. They're usually reliable and will cause less of a stir among the ones that live there. They have proved to be deceptive and cunning, so remind them that it is I who am seeking their assistance." Then, turning his head toward his subordinate, he growled, "Roozen. You will accompany him."

The giant lizard laying on the rock beside the king looked up and blinked. "Ok, but where?"

"To find Scalar, you idiot!"

Roozen crawled off his boulder reluctantly and joined the messenger while thinking how nice it would be if he could find Scalar himself and take the glory.

The two slowly ambled away down the path and disappeared into the forest. The two other lizards watched them leave. One said to the other, "The king worries. Perhaps this is an opportunity."

"There will be many opportunities," replied the other, "many that may include Scalar as well. We will wait for further news."

They both lowered their heads and returned to enjoying the warming rays of the sun.

# 5. MOSS ROCK

TENARA PULLED JOEN FURTHER INTO THE GRASS FOR COVER.
The figures on the high bank continued to stare at the water.
They were much taller and wore suits of green and black woven
from some plant neither had seen before. Each held a single
spear motionless and stared unblinking into the distance. Joen
grabbed at Tenara and whispered, "Why do they not move?"

"I don't know. Perhaps they're supposed to be like that."

"Should we call to them?"

Suddenly, they heard multiple voices. Looking up, they both
saw at least twenty of the same strangely dressed figures moving
as one and chanting in a strange dialect on the other side of a
tall willow tree.

"Get down, Joen."

"Maybe we should go back home," whispered Joen.

"I'm frightened too, but what would we say to the ones we
left behind who want their family and friends back?"

Tenara looked up and saw the creatures marching around
some large rocks and then disappearing.

"Where did they go?" ask Joen.

"Let's get closer."

They had moved through the grass to the side of the bank and were carefully climbing when they suddenly heard the soft rustle of water behind them. Freezing, they both turned and saw a shadowy shape moving just beneath the surface, coming in their direction. Joen jumped back at once, forcing both of them to fall back to the slick mud that lined the water's edge.

Both Tenara and Joen turned around and saw a serpent slowly emerging from the water, revealing two menacing eyes. Panic immediately overcame Joen, who began to flail at the muddy bank while trying to escape. Tenara tried to push her friend up, but the two of them kept sliding down until the snake was almost upon them.

*Bang, bang, bang!* The sound came from somewhere above them. *Bang, bang, bang!* it sounded again and, with a start, they found their arms encircled with ropes, which jerked them up over the top.

As their shock fell away, they looked up into the face of the guards they had seen on the cliff.

"All's well captain," said one, looking at another. "Aye, we got 'em, sir."

"Very good! Bring 'em to the Colonel for a viewing."

"Yes sir."

After the ropes were removed, they were pulled up on their feet and marched off.

Tenara turned around, saw Joen shaking from the recent attack, and tried to calm her down. At the same time, she noticed the stream had split in two. "Joen, we're on an island!"

Each felt themselves being pushed forward gently. Everywhere they looked was a deep carpet of green moss interspersed with strange trees that cast deepening shadows from the setting sun. One in particular was enormous.

Joen looked up. "Tenara!" She pointed.

They stared in awe at the heavy limbs that reached out to touch the ground in every direction. The guards ducked under one that was covered by velvety lichen. And then, within moments, they smelled a particular sweetness that drifted by, forcing their feelings of dread to fall away. Tenara glanced back and saw Joen wriggling her nose.

"Halt!" yelled the captain.

Tenara saw a well-dressed figure twice her height walk over to the lead guard. He wore a broad hat of stitched bark with two red and yellow feathers protruding from the side. This contrasted with his green and brown suit, which was held tight with a belt made of the same willow leaves. Around his neck was a rock that glowed in the setting sun and in his hand was a wooden staff.

"Report."

"Sir. We have some uninvited visitors. They were plucked from the water just before one of the two-teeth could get 'em."

The Colonel looked them over with a serious face. "So. What shall we do with you? Throw you back?"

Tenara looked over to Joen and saw that she was dizzy with fear. She grabbed her hand and squeezed it.

"Well! Speak up!" said the Colonel, making the word speak sound like squeak.

"See here," blurted Tenara, mustering up some courage. "We were not meaning anything at all. We are on a journey and accidently saw your encampment, or village or whatever this is. We didn't do anything at all!"

The Colonel leaned forward and stared a moment. "How do we know you're not spies, eh?"

Joen's mouth fell open in astonishment at the question. "We're no spies, you old—"Tenara kicked her leg.

"Well then," said the Colonel with a half grin, "I don't see any spy hats, so maybe you're ok. Don't recognize your kind though. You from the lower stream, eh? Why are you so far from your home?"

"Many from our village have been taken. We are on a journey to look for them," she said, gaining some courage. "We were told there was a place called Moss Rock where others could help us."

The Colonel leaned closer and asked slowly, "Where did you hear that name?"

"From a turtle," Joen replied.

Straightening up, he glanced at the captain and then at the newcomers. "A turtle, eh? Hmmm. Got to be Borgannell. Very good. Well then, welcome strangers. This here and all around is Moss Rock," he said with a wave of his hand. Then, turning to his aide, he said, "Captain! See to it that they are properly fed and housed. The little one looks a little droopy."

Joen squinted her eyes at the remark.

"Yes Sir!"

The captain turned and pointed. "This way. Come along."

Tenara fell in behind the captain and looked back at Joen. "You ok?"

"Droopy?!" she whispered. "Why, that ole pittering…I'm just

hungry, that's all." Brightening up, she said to Tenara, "You got some courage talking back to him like that."

Her friend laughed. "You do too. I heard what you wanted to say to him back there."

Tenara gazed in the distance at the many little fires that illuminated the wooden homes they passed. Each one looked as if had been carved by an artist and set down on the carpet of green that ran the length of the island. The village was alive with the noise of cooking and conversation, and each person they passed politely greeted them as they walked by. It was a strange sight. Most of her kind, thought Tenara, spent their entire life in the water, but these built great homes at its edge. She wondered how long they had been here and where they came from.

"Here ya are, my friends," said the captain as they came to an unusual house made of woven vines and stones neatly wrapped around each other. In front was an imposing door of carved wood, decorated by small white flowers and a single white stone in its center. The colonel stepped up, pulled out his own stone from his pocket and then tapped the one in the door lightly. When the two stones met, there was a soft sound, like a single note plucked on a harp. "Mrs. Gilgatop, Colonel sent me," he said to the closed door. "Can ye see to some refreshment for some newcomers?"

A moment later, a tall slender female emerged, impeccably dressed in a robe made of stitched leaves that gave off an almost royal air. Around her waist was a colorful sash of woven moss that perfectly matched her purple shoes made of acorns and bark. Smiling broadly, she nodded. "Of course. And bid the Colonel a good afternoon for me."

The captain saluted and promptly left.

Tenara noticed the woman looking curiously at them and then saw her point to a fireplace outside. "Now you two sit by the fire there while I bring you some good soup from the pot."

Tenara and Joen watched her disappear within the small house of earthen wood and then sat down on thatched chairs beside the fire. Almost as if by magic, the woman suddenly emerged with a pot in her hand.

After ladling the soup in some small bowls, she asked them with a quizzical look, "Where are you from? I have met many visitors who have come and gone, but I don't recognize you. How did you come to find us?"

Tenara told her of the disappearance of her friends and her journey to Moss Rock. At times, the woman leaned closer to hear about the friends and creatures the two had met along the way. But when Tenara mentioned Borgannell, the woman jumped up. "I know that turtle! He's been a good friend of Moss Rock for quite some time. It is said that he is very old, perhaps older than Moss Rock. You are indeed lucky to have him as your friend."

"Mrs. Gilgatop," Tenara said, interrupting her, "you referred to the Colonel a moment ago. You know him well?"

"I should say so! We share the same pad."

"Really!" said Joen, almost choking on her soup as she remembered when the Colonel had said she was 'droopy'. She coughed. "And he was so nice too," she said, still choking.

"Thank you, my dear," said Mrs. Gilgatop, standing up. "But it's late now and you're tired from your long day. Finish your dinner and come into my house."

The two enjoyed the remainder of the meal in silence, and then dropped their bowls beside the fire. Inside, they were met with a delightful odor of wild flowers that seemed to permeate everything. On every wall hung objects both curious and strange. There were sticks whose ends seemed to curl back and forth by themselves, rocks that changed from black and white, and an acorn the size of a head! All of them were covered in what looked like medals, each inscribed. "For the Colonel," said one, a rock of dazzling color, continuing, "Your mentor and friend, Fladon."

It was that rock that caught Tenara's attention. Never had she seen something so incredible. "Who is Fladon, Mrs. Gilgatop?"

"He was a dear friend to us both." She paused and looking out the window. "He disappeared a long time ago." Recovering, she turned and smiled. "Come with me now."

She led the way to a short hall and pointed to a room at the end. "You must rest now. I am sure tomorrow will be long day for you both."

"Thank you for being so kind!" said Tenara. And with that, Mrs. Gilgatop disappeared down the hall, leaving the two of them standing on a stone floor covered with soft leaves. Joen looked up and saw a round window high above, where streaks of red light were faintly visible from the sunset.

As they lay down, they also noticed tiny rainbows suddenly dancing around overhead. Looking up, they followed the light to its source, a broken rock that was wedged neatly into the corner of the room. Looking ever closer, they saw it had a hollow center filled with hundreds of little crystals that reflected the light of a tiny fire burning within its center. Both of their mouths were agape when they saw its light form twinkling stars that danced on the ceiling overhead, making it look as if the roof itself had vanished. Tenara was so mesmerized she never heard Joen say good night. She just lay there and stared at the miracle until she fell asleep, dreaming of her home and the friends she missed.

The next morning, however, they woke to an empty house.

# 6. THE SERVEYANS

"Mrs. Gilgatop?" Joen asked loudly. No answer. "Where is everyone?" She then joined Tenara, who was standing outside the door with her head cocked to the side.

"Listen. You hear that?" asked Tenara. "It sounds like someone's talking in the distance. Let's get closer."

"You sure that's right? I remember the Colonel saying something about spies yesterday. I don't want to be a spy," said Joen.

"You're not a spy, Joen," Tenara said, shaking her head. "We're guests just looking for our hosts. Whatever they're talking about may affect us as well. Come on. Hurry!"

They walked up the long path, passing houses of different construction, until they reached the open area where they had been first brought to the Colonel. No one was in the yard or on the street, which made it all the stranger. Slowing down and taking shelter behind a tall bush, they saw the Colonel. He was dressed in a formal looking jacket with bark buttons, light brown trousers made of stitched leaves, and shiny shoes made from acorns. He was addressing a large crowd, and both noticed he was wearing the same green leaf as yesterday, along with a weapon held tightly in his hand.

"As you all know," his voice echoed over the ground, "our good scouts have been watching the lizards for some time."

In the crowd, three of them raised their spears. Noting the motion, he smiled and raised his own as well.

"We have learned recently that one of 'em left their home in the North. This is serious, but moreover, and most disagreeably," he stamped his spear on the ground, "we have seen others wandering the western woods. This should be a warning for everyone to prepare for the worst, which brings me to a new topic.

"Yesterday, two visitors came here and were offered food and shelter by my good wife." He turned, holding his hand out. "Thank you, my sweet." She beamed at him.

Turning back, he continued, "Surprisingly, we were not aware of their presence until they were about to be attacked by a serpent. They survived thanks to the guards, who rescued them."

Two soldiers, dressed in green felt trousers and red sashes, stood up and bowed.

The Colonel continued, "Umm. Yes, yes. These strangers told us of their great village, far downstream where the water is lazy and many of our cousins live. But in this place, a terrible crisis has happened. Members of their clan have disappeared, so their leader sent their greatest warriors on a journey to find them."

Tenara's jaw dropped.

"And they made it far into our realm and surprised even our best sentries. Initially, I found them small, almost unworthy of being here except for their courage and stealth. But for that, they would have been turned away, but, at this hour, they will be of use to us."

Joen drew a sharp breath. Tenara held a finger to her mouth, but it was too late. The ears of a sentry caught the sound and he turned, spotting them behind a bush. "Hey, you there, out with ya."

The Colonel stopped talking and looked over at the two as they were prodded to the front.

"So, you do spy on us when we give you good food and shelter!" observed the Colonel.

"N-no," stuttered Tenara. "We woke and found your home empty. We were fearful that some terrible tragedy had befallen your village and so we went looking for you. We meant you no harm and hope that you will help us in our journey. Or that we may help you."

The Colonel closed his eyes and then opened them again. "The tragedy that happened to your village cannot be allowed to spread beyond its banks. Therefore, you two must leave Moss Rock and continue on your quest for those missing."

Tenara looked down in despair and shock. She glanced at Joen, whose mouth was agape. Neither expected this after the warm bed and good food they had been given.

The Colonel continued, "You will leave in two days when the light first touches the eastern bank. However," he leaned down closer and smiled, "you will not go alone. I have ordered two of our best scouts, Blendefest and Frondameer, to accompany you. There are many things, eh, that you can learn from them and, not surprisingly, they can learn from you as well. Joen and Tenara, though you are small, you have the makings of scouts yourself, as your feet are silent on the moss and nearly on the water. It is for this reason that, when you go forth, you will report to us as well."

He then looked over at the two scouts standing in front of him. "Ready them."

After the crowd dispersed, the two scouts ambled over to the visitors and introduced themselves. Tenara looked up at both and noticed the same dark eyes and stature everyone she'd met in Moss Rock had. Each was dressed in a green shirt made from the knots of hundreds of leaves, which looked like chain mail hanging from their necks. Below that hung brown pants that fell to their shoes, which resembled small canoes missing their paddles. Around their waists were green sashes that shimmered in the light while floating lightly at their sides.

"I am Blendefest," said one in a deep voice. "This is Frondameer," he added, pointing to his partner, who took a position next to Joen.

"We have been looking forward to meeting you," said Frondameer.

Tenara looked up and nervously extended a hand "Thank you. We worried you would make us leave." She paused. "May I ask a question?"

"Of course."

"What did the Colonel mean when he said, 'You will report to us'?"

"We have recently learned about creatures that have not been seen in the forest for a lifetime. He is concerned about this news and saw that your quest may be related. But mostly he was impressed by your courage and guile when you decided to risk everything, including your lives, to find your friends."

She started to speak but he held his hand up. "I will answer more of your questions later. For now, we must begin preparations for the journey ahead. Come."

Tenara saw Frondameer glance at Blendefest. "Do you have a question for us?" she asked.

"Yes. We are both puzzled about how you made it so far into Moss Rock without being seen."

She watched him look down at her clothes and over at Joen. "Perhaps because we are small."

"Come with us." The scout pointed down the lane toward a moss-covered cabin that lay just beneath one of the willow limbs. The structure seemed to be ageless, many times older than anything Tenara and Joen had ever seen before. But it was the windows that caught their eyes the most. Each was graced with some kind of flag or cloth with markings similar to what hung from the waist of their escorts.

As they got closer, they noticed the entrance was covered in detailed carvings of strange birds and animals. Just above was a mounted sword with runes etched beneath it that said, 'We Take Risks for Those Who Can't.' On each side was an eye carved into the wood that stared at them both.

Tenara touched Frondameer's back. "The sign above the door, it's written in strange symbols, not like ours."

"Because it's the language of the first ones to arrive here," he replied.

"What are those things that hang in the windows?" asked Joen.

"Family crests. If you look closely, each one is unique and represents a different scout who has learned his trade from years of service. There are only ten of us. Eight are absent for the moment, deep in the forest as we talk, gathering information and other things that allow us to be safe and vigilant here in Moss Rock."

Tenara looked up at the runes again and turned to Blendefest. "How long has the village of Moss Rock been here?"

"Here?" Blendefest replied in a deep voice. "We are not sure. There are runes on the wall of stone next to the willow tree that describe the founding of this place, but no one has been successful in understanding much of it so far."

"What do you call yourselves?"

"Serveyans. Now follow us in, please," said Frondameer.

They took a few steps while staring longingly at the unusual door as well as the strange symbols on the flags that hung from the windows nearby. Inside, the lodge was even more magnificent. Everywhere they looked, they saw unusual and exciting objects that hung from the walls and graced the floor. Some even glowed and shimmered in the light of the morning sun.

"Welcome to the Lodge of Knowledge," said Frondameer, waving his arm around the room. "Here, before you, are the things that Moss Rock scouts have brought back from their adventures and quests."

Tenara spoke up immediately. "How did you come by them?"

Frondameer smiled. "As we traveled, we learned from others how they defend and disguise themselves from danger. Some of the things you see, we found ourselves and others were given to us as gifts. Each is one of a kind and all were brought here for one purpose: to understand how we can use them to defend ourselves, our home, and others if necessary. I now offer one to each of you."

His demeanor turned more serious. "Because this house is a place of honor and courage, few are invited. But you deserve to be here, as you have impressed my Colonel with the risk you took by leaving, not to mention the stealth by which you came. Many of us have worked for years to pass unseen. You appeared to do it with ease, which is both curious and useful to us. As I said before, it is the reason the Colonel ordered us to join your quest and why we leave Moss Rock together in two days."

Blendefest interrupted. "They need to know more Frond, about what they will face. Tell them of our recent outing."

The other scout hesitated and then nodded. "Look to the wall on your left." He pointed at what looked like a simple rope laced by brownish and gold threads running down its length.

"Blend brought that back on recent trip. It is known as a Chatter Berry root, found only in the dry fields at the northern end of the forest, which is," he frowned, "a most distressing place for our kind. We discovered it by accident following one of the great lizards to its home in the northern desert.

"For a moment, we had forgotten about that lizard and focused on the Chatter Berry root. You must know that this is a very special tree. It is rare and seeing it once in your life is considered a gift. Blendefest insisted on retrieving the root, even at our peril and so close the giant lizard."

"Excuse me," interrupted Blendefest again. "I think Frond is having a moment here. I want to remind him that we *both* wanted to remove it."

"Eh? Yeah, well uh…." he said, clearing his throat. "We both quietly began the tedious work of digging it up, while at the same time protecting the tree it once grew from. Chatter Berries have multiple roots, some of which are no longer used as they age." Frondameer then picked it up. "It is unique and makes the sound of rain when you shake it."

Tenara and Joen watched him move it slowly back and forth until they could hear the sound of a light shower. Or was it a hundred people talking in the distance? To them it was amazing, enchanting, and marvelous at the same time and made them shiver at the mysteries that might be found elsewhere among the objects that surrounded them.

Tenara asked, "So where did the lizard go?"

Blendefest laughed. "It's typical for Frondameer to go off topic."

Frondameer shook his head, trying to ignore his partner. "Yes, well, ah…moving carefully through the trees, we tracked it until it left the forest and joined the others of its kind that lay sprawled across the hot rocks. Hiding carefully, we noticed that it approached an even larger one lying on a huge boulder. We could only hear a few words, something about one of its own disappearing."

"We believe they are searching for it," interrupted Blendefest.

"Yes," added Frondameer. "Apparently the one we were following was acting as a scout or a spy. We're not sure."

"But lizards do not scout," Blendefest murmured.

Frondameer grimaced. "No, they do not. They are lazy and lie in the sun all day. And rarely leave their desolate territory in the north for shade of the forest. The fact is that this one did and became a threat to Moss Rock that we cannot ignore. It is the reason we returned to report it to the Colonel."

Blendefest walked away from the window and pointed to some chairs beside Tenara and Joen. "We will tell you more about where we will go and the danger it holds for us. But for now, you need a weapon for defense."

Tenara winced. "We do not use such things. No one of our village has ever had need of one."

"Do your kind not wander from your home and explore and then later come back to report their findings?" asked Frondameer.

"No," replied Tenara weakly. "Only a few have done that." She noticed Joen looking away.

"Then it is important," stated Blendefest, "that you understand the need to defend yourself and those at your side. The forest is dangerous, as you have found, and filled with many surprises."

"Joen?" Frondameer commented, interrupting her thoughts, "that red sash will not do. Remove it. This is your new companion," he said, handing her a long tooth off the wall. "Use this as a dagger." In a flash, he struck the air in front of Joen, nearly causing her to fall backwards in fright.

"Keep it close."

"Was that necessary?" Tenara asked loudly, seeing that Joen was in shock.

He looked over to her. "Your first lesson. Always be ready for danger. The forest does not forgive."

She looked to Blendefest, who was nodding slightly while looking down.

Frondameer handed Joen a sash made of a fur mottled with black and brown spots. "This is for the dagger tooth. It fits to the pouch here," he said, pointing to a pocket on the side. "Pull it out only when you intend to use it. A warning: it will glow in the dark when it's near the belt. But take care. There will be times even darkness is your friend."

She held the weapon in her hand and suddenly felt braver. Maybe she could do this after all…or maybe not. She slumped back in the chair. Blendefest leaned down and whispered in her ear, "You give up too easily."

Joen grimaced and started to say something but was cut off by Frondameer.

"Tenara, this is yours," he said, passing her a large vest made from the skin of some animal. "We call it 'Serpents Fool.' It will blind a snake for a moment and if it strikes, it will lose a tooth."

She picked it up, noticing that it was light as a feather and dark gray. Frondameer took it back and then walked over to a window. "Watch its colors change in the light." She noticed it start to shift back and forth from green to brown. "Now look," he exclaimed, stepping away from the window. She saw it turned to gray again. "Different!"

He handed it back and then gave her a small wooden knife. "I can see in your eyes that you doubt a weapon made of wood."

Tenara looked up. "Yes."

He nodded. "You should. But this one comes from the Erinoak, the one tree that beavers never touch. It's as hard as stone

yet light for someone like you. This is the sash to carry it. And as
I said to Joen, only draw it when there is no other choice."

Tenara stood up. "I don't know if I can do this."

"When your mind is ready, your body will follow."

He ushered them over to a long decorative table in the center
of the room with ten intricately carved chairs. In front of eight
of them were the carefully folded sashes that uniquely identified
each of the scouts by their runes and symbols.

Frondameer and Blendefest stood before the table. "And
now we lay ours upon the table as well."

Tenara and Joen watched the scouts remove their own sashes
and carefully place them on the table in front of their personal
chair. Then, they each reached down and lifted a short sword and
scabbard from the seat and tied it to their waist.

Frondameer brightened up. "We leave now to begin your
training near the great tree. There, you will learn to use tools we
have given you to protect and conceal yourself. At the end of the
day, there will be a festival in your honor. Come!"

For hours, Tenara and Joen parried with the scouts, learning
the ways of defense and cover. The hiding part was easier, as they
played this game often at home, but the fighting was another
matter entirely. Both were fearful of using their weapons on the
chance they would harm the scouts.

"Strike at me, Joen!" ordered Frondameer. "Or are you just
droopy like the Colonel said?"

"I'm not droopy!"

"Sure you are. You just want to give up, you poor little thing."

Joen gritted her teeth and slashed forward, nearly striking

Frondameer's leg and causing him to jump back. He was surprised at her speed as he parried her weapon to the side.

She looked at him hard. "You said that just to get me."

Frondameer just smiled again. "Did I?"

The best part of the afternoon was 'the search'. The scouts hid in the grass and trees and repeatedly moved around to confuse them, but Joen and Tenara, using their own skills, found them every time. And, for a brief moment, they forgot the dangers that lay before them.

As the afternoon progressed, they saw the shadows of the trees begin creeping across the island. Their short training had come to an end when Frondameer and Blendefest suddenly waved them off to join the gathering in front of the Colonel's house. Word had traveled throughout the village that the two visitors had come from the 'Quiet Water', the name they had given their home downstream. Many whispered about the ones missing from their village and wondered if something like that could happen to them. So it was no surprise when everyone crowded into the Colonel's yard for dinner wanting to know more about who they were and what they planned.

The Colonel stamped his foot for everyone's attention. "Eh, my fellow villagers, tonight we celebrate the bravery of these two intrepid warriors who left the safety of their home to look for their lost friends. We honor their cunning and skills and are grateful that they have come, on purpose or by accident, to our shores to share their stories. Unfortunately, more adventure awaits them when the light returns tomorrow. So let us celebrate and wish them and our fine scouts a safe quest!"

To Tenara and Joen's surprise, they all bowed once and then immediately began eating.

Soon after the sumptuous feast, the Colonel and Mrs. Gilgatop sat among the other officers of Moss Rock and listened attentively to Tenara as she described Rippleshy and the people that lived there. They were especially curious about the snake that befriended them on the way, as well as the impertinent turtle and the gossipy catfish. When she stopped, the Colonel stood up and waited for the conversation to die away.

"You all know that we would have them share their stories and their fellowship for as long as they want."

Several watching started to nod and stomp their feet.

"But," he said, with his hand raised in the air, "there is another subject that I must speak on that concerns all of us in Moss Rock, as well as our new friends."

He took a moment and continued, "It has also come to my attention that one of the giant lizards of the North was seen moving through the forest. Many of you are familiar with the runes written in the Lodge of Knowledge that describe them as Saurians of the Sun that never stray beyond the Place of Fallen Stones. The willow runes describe them as horned monsters and enemies of the fire demons that walked the forest long ago. No one knows where either came from or what their intentions were."

The Colonel waited for the conversation to die down. "As a result, all of our scouts, except the two before me, have secluded themselves within a day's travel of Moss Rock to give warning if one is sighted. Tomorrow, Frondameer and Blendefest will join our new friends and leave as well. However, this time, I send them deeper into the forest than any other scout. They are to find the missing ones of Rippleshy and to seek clues on the Saurians sudden appearance.

Frondameer stood up. "We have seen them ourselves. And there is no hope in fighting them alone."

The Colonel nodded. "Therefore, if their intentions are cruel, these four must seek alliances with others to defend our home if necessary. They carry Moss Rock's future. We honor them tonight for the courage they have in facing the threat before it faces us. Good hunting!"

With that, both scouts stood up and shook their fists while motioning for the ones from Rippleshy to do the same. Tenara looked around at the cheering faces and noticed the young ones that clung to their parents. She felt a dread crawl up her spine and turned to Joen, who was staring back with the same fear. Soon, it would be time to leave again.

Blendefest motioned them forward. "We must return to the Lodge now, where we will rest before crossing the river."

Tenara stepped in front of Frondameer. "The Colonel is asking more than we can give."

"You haven't even started," Frondameer replied, looking at her in shock. "How do you know what you can give?"

She asked, "You know the way?"

"We both do."

"Well, Joen and I have a right to know what faces us." She suspected they were being quiet about their plans on purpose.

The two scouts started off down the path without replying, leaving Tenara and Joen wondering what had been left unsaid.

# 7. CROSSING THE RIVER

TENARA SUDDENLY HEARD A SCREAM AND HER BLOOD FROZE INstantly. The beast was just behind her now, but she couldn't move her legs. She looked back and yelled, "Joen, RUN!" but it was too late. The paw touched her head and she screamed again.

"Tenara, Tenara!" repeated Blendefest, pulling his hand back and shaking her. "You must leave your dream now. It is time to go."

She jumped up, feeling her heart beating wildly, and then looked around, realizing she was still in the scout's lodge.

"Are you ok?" asked Joen, already awake and pushing her dagger tooth weapon into her belt.

She nodded.

"Good," Frondameer said, walking over. "We must leave now before the light touches the river."

She silently picked up her vest and wrapped it tightly around her, while hoping the walk to the river would clear her head. Upon arriving, she saw Frondameer standing on the bank. She looked up and noticed the first rays of the morning sun striking the tops of the trees. "We cross the water here."

She glanced in the direction he pointed on the far bank and noticed the cypress trees towering above the crystal-clear water. Then she noticed that the crossing was much wider than the section they first arrived in. She shook her head and looked at Blendefest, who was nearby, talking quietly to Joen about some curious things the scouts had discovered in their recent adventures.

"Tenara, the water is nice," said Frondameer cheerfully, looking directly at her for a response. "Would you like to go first?"

"No thanks!" She stepped away from the bank. "Why do you make it sound like fun anyway? There was nothing fun about it when we first arrived," she said mournfully, gazing back at the scout.

He smiled. "I understand that you are both new to the forest, so let me ask you a question. Do you wish you had never ventured to Moss Rock, or met the turtle who guided you to our shore? What about the stories of my people we shared with you and the new friends you have come to know? Each of them took a first step."

"Perhaps," she countered, "but I'd rather be second."

"Hold up," Blendefest interrupted. "Frond, he's back and has a friend," he said, pointing in the direction of a large cypress tree on the far side of the water.

Tenara looked around. "Friend? Who? I don't see anything."

"We call them Two-Teeth: serpents. They often watch us crossing near the knobby knees at the bottom of the trees," Frondameer commented.

Remembering their encounter with the vicious snake when they first arrived in Moss Rock, both Tenara and Joen jumped back from the water. "I don't see it," Tenara said, frustrated. "Maybe this is not a good time to cross."

"It's because you look but don't see." He pointed across the river. "Notice the water moving around the tree over there?"

She replied, "The water makes a U around that tree, but a V around the others. Is that it?"

"That's it! The snakes are just upstream of the tree. Blend and I have a strategy for crossing. We've done this before." He looked over at his partner. "Watch for my signal."

Frondameer slipped under the surface and began paddling against the current to a point just downstream of the two serpents. At the same time, Blendefest grabbed a vine, tied it to a tree nearby, and slipped into the water as well. Careful not to create a ripple, he paddled slowly toward his companion while gently pulling the vine. It bobbed slowly across the surface. Tenara and Joen watched the snakes and for any sign of Frondameer but there was none. They turned their eyes toward Blendefest, but he too had disappeared.

"I don't see any of them, Tenara," Joen said anxiously.

"Shhhhh," she ordered.

Tenara had her eyes focused at the base of the tree where they had first seen the snake. As long as the motion of the water remained the same, she knew the snakes had not moved.

Joen whispered, "There!" Tenara saw it too. Frondameer's head broke the surface and slowly moved back toward them.

The scout swam up and pushed the vine up with his hand. "Tenara, take hold and pull yourself across…slowly." Then, he lowered his voice. "Focus on the vine, not the snakes. We have done this before and I will be in front of you the entire way.

"Also, do not look for Blendefest. He already crossed the water downstream of the Two-Teeth, and securely tied the other end to a tree. One more thing before you begin," he cautioned. "The snake can feel the water with its tongue. Be silent while you move. If you have to leave the vine, make sure you remain downstream of the tree and, if at all possible, beneath the surface."

He took Tenara's shaking hand and gently guided her into the water, Joen following just behind. Once the three were holding fast to the vine, they began quietly pulling themselves under the surface while keeping as close together as possible. Frondameer looked down at the river bottom and was grateful for the clear visibility from the morning light.

Nearby, one of the Two-Teeth had become bored waiting for the scouts to cross and left to seek prey upstream. Its sudden motion disturbed the other one just enough to turn its head in their direction.

"Long I have waited," it hissed.

At the same time, Tenara was focused only the vine, keeping it as close as possible. However, Joen had become distracted by the fascinating undersea forest of strange tree stumps and grasses that she passed. She fell back slightly, just enough to look but still remaining close to the others. All around her were a mix of dancing shadows that galloped along the river bottom, some from the tall trees that grew on the sandy banks and others from the crazy fish whose curiosity followed them along the vine.

It reminded her of the Shadow Game back home, where she would guess which of her friends swam above her from the shadows they cast on the bottom of the pond. That's when it struck her. She immediately glanced down again and noticed one shadow was moving rapidly toward her and did not belong to any of the creatures nearby. That meant only one thing. She glanced up, saw a familiar shape, and nearly froze.

In a panic, she jerked the vine and slapped Tenara on the leg. But there was no reaction other than an annoyed look. Joen slapped her again while desperately pointing up, but there was still no response. It was at the third slap that she understood and looked behind her, seeing the large silhouette coming fast. To protect Frond, she immediately released the vine, motioning for Joen to do the same, and pointed to the left. Splitting up was the only way to save at least one of them.

The snake saw them as well but took the third option; it bore down on Frondameer. With glee, it began opening its mouth, revealing its fangs, just as the scout looked back for Tenara. In a panic, he began thrashing through the water, trying to get away. But it was too late, so he turned to fight a hopeless battle. Then, to his astonishment, the snake suddenly jerked backwards. Shocked at his sudden luck, Frondameer recovered and saw the reason: Joen's dagger tooth had been driven deep into its spiny tail.

Enraged, the snake twisted around and saw the one who had attacked it swimming away. But that was not the one it was after. It wanted Frondameer. It whipped around to face the scout again, who took that short moment to dive to the river bottom. Immediately, he began flailing his body against the sandy floor, causing a haze to erupt that swallowed him in a fog of murky brown water. At that same instant, Joen dove for the snake again.

Tenara raced to her side just as Joen withdrew the dagger.

But before the snake could turn around, they both plunged to the river bottom and raced into the cloud as well. The serpent angrily swept its murderous eyes around, searching for its original target before noticing some tracks on the river bottom that led directly into the drifting fog. Pulling its girth together, it plunged in. Tenara and Joen, at the same time, flew out the other side and instantly saw some cypress roots to their left. Both turned abruptly, just as the serpent exploded out of the cloud, missing them by inches.

Tenara grabbed Joen and darted for the ghostly outline of the roots, clinging to the river bottom as they went. Swimming as fast as possible, she raced toward the cluster of roots and then released Joen, who erupted out of the water and landed on one of the knots at the base of the tree.

Just below her, Tenara had successfully driven herself under the cypress tree and now stood transfixed in horror, noticing that Joen was missing. She quickly pulled the Serpent's Fool vest to her body and hid behind one of the larger roots just as the snake came into view.

Its scaly body slowly moved around, checking each crevice its quarry might be hiding in. And then it looked straight at her. Resisting the impulse to run, she saw the rest of it coalesce out of the remaining cloud. It was a fearsome monster whose eyes were as black as night. Slowly, it slithered closer, testing the water with its long tongue, until it was mere feet from the roots.

It was all Tenara could do to not flee in terror. But she knew if she did, she would be abandoning Joen. Instead, she remained rigid, staring back at the monstrous head while pulling her vest closer.

The snake was sure its prey was here. Its tongue raked the water again and again, searching for the faint smell of it. Frustrated, it could see nothing but the outlines of the pillars that held the tree to the river bottom. With a jerk, it turned away and floated slowly out of sight to wait patiently for another clue.

Further upstream, Frondameer swam around, exhausted from creating the muddy fog. He carefully searched the area along the river bed for the serpent and then spotted it drifting away from the base of a cypress tree.

He immediately shot for the surface and began looking for Blendefest.

"There you are," his partner observed casually from the shore. "Playing with the Two-Teeth again, eh? One left several minutes ago. Guess the other one found you."

Frondameer ignored his friend's casual indifference to what had just happened. "You gathered the balls from the tree?"

He nodded. "Their scent is all over 'em. By the way, Joen is over there." He pointed.

Relief swept over Frondameer. He knew that Tenara had to be just beneath her. "Excellent. Toss the balls in the water, there and there." He pointed upstream. "The fish will do the rest."

As soon as they started bobbing in the current, Frondameer slipped beneath the surface with Blendefest close behind. They both waited patiently. Less than two minutes had passed since he last saw Tenara. It felt like an eternity.

Years ago, the scouts discovered that cypress balls attracted the local fish because of their resemblance to large insects. They knew it wouldn't be long before the larger ones began to tear the balls apart. Inside each were bits of scales and skins of serpents that the scouts had carefully packed the night before. The snakes that prowled this water were territorial, so when the scent of one of their own kind was detected, they would find themselves more pre-occupied with a possible burglary than with lost prey.

At the same time, Joen noticed the scouts tossing something in the river, but her mind was focused on the absence of Tenara. She felt guilty about abandoning her but realized there was not enough room for both under the cypress tree. She stood up, holding her dagger tooth tightly in her hand and was preparing to jump back in.

By now, several large fish had started thrashing at the wooden balls. Frondameer shifted his eyes downstream to where he thought Tenara was and waited patiently. There! The serpent lifted its head above the surface and looked straight at its den. With a loud hiss, it whipped the water with its body and flew across the surface at high speed.

Taking advantage of the moment, Frondameer slipped under the water and swam as fast as possible toward Tenara while pointing up.

By now Joen was dizzy with fear, especially after listening to the noise of the fish upstream. She was preparing to plunge back in when she heard the water stir beneath her feet. Holding her dagger tooth up, she readied for another attack when the water exploded upwards, nearly forcing her backwards into the water.

"Joen, it's me," Frondameer exclaimed, fending off the knife. "Tenara's just behind. Come. We must go now. Quickly! The snake won't be fooled for long."

She looked dumbly at him.

"We distracted it. By now, the serpent knows that he was deceived."

Joen was still confused but paddled behind him to the other side of the river with Tenara following.

After arriving on the far bank of the river, Frondameer turned to Joen and shook his head. "Both of you have been lying to us."

Tenara and Joen looked up. "What?!"

"You said before leaving that you were unprepared for the forest, yet you were the ones who distracted the serpent and saved me. You have not been honest with us!"

Blendefest half smiled. "What do we do with them?"

Frondameer looked over at his partner. "We could throw them back in the water. But I guess that would be cruel to the snakes. I guess we better bring them along. Perhaps they can save us again, Blend," he said indifferently and walked off.

Tenara and Joen both smirked and quickly caught up with them.

# 8. An Uninvited Visitor

By late morning, the warmth of the forest had been replaced by a cool breeze and a rocky path. Wispy clouds had now covered the sky, giving it a barren and forlorn look, which only aggravated their mood further. No one had spoken since leaving the water. It had been more than four hours since they huddled together against the wind to eat lunch. But it would be late afternoon before they neared the top of the mountain.

Since she left the river, Tenara had been thinking about the snake that nearly took them both. She shivered at the memory and the breeze that kept buffeting them as they walked along the path. Occasionally she looked back at Joen, who kept staring at the lush valleys and snowy mountain peaks. In that moment, she understood why the two scouts chose to leave the comfort of their homes and explore their world.

Frondameer motioned them to stop and pointed down. "That is a Noptis plant. Its leaves taste like cake! Gather some. You will want them later."

Joen bent down and took a bite. "I think I want them now."

It was well into the afternoon when Frondameer stopped again and pointed to a different flower with a red stalk.

"That's called Fearsome Root. You will find it only among the rocks at the summit. This one is not for eating. The smell is quite unpleasant, but for those creatures that live on the mountain and hunt at night, it's much worse. We will use it as our first defense when we sleep tonight."

Frondameer saw Tenara looking at the setting sun. "Hurry. The first shadows of the night begin to crawl across the ground. Blendefest and I have agreed to use Sirasoar cave for the night. It is unknown to most creatures and should provide the shelter we need."

Tenara interrupted, "Why is it called that?"

"Sirasoars were the great birds that once nested on this mountain."

"Where did they go?" asked Joen.

"We don't know. Legend has it they left for the North during a great war." Frondameer then put his hand up. "But enough of that. Hurry. We must be moving now. It will be night soon. Our food is sparse, so eat what you have. When the light comes again, we must hasten to the bottom of the mountain."

Joen looked at him. "Are there any snakes around here? Just asking."

Frondameer shook his head, smiling. "You ready to battle another one?"

"There's one here?" she asked nervously.

"No. But we can let you watch for one tonight."

"Funny!" She saw Blendefest grinning.

Frondameer turned serious. "Joen, it's not the animals on the mountain we worry about. It's the ones we may see in the forest tomorrow morning. We must be well beyond their reach if we are to cross the Whispering Woods and Ildon before night."

"Ildon?"

Frondameer replied quietly, "It is an ancient place, a swamp that existed before the forest arrived. It was once home to Ildon, a great serpent that roamed its waters. But that's just a legend."

Joen interjected, "Well, maybe we should go another way."

Tenara looked hard at Frondameer, waiting for his answer.

Blendefest spoke up. "It's the fastest way."

"Why?"

"Because whoever took your people would not have risked crossing its black water. And we have seen no tracks on the path since leaving Moss Rock. We believe they forced them through one of the two valleys that border this mountain."

"But isn't the swamp dangerous?'

"Yes. There's risk in both choices. But we feel the greater one is being seen by whatever took your people."

"What is this Whispering Woods you speak of?"

"It is a part of the forest that's strangely quiet. Nothing chooses to live there. In fact, the only sound you will hear is the wind that tiptoes through the canopy above. And I'm sorry to tell you this, but it's also the home of many serpents—a place where any noise might reveal our presence to the Two-Teeth that prowl its ground."

Joen jumped. "Snakes? You said there were no snakes!"

Frondameer looked despondent. "Did I say that?"

Joen looked at Tenara and then the scouts. "I'm going to

sharpen my dagger-tooth for both of them now," she replied, pointing to Frondameer and Blendefest.

The scouts grinned. Frondameer set off, purposely leaving Blendefest behind. The last light of the sun now began to disappear just as the moon came up. "As I was saying, once we cross through Ildon, we will then make for the Dismal Woods of the Eastern Forest."

"Dismal Woods?" asked Tenara.

"Yes, a name given to it by one of the scouts long ago. We only know about it through shared tales, most of which," he said, grinning, "we suspect came after drinking too much nectarhol."

After a few minutes, he stopped in front of a dark entrance, carved into the face of a cliff, that looked foreboding to Tenara and Joen. "This is Sirasoar Cave. We will remain here for the night. You two will sleep first. We will take the first watch."

Tenara gazed at the impenetrable darkness. "Perhaps we should join you for that."

"You will have your chance."

"What if something is in there?"

"If there was, it would have already attacked."

Tenara and Joen both felt for their weapons and then slowly stepped into the darkness. They looked back and could see the moon fighting its way to be seen through the jumble of rocks outside.

Blendefest sat down beside Frondameer. "The Fearsome Root is in place."

"Let's hope it's enough."

Both scouts watched the forest as the moon continued to shine its feeble light down on the craggy landscape. Closing their eyes occasionally, they listened to the buzzing sounds of insects that echoed off the rocks nearby.

But after a few hours, it suddenly stopped.

Blendefest was the first to notice and motioned to Frondameer, who was half asleep. They both stood up and moved to the entrance silently, straining to hear something that would alert them to a threat.

Frondameer saw it first. "There!" he whispered. Two large red eyes suddenly appeared several yards in front of them. Blendefest saw them as well and nodded his head. He then carefully reached down for a stone and tossed it quietly just beyond the creature. The eyes vanished but there was no noise of retreat.

"Blend, did you think to bring some fire rocks?"

"Yes, one, but it's the last one we have."

Long ago, they had found several buried near the willow tree in Moss Rock. No one had any idea who put them there or why.

Blendefest tossed the stone directly toward where the red eyes had first appeared. As soon as it hit the ground, a flash of light appeared and, for an instant, they saw the form of a giant lizard glaring their way. Then the light was gone and with it, the sound of footsteps being swallowed up in the night.

"A Saurian! They never travel at night," Frondameer exclaimed quietly.

"Apparently, this one has a reason too."

They resumed their original positions on the floor of the cave and waited. Before long, they heard the insects again. Blendefest whispered, "Wake them now?"

"No."

"Should we tell them what we saw?"

"No, only what they need to know. The Saurians are the first real threat to Moss Rock. The Colonel believes the Willow Runes have the answer. They say go east."

# 9. THE WHISPERING WOODS

TENARA WOKE TO THE EARLY MORNING LIGHT FILTERING INTO the cave. She yawned, pulled herself up, and noticed that Joen was still asleep. Nowhere did she see Blendefest or Frondameer. She called out to them but only silence returned.

A moment later, they walked in. "You gave me a fright!" she exclaimed. "Where were you?!"

"Apologies, we needed to ensure the path down the mountain was free of danger before leaving. Are you ready to leave?"

"Yes. I hope the way down is warmer." She turned to Joen, who was now staring at Frondameer.

"It will be."

As they began their descent into the forest that bordered the Whispering Woods, they noticed the early morning fog drifting down the mountain. Frondameer determined the best choice were the paths that led between the ridges. They offered the least exposure from any prying eyes that might follow behind. Blendefest brought up the rear to ensure none did. Still, of all the trails they had taken since leaving Moss Rock, this was the most worrisome.

After a few hours of hiking, Frondameer led them between two high stones before pausing a moment. The soft wind pushed the cool mist away from their bodies. All at once, they felt the early morning sun break the grip of cold that had followed them all the way from the top of the mountain.

A minute later, he stopped at an overlook. "From here it is a short walk to where the forest begins. In the distance," he pointed, "where the eye can barely see, lies Ildon. You will see it as a dark green smudge against the forest. Just beyond is Songentrope Creek, where the water flows from the hills of the Anduin Mountain of the north. Once again," he said, looking at Tenara and Joen, "when we enter the forest, you must walk light and make no sound."

After an hour of silence, they entered a shallow valley containing hundreds of rocks, each covered by a luxurious carpet of green and purple moss. Joen took notice of one and leaned down to rub its velvety face when she suddenly saw Blendefest's foot between it and her fingers.

"It's called Eyeglass. It wants you to touch it," he whispered.

She jerked her hand back. "What?"

"Its scent is the first warning to the forest that we have entered its domain. Quickly now, we must walk fast to catch the others."

After a few hours of walking silently, Tenara began to notice several trees that had long strands of thick moss, almost like rugs, that covered their limbs. A moment after that, Frondameer motioned everyone together. In the quietest whisper possible, he leaned close and said, "This is the edge of Ildon. It will try to confuse you whenever it can. When you see the first signs of water on the ground, look for a log to step over it. Do not allow the water to touch you."

Tenara was not at all prepared for this. She was becoming increasingly nervous. At first the walk was pleasant except for the buzzing of insects nearby. But that soon was replaced by a soft sigh of the wind in the canopy overhead that reminded her of better times. By noon, however, the hard ground had turned mushy under her feet and dead logs began to appear everywhere, surrounded by strange pinecones, each sporting multiple needles that glistened in the light.

At least the logs were covered in a rich moss and leaf mix that would make the walk easier. She started to step up on one when Joen touched her back. "Careful, the moss!"

Blendefest shook his head. "It's ok. It's ordinary moss. The Eyeglass Moss only grows at the outer edge, not within the Whispering Woods. Like so many other plants and creatures, it avoids Ildon." Relieved, Tenara and Joen followed the scouts across the log until they reached the other end, where they carefully checked for puddles before continuing to the next.

After a few hours, they became weary from the steamy mixture of heat and humidity that permeated the path. It seemed their energy was being pulled away somehow.

While crossing between two logs, Tenara closed her eyes for a moment to rest. No more than two seconds went by before she felt a terrible pain, as if she had been stabbed by a sharp knife. Glancing down, she saw the reason. One of the pinecones had barely touched her, but it stung. In a panic, she tripped over a log and rolled down a small hill, completely disappearing in the lush plants below.

When she came to a rest, her first impulse was to yell, but she knew the sound would expose her friends to further danger. So, instead, she pulled herself up and had started to untangle the vines around her feet when she heard a loud hissing sound. Her heart began to race. Slowly she turned her head and saw a long black snake with a huge head and body that wound back along the forest floor and into the bushes beyond.

"I don't recognize you," it said sweetly, moving closer. "You are not from my woods, but you look tasty all the same," hissed the snake. "Soon you will be a memory and them as well."

Tenara's eyes got big. She turned around, listening for her friends, and noticed her wooden knife was missing.

"You didn't think I heard them, did you? Nothing passes this way that escapes my tongue. In a matter of moments, they will be gone as well."

In a flash, the serpent leapt at Tenara, who immediately felt a crushing pain across her chest as it bit down. But to her astonishment, the head just as quickly jerked back.

"What have you done to me!!!" it yelled in agony. Then she noticed a fang on the ground, still dripping with venom, and suddenly realized what had happened. Her vest had saved her. She looked up and saw the snake twisting its head from side to side. It then backed up, preparing for another strike.

At that same moment in the swamp, Joen stood ready to chase after Tenara when she was suddenly yanked back by Blendefest. "No," he whispered, shaking his head.

She angrily turned her head to suddenly see both of them pull their swords out and carefully step down on the spongy forest floor. Joen calmed herself and followed them off the log, pulling her dagger tooth out as well.

Just below them, Tenara continued to move away from the serpent until her back was against a tree. She quickly looked around for a weapon and noticed a stinging pinecone nearby. Using a stick beside her, she flicked it into the snake's mouth just when it opened up again.

Immediately, it began to gag on the foreign object, slapping its tail repeatedly against the ground. At the same time, its eyes began to flutter as it tried to cough the pinecone out. But it didn't last. Within moments, she heard the sound of the bristles cracking under the pressure of the snake's one remaining tooth.

Tenara knew it was not possible to fend off another attack. It was just a matter of time before the snake finally crushed the pinecone, so she braced herself.

# 10. ILDON'S SWAMP

TENARA WAS ABOUT TO YELL OUT WHEN SHE HEARD ANOTHER hiss followed by a second snake suddenly crashing into the side of the first. She watched in horror as its mouth opened and its fangs sank deep into the side of the first. Then all was quiet.

"Youssss a difficult frog and isss strange that you come here," said a familiar voice. She immediately recognized it as the one that gave her and Joen their first hint at finding Moss Rock.

"Oh, you gave me such a fright, Butiss. How did you come to such a wretched place? We have traveled so far!" panted Tenara.

Just then, Blendefest and Frondameer burst through the foliage with their swords at the ready.

"No, no!" She moved between them and Butiss. "This one saved my life. He is a friend, from the Western Forest where my village lies."

"You have made a friend of a serpent?!" Frondameer said, aghast. He then remembered her stories of a snake that had suggested she come to them for help. He looked down at her vest. "It shows teeth marks. You have been attacked!" He put his hand to his sword again.

"Yes," she said, pushing his weapon away. "But not from this one. It's the other, which lies still on the ground beyond." She pointed.

Frondameer shook his head in amazement and then turned and bowed low to Butiss. "I apologize for my reaction, as I was unaware that your kind …."

"Are not all the sssame…?"

"Yes, as a matter of fact." There was a long pause. "May we ask a favor of you?"

"Yesssssss?"

"Would you do us the honor of accompanying us across the forest for our protection? It is a perilous walk for us and, although we have been this way before, speed is of the essence."

"I will be near, but you must take caution yourselves. If there is a warning to be had, I will givesss. The forest isss no friend, even to me."

Frondameer looked at Tenara and then the snake. "How did you know…" but before he completed his question, the snake disappeared in the vines.

"Know what?" asked Tenara.

"To find us here—never mind. We need to be moving now." She caught up with him. "You seemed to be surprised."

Frondameer ignored the comment for a moment and then turned back. "We can't talk about it now."

The group continued on in silence, stepping from log to log through the dense forest, all the while taking note of their surroundings and any signs of Butiss. But there was none, at least none that they could see.

Frondameer turned around and whispered, "Very soon, the ground will be covered by water. In order to…."

"How do you know that?" interrupted Joen.

"Have you been asleep as we walk from log to log? Have you not felt the ground?" asked Blendefest.

"Yeah, I guess. It sort of feels the same."

He pointed off to the side where they stood. "Stand on that."

Joen stepped down and grimaced. "I'm sinking!!!" She jumped back.

"Yes. The swamp is subtle and will grasp you when you're least aware."

Frondameer held his hand up. "We need to keep moving. The shadows are getting longer. We must hurry."

Soon, the ground under their feet felt like a sponge and the puddles because larger. Tenara looked down at one of them and saw the reflection of the trees high above painted a blood red color, which sent chills down her back. This was the beginning of Ildon. Even the leafy vines they had seen on the ground now climbed to avoid the water.

Frondameer walked over to one. "We go up now."

"Are you kidding?" asked Tenara.

He shook his head. "We cannot cross the water, so we must walk above it. See how this vine grasps the tree on both sides? Watch." He stepped up to the tree and began climbing it as if he had done so all his life. "Come now. This should be no problem for you." He waved at them, looking down.

Tenara was not convinced. She crossed her arms and stood still. "Come back down and tell me again why we're doing this."

Frondameer reached up and pulled himself onto a limb. "It's quite comfortable up here."

Tenara just shook her head.

There was a splash in the distance.

Startled, Blendefest came up behind her. "We will not survive if we remain on the ground. Trust us. You do not want to meet any of the creatures that live here." He moved around and looked directly at her. "It is ancient and filled with things that hunger all the time. Frond and I have been this way before. Climb or die."

Joen's eyes got wide "And if we fall?"

"That will not happen," said Blendefest behind her.

"How?" she asked nervously, still looking up. "Do you intend to tie us together?"

"Exactly!" whispered Frondameer, lowering himself softly from the limb.

Tenara watched Blendefest remove some short vines from the forest floor and cut them into two pieces with his sword. After tying one end to Tenara, he tossed the other to Frondameer, who subsequently tied it to himself.

Another splash was heard, this time closer.

Tenara jerked on the vine.

"It will hold," Frondameer commented blandly.

"Uh huh." She saw the water rippling nearby. "Just making sure."

She then followed Frondameer up with Blendefest and Joen just behind. At first, she was hesitant, but after several more minutes, they all found themselves in the canopy, far above the murky swamp.

"Before we begin," Frondameer pointed out, "choose the wide vines that run from tree to tree to walk on. They are the least likely to shake in the wind."

Tenara looked suspicious. "Shake in the wind?"

Frondameer ignored the remark. "If necessary, hold on to the ones that hang above you but do not trust them."

Tenara leaned over and tried to see the ground, but thick leaves stood in her way. She didn't like this at all.

"Time to cross now," said Frondameer, stepping on a particularly thick vine that stretched to the next tree. At first, they all took small steps but later increased their pace, seeing that everyone was doing well. About halfway across, Tenara noticed the vine she was on begin to move with the wind.

"Frondameer, is it supposed to move like this?" she asked in a squeaky voice.

He turned around and took her hand. "Yes. You will be fine."

"Why do you keep saying that?"

He shook his head and continued across the vine to the next tree while the others followed at their own pace. Along the way, one of the many territorial birds perched on a limb and stared at them. Tenara had never been this close to one and started to reach out when it suddenly squawked loudly. The shock of it caused her to miss a step, but before she could grab the vine, she felt someone pushing her back. "Quit playing with the birds," said Joen.

"I was not playing," she said, quickly glancing back.

"You were, and you almost tripped."

"I was just testing the vine." Hiding her smirk, she said, "Seeing all of this, don't you wonder what you've been missing?"

"Sometimes, but that nasty place below is not one of them. You finished testing the vine yet?"

"You want to get in front of me and lead?" Tenara moved her hand forward on the vine while turning back to Joen.

"I can't. I have to make sure that Blendefest is ok." She winked.

"Excuse me?" said a voice behind Joen. "You must proceed if we are to make it to the river before the day is gone."

"Why do you talk so formal?"

"I do not understand," replied Blendefest.

"Never mind," Tenara echoed back, shaking her head.

By now, Joen and Tenara had lost count of the number of tress they'd passed. After a few hours, the leaves below them began to thin and visibility improved, but darkness was coming soon. They continued passing slowly above the swamp, but the vines they held to were becoming fewer and fewer.

Then Frondameer stopped. "We will cross one or two more trees before we descend. Very soon, we should hear the noisy water of the Songentrope Creek."

After carefully making their way to the next tree, the faint sound of rushing water came to their ears.

"We go down now," Frondameer ordered "At the bottom, you will find the ground hard. It is a high spot in the swamp that borders the river and should be safe."

Once down, they untied their vines and made for the river just beyond the trees. From there, they walked downstream along its length until the water began to slow and form a pool.

Frondameer turned to the company. "This is Darmok's water.

It's too close to Ildon to cross. Therefore, we will cross the dam instead."

Joen looked down and saw her feet covered by something sticky.

"That is the sap of the tree," Frondameer explained. "Remove it before we continue."

"Can we use the water?" Tenara asked, looking at the same on her own legs.

"More than that, you can swim if you want. The water is fast here and the noise will not be heard. Do it before the last rays of the sunset are gone. We will rest here for the night but must cross just before the light returns. While the water is safe, the forest beyond is unknown to us. It's the reason we wait."

Abruptly, the scout stepped into the water and was gone. Tenara looked anxiously at the stream, wondering if there were hidden dangers he hadn't mentioned.

Blendefest walked up behind her. "The stream is safe. If it were not, the beavers would have left." Then he too dropped into the water, leaving Tenara and Joen alone.

More than an hour passed and there was still no sign of the scouts.

# 11. TEALICK'S PLAN

As the sun began to cast long shadows across the forest floor, the skinks left their posts to march their captives back into their dark hole for the night. One by one, they were pushed and prodded into the cave, which was partially lit by the thousands of glowing insects that lived on its walls. Inside, most of the captives fell to the floor, exhausted, while the entrance rock was slammed back into place and their guards assumed their posts.

All at once, everyone started murmuring about the day's events and how Tealick stood up to the dragon lizard. But it lasted only a few moments before the entrance rock was pushed away again and Tealick was thrown inside the cave. Their captors glared at them and quickly slammed the rock back.

Parsnippy ran over and helped his friend to his feet. "What did you do?" he asked, shaking his head.

"He probably antagonized the guards," said one of the others standing nearby.

"Or maybe Tealick did it to help us," echoed another beside him.

"That's enough!" said Parsnippy, holding his hand up. "Give him some rest."

The chatter subsided, but the crowd kept staring at him for an answer.

Tealick said quietly, in the hopes the guards would not hear, "One of the skinks said that we would never be rescued, even if someone did leave our village to look for us."

Once again, there was the bedlam of multiple voices. Parsnippy shushed them down.

"You think someone is?" asked one.

"Probably not - I know of nobody willing do it at Rippleshy."

Parsnippy interjected, "But if it's true, we must find a way to help them."

One of the others stood up. "How can we do that? They lock us up at night and watch us during the day."

Tealick met his eyes. "He's right. One of us has to escape when the guards are not looking."

A gasp was heard around the room. Parsnippy turned to his friend, astonished at his gall. "The risk is too great for that."

"I see no other way. What do you think the lizard will do when they finally have no more need of us? Tell me!" There was only silence. "If we have any hope of returning to our families or of surviving, one of us has to take the risk. I choose me!"

No one spoke for a long time.

"You will not!" boomed a voice in the darkness. "I will find them."

Everyone jumped back, fearfully looking around, but the owner of the voice remained hidden in the darkness. Tealick squinted with a combination of fear and curiosity. "If so, how will you make it past the skinks? They watch our door, even now."

"Because I am not one of you," said the voice, softly laughing.

"I don't understand."

Out of the shadows, a large silhouette appeared and began moving toward them. Several around Tealick backed up while others jumped to the other side of the cave in shock. Ever so slowly, the subtle light of the insects fell upon the creature until it was fully lit. Standing before them was an animal three times their size with thick fur and a large flat tail.

"Sorry," he said, waving his hands all about. "Don't be afraid. I don't work for the lizard. I do as it says, but it does not own me."

Tealick gazed up at him. "What is your name, beaver?"

"I am called Brondanur. I came to listen and to help."

"How did you get in here? Is there another entrance?"

"Yes. It is deep in the cavern and dangerous for small ones like you. I am here as an ally."

Tealick took a step forward, watching him scratch his back. "I remember. You were standing on the dam when we first arrived. What can you tell us about the lizards? We never knew such monsters existed! Where did they come from?"

"I am not sure." He scratched his back again. "My father once told us stories of demons that lived in the northern hills whose skin were like rocks. Perhaps they have come from that place."

"Then they do not live in the forest?"

"I cannot say," Brondanur replied. "He told us little. What I know is this: they have not always lived within Anzenar."

"Anzenar - I know that name. It means 'everywhere' in our village."

"For the beavers, it means 'all the wood.'"

Tealick was puzzled. "How do you know they come from somewhere else?"

He rolled his shoulders, scratched, and fidgeted even more. "There is a great recollection handed down…from beaver to beaver…about the first of our kind, who created a mighty lodge at the foot of the northern mountain. The story goes that the first beaver to arrive in Anzenar turned a thunderous river into a mighty lake, which stretched as far as the eye could see. His name was Canadensis and some believe he came from a place beyond the mountains.

"Beavers learn early in our life where the running water is for possible lodges, but none has found a lake such as that." He shook his head and fidgeted again with his hands. "Sorry. I sometimes talk too much." He scratched again.

"No. You honor us with the risk you take by being here."

The beaver bowed. "Know this. Their scaly kind cares nothing for the forest. It is why my family was forced to remove the trees."

Tealick could only nod.

Brondanur continued, "The skinks and chameleons showed up two weeks before you arrived. One week ago, we saw them again with you at their side."

Tealick was curious. "You said there are other beavers?"

"There are many within Anzenar, but the one who lives closest is called Darmok. He shares the same water as my lodge."

Parsnippy interrupted, "You have been watching us the entire time then."

The beaver nodded.

"So why come to us now?"

"Because of the courage I saw in that one," he said, turning to Tealick. "You took a grave risk when you faced Scalar."

Tealick replied, "I had to see its eyes to know our future."

"And what is that?"

"Death." He waited for a response, but heard only the distant drip of water splashing rhythmically on the rocky floor.

Brondanur looked up at the dripping water. "There is one more thing. Do not look to the water to find an exit from this place. The cavern extends far back under the mountain that towers above us, possibly further. There is a story told to me by a crazy river otter that says it pours from a fountain in the shape of your kind. I believe it a fable, as they don't live in caves."

"Our kind?" Tealick looked at Parsnippy with an astonished face. Then, turning back and regaining his composure, he said, "Thank you, Brondanur, for taking the risk and coming to help us. One more question. Can this Darmok help us?"

"It is a question I have as well." He glanced to the door of the cave. "I'm sorry, but I must return to my lodge now. The moon becomes brighter every night, and I can be easily seen outside. My family and I will discuss your question soon. Listen for my tail to slap the water three times if the answer is yes."

Tealick interrupted, "And then you leave to seek his help?!"

The beaver glanced at the stone door and said quietly, "Yes, when you see me on the dam with two sticks pointing up, that night I will leave. The lizards and skinks should be unaware of my absence, unless I do not return within two days. Several times I have seen them sleep at their post. However, if they ask for me, you must give them a reason not to search."

"How?" Tealick asked. But the beaver had already pulled back into the shadows and was gone.

# 12. ACROSS THE BEAVER DAM OF DARMOK

IN THE EARLY MORNING HOURS, TENARA AND JOEN FELT THEM-selves being shaken. Both instantly jumped up, ready to run.

Frondameer held them back and whispered, "Sorry. We must leave now. Gather your things."

"Where have you been? We were worried that something might have happened to you."

"We apologize. But there is something you must know that we did not share with you last night. We saw a saurian on the mountain, near Sirasoar Cave, while you slept two nights ago and another a few hours ago on the other side of the Songentro-pe Creek. It forced us to delay our return for fear of being seen. Again, we apologize."

"Is it gone?" she asked, looking up at him.

"Yes." Then the scout abruptly walked off, leaving Tenara staring up at the stars peeking out between the drifting clouds.

Joen looked over at her. "Why have I got the feeling that they're not telling us everything?"

Tenara did not have an answer. She stood up and saw the

scouts quietly talking beside the water, barely lit by the partial moon above. Though the four travelers were awake now, the forest remained eerily silent. But they knew that silent did not mean safe. Joen was right. Their behavior seemed at times erratic.

Frondameer interrupted her thoughts. "Ready?" She nodded.

Joen, still grumpy from being woken so early, moved up behind Blendefest. Suddenly, without warning, the scout slapped the air, followed by the sound of a small splash. Joen instantly fell on her backside in shock while at the same time looking up, petrified as to what just happened.

He turned around and grimaced. "Sorry. A spider and I came to a disagreement."

"Y-you could have let me know!" she stuttered quietly.

He pulled her up, smiling. "As we said, you must be ready for the perils you cannot see."

Tenara put her hand on Joen's shoulder and asked, "How can we be ready for something we can't see?"

Joen just growled quietly.

"No more talking until we cross," whispered Frondameer, ignoring the remark. He turned around to face Tenara. "We know little about this beaver other than his name: Darmok. Some say he is vicious, others kind. To be safe, we must cross quietly."

Joen looked at Tenara, confused. The beavers they knew were good friends.

They resumed their walk behind Blendefest until they reached the dam.

After he inspected it carefully, Frondameer walked up to Joen and Tenara and pointed to some loose sticks on the ground nearby. He then placed his foot just above them and shook his head, and then pointed to a solid log to the right. Then he whispered, "No sound."

They understood.

Hearing nothing, they began stepping carefully across the thick logs that comprised the lodge. After reaching the roof Frondameer noticed a set of small logs mixed with sticks and brush. He glanced up at the waxing moon, wishing he had more light. He was about to take the next step when Tenara pulled him back. He looked down and saw a small stick just beneath his foot.

He nodded his thanks and thereafter checked with Tenara for each additional step. She realized they were all tired. The tedious process of crossing the dam made it all the worse. The descent was easier since the logs were larger and spaced closer together. Just at the end, after the first three had stepped down on the hard ground, they heard a crack from behind. Blendefest grimaced and rushed forward with the others to hide behind a large bush that jutted out from the bank.

Like a rocket, one of the beavers blasted up from the surface and looked around slowly. After swimming back and forth several times, it quickly withdrew to join its family below.

Frondameer looked hard at Blendefest. Joen whispered, "I think a bird did that. Don't you, Blendefest?"

He looked down at her for a long moment. "Perhaps it was."

Frondameer looked back and forth between the two girls. "Uh huh—it must have been the kind that makes their nests on beaver dams."

He then turned around and made his way carefully downstream, well away from where they crossed, and then turned to the others. "We are making too many mistakes. We will rest here until sunrise."

At dawn, Blendefest was the first to feel the sun's warmth cross his face. He looked up and noticed the fog drifting away, leaving its watery dew behind like a scattering of sparkling diamonds that covered the leaves and bushes nearby.

He noticed the others, who lay quietly nearby, and decided to let them sleep. Right now, he wanted to follow the water back upstream and watch for the beavers' morning ritual.

They were his early warning system for anything else nearby. After secluding himself, he watched them swim the length of the pond several times before returning to their lodge. However, at one point, his heart skipped a beat when he noticed the last one carefully inspecting the top of the dam. However, after a short moment, it too disappeared into the water, leaving the scout to finally breathe again. He turned around immediately and walked into the Eastern Forest, where he was swallowed up by the lingering mist.

A short time later, Frondameer opened his eyes and saw Tenara and Joen talking among themselves near the water. After standing up, he noticed that Blendefest had gone but then remembered that it was his turn to ensure the path ahead was safe. He started to look for him but noticed his companion coming out of the shadows.

Frondameer walked up to him. "Ready to leave?"

Blendefest just stared at him blankly. Frondameer looked closer and saw something he had never seen in his friend before.

"You ok?"

"Before we left, we were told to search for signs of the lizards as well as the missing ones from Rippleshy. You remember that the Colonel included the Dismal Woods as well?"

"Yes."

"We're in that forest now."

"How do you know?" asked Frondameer, taking a moment to look around.

"You didn't notice how the trees changed after we crossed the beaver dam?" Blendefest asked in a low voice. "Remember the rhyme shared by the scouts of old?

*And in this forest,*
*Where the trees grow tall,*
*A presence unknown*
*Protects them all?"*

"Yes," Frondameer said quietly.

"I think we're being watched."

His companion gazed up at the trees.

Dropping his voice further, Blendefest knelt and scratched at the dirt. "We only remember stories of giants that roam these woods and glowing objects that mystify those who gaze upon them."

Frondameer paused a moment while looking into the distance. "Should we believe in those tales?"

Blendefest looked away and said nothing.

"Are we ready?" asked Tenara, interrupting their thoughts.

Both jumped from the sudden intrusion.

"I'm sorry. Did we scare you?" asked Joen.

"Not possible," said Frondameer, regaining his composure quickly. "However, we are impressed that you have learned the importance of a light foot. Actually, we sensed you both coming before you walked up. We thought it an opportunity for you to prove your skills." He winked at Blendefest.

Joen wore a dubious expression. Tenara just stared at both of them. "You are saying that you were aware of us standing behind you?"

Frondameer replied blandly, fighting the urge to grin, "I'm just saying that Scouts are never without their senses of what's nearby."

"Sure. But perhaps the one that sees behind was not working so well."

Frondameer couldn't help but laugh. "Blendefest, we need to watch these two more closely."

"Indeed—they are wily and cunning." He smiled faintly and then turned abruptly and set off into the Eastern Forest.

# 13. THE DITHER TWINS

FOR SEVERAL DAYS, TWO SKINKS CONCEALED THEMSELVES WHILE spying on some beavers that were fussing about with their dam. Unfortunately, they had heard nothing other than the twittering of gabby birds claiming their territory. And now, they were bored, bored out of their minds doing the job that Keltar commanded: seeking clues on the whereabouts of one like him. And if no information came back, then there was that other thing about being on his menu.

"I am not enjoying this at all, brother," said the one of the Dither Twins, tail moving slowly across a log.

"How long we been watching these miserable beavers?"

"Four days and we've seen none besides them!"

"Maybe we should just go back home to Grivelridge."

"Yes. Of course," he spat. "Our sister would be the first to leave and profit by telling Keltar. They're all devious. Besides, you remember what the king said. It'd be more than our tails if we come back with nothin'."

"Perhaps they know something," he said, pointing at the beavers while grabbing his blue spear.

"We need to get closer…" the other replied with his red spear in his hand. He stepped off a rock and started down the leafy path with his brother just behind.

As they silently crept forward, they suddenly heard some crunching sounds and quickly concealed themselves under a holly bush. Just a short distance away, they saw a small beaver chewing on a piece of wood with a much taller one standing to its side. After covering themselves carefully with leaves, they lay quietly and strained to hear the conversation that drifted their way.

"… I don't know if it will be completed or not," said the smaller one.

"You mother said we have two days to finish it. You're doing fine," said the much larger one.

"Two days. That won't be enough!"

At that moment, Blue Spear felt a holly leaf prick his back and grunted out loud. His brother socked him, but it was too late. They saw the larger beaver turn around and look directly toward them.

"I know you are there," it said, growling out loud. "Show yourselves!"

Red Spear immediately jumped out and held his weapon high. However, his brother, forgetting his own, ran back to the bush and returned with it a minute later. Red Spear glanced at him with a menacing face.

"What is this?" the beaver boomed.

"We got some questions for ya, beaver."

The smaller one shook with fright when Blue Spear pushed

his weapon against its fur. Enjoying the reaction, he did it again until the beaver fell to the ground and began pushing itself away.

"About what?!" snarled the larger while looking down at his son.

Red Spear, believing he had the situation under control, blurted out, "Far to the north of us is a great king who rules the Northern desert. His name is Keltar and he seeks a member of his clan who disappeared."

The adult beaver flinched but then in a calm voice, he replied, "How does that concern me? I know nothing of the North or those that live there. What does this creature look like?"

Red Spear looked dumbfounded. "You don't know of 'em?"

"Why should I?" he asked, leaning over slightly "And I suspect you know little about beavers. We are not wanderers of the forest, nor do we seek knowledge except for what serves our family and their protection. We build our homes once and thereafter, remodel them when we see fit."

"Then I will tell you," Red Spear said, pushing his spear toward him. "Keltar is one of them lizard dragons that rule the Anduin Mountain and maybe more. You scared now?

The beaver looked indifferent.

The skink droned on, "He has no time or patience for dumb furry creatures like you. Soon, we will see him again. And when we do, we'll just say that you didn't want to help. We may be punished for our failure. But you will fare worse. His army will come into the forest and he will ask you the question himself. So don't enjoy living here for long."

The beaver looked away and contemplated the warning. Contrary to what he had said, he had indeed heard of the demons of the North but had never met one. When he was young, he dismissed them as fables; however, he had now come to know they were true. He was the fifth generation and descendent of the clan of Darmok, who built the first lodge on Songentrope Creek. It was well known throughout the middle woods as a place of magnificent vistas and clear water.

He looked back and carefully asked, "You are asking me if this creature you look for, whose home is under a bright sun, is walking the forest somewhere as we talk? You would have me believe this is true? In the many years I have lived here, no saurian has ever been seen in the forest. They walk the world beyond the northern edge. However," he said, noticing his son quivering on the ground, "I will tell you this. My family and I will watch for it. What name is it known by, skink?"

"Scalar," Red Spear replied, "and he's got two friends with 'em named Borgjump and Barkchew. And if I was you, beaver, I wouldn't talk about this with nobody; for if it gets back to Scalar you did, Keltar is your only hope." The skink pointed his spear at him.

The beaver contemplated this and replied, half smiling. "Then perhaps the one you seek can be found within the Whispering Woods," he said, pointing in that direction.

Blue Spear looked up and about fainted. His voice wavered. "Nobody goes there. Even we have never been there."

"Then perhaps you should choose the other way," said the beaver, glaring and pointing east.

Red Spear turned his head. Neither he nor his brother knew anything about those woods or what lived there. He glanced over at his brother, who was loath to choose that path. But they also had nothing to report to Keltar.

"What do you know of that place?"

"Nothing," he said, smiling.

Red Spear motioned his head at his brother and both backed away. The beaver smiled and watched them scamper off into the Eastern Forest. Just as they ran under the first trees, Blue Spear looked up and shivered before following his brother deeper into the shadows.

Darmok's son jumped up. "Father, I'm scared. Are the terrible lizards going to come here?"

He looked down and said, unsmiling, "Speak no more of this. Return to the lodge now."

The younger beaver nodded. Just before he plunged into the water, he thought he heard his father whisper, "Do not worry about them. It's not us they should be worried about."

# 14. THE WOODLAND OF THE EAST

IT WAS NEARLY MIDDAY BEFORE TENARA, JOEN AND THE TWO scouts spotted a clearing under the tall trees. Since crossing the Songentrope Creek, they had been walking in silence under a thick canopy of leaves, hoping the sun would appear to improve their mood. But that didn't happen. Along the way, they looked for flowers and small streams, but none could be found. It was as if they were in a desert of giant trees, all the same, everywhere they looked.

Tenara also noticed that Blendefest's behavior had changed since entering the strange forest. At times, she saw him staring at the trees as if something ominous was about to happen. He had certainly not been himself since leaving the creek.

Frondameer broke the silence. "The light appears to be coming from all directions, offering us no clues as to which way is east now. We will stop there," he said, pointing to a clearing just ahead surrounded by several boulders that appeared to have been placed intentionally in a circle.

Tenara arrived first and pulled herself up on one. She peered up at the canopy overhead. "Joen, do you remember the cave on the mountain in the Western Forest where we slept the first night after leaving Moss Rock?"

"Ughhhh," she replied, looking back.

"I know. But I think I would take it over this dismal place. Did you notice the tops of these trees?"

"No. What about them?" she asked, looking at Blendefest, who was also staring in the same direction.

Tenara replied in a slow voice, "They seem to be alive at the top. But down here, there's nothing. And where are the leaves under our feet? Surely some must have fallen. Blendefest, did you notice it as well?"

The two scouts looked quizzically at Tenara. "No, I didn't," Blendefest replied in a distant voice.

"You ok? I saw you looking around a lot on the way here. Should we know something?"

"No. This is just new to me as well."

Frondameer stared at him for a moment.

Joen looked down at her feet. "Yeah, it's strange. While coming here, I felt like I was walking on something, but perhaps it's just how the ground is."

Tenara jumped off the boulder. "That's it! I felt it too. You don't suppose…." and with that, she walked into middle of the clearing while scuffing her feet along the forest floor. Then she felt something move against her leg. An outline of a leaf appeared and then disappeared just as quickly.

She kicked harder and the ghost of a leaf appeared and faded again. "Frondameer, Blendefest, come over here and look at this!" She motioned.

"You found something?" Blendefest inquired.

She nodded her head. "Put your foot here, and give it a hard kick like you're hitting a rock."

He did and suddenly all three of them saw a leaf with seven points float off the floor of the forest and fall back slowly to the ground. But then, something extraordinary happened - it disappeared.

Frondameer's mouth fell open. "It's a Camelio leaf! There is one on the walls of our cottage at Moss Rock. It was brought back by another scout long ago when I was very little. Do you remember it, Blend?"

Blendefest squatted down and waved his arm across the ground. "Carried back by the one who was my mentor, the reason I joined the lodge. He said his greatest adventure would be his last trip."

"You think he found it here?" asked Tenara, still staring at the ground.

He shook his head slightly. "I only remember him talking about when he was chased into this forest by a vicious woods mole at sunset. While running, he stumbled into a pit and then readied his weapon. But nothing came. In the last rays of sunlight, he said he saw some leaves float down and eerily disappear. But what happened next was even stranger: a sudden flash of light above followed by an anguished cry."

Joen's eyes got as large as saucers. "What happened then?!"

Blendefest looked over at her with the faintest of smiles. "He fell asleep."

Joen said loudly, "He fell ASLEEP?! That's it?!"

The scout nodded once. "The next morning, he climbed out to find the woods mole had gone. But there was something else.

He saw an arrow driven into the ground that pointed in the direction he needed to go to find his partner."

"So he got back ok?" Tenara asked with an anxious voice.

"Yes. They later returned to Moss Rock, without finding the owner of the arrow."

Frondameer looked at Blendefest. "This is why you have been so quiet."

Blendefest stood up and, without any words, returned to the rock circle.

Joen followed him back. "You think there are any of those woods moles nearby?"

"If there are, there is little we can do about it."

She fell back against a rock. "That wasn't very reassuring."

Frondameer came up behind her. "You have your dagger tooth."

"You're not helping."

Tenara spoke up. "Where is this mentor of yours now?"

Frondameer answered from behind her, "He left to find the owner of the arrow."

"Did he?"

"We don't know." Frondameer looked over at Blendefest, who turned away. "He was never heard from again."

Tenara nodded. "So there was another scout who's been here before. You didn't think to mention that?! And the fact that you have not been here either?"

Blendefest turned to her. "I remind you that this quest is more than just finding your friends. The Saurians of the North have been found in the forest. We must know why."

Frondameer walked over. "Do you remember anything further?" Blendefest sighed loudly. "Only that the arrow was made of an odd-looking wood with a glowing point at the end. And that it contained glyphs that were similar to the inscriptions at the foot of the willow tree that shades Moss Rock."

Tenara saw the look of surprise in Frondameer's eyes. She started to ask another question, but he held his hand high. "We have a problem."

Tenara spoke up. "Something else you didn't mention?"

Frondameer ignored the remark. "We need to search north and east to look for signs of your friends as well as the lizards, but I have found no clues on which way that would be." He glanced at Tenara. "You must help as well. Look for birds. Normally they are good guides for direction, but I've seen few since this morning."

Tenara asked, "Look where?"

Frondameer laughed. "We are a lot alike, Tenara. We ask a lot of questions. When I was young, I was taken to the woods to learn the ways of the forest. Many times, I was asked, 'Did you see that?' I would answer, 'No.' My father, who was a scout himself, then pointed to the things I missed. Be patient."

Joen interrupted, "You saw some birds?"

He smiled, walked over to a tree, and knelt. "Early this morning, I saw some fly into these woods and flutter around the bottom of the trees, as if they were looking for something. I was distracted at that moment and when I looked back, they were gone. My intuition tells me they didn't leave. Perhaps their nest or burrow is on the ground or near a tree."

Tenara looked down. "How can a bird give us directions?"

Frondameer stood up, allowing some dirt to fall through his

hands. "They must have water, like us, but I have seen none since leaving the river. My assumption is that they fly back west. If we see one, then finding northeast will be simple.

"Please choose a tree and look around. But do not go beyond sight, and make no noise while you search. We do not know what lives in these woods or what may be lurking about."

Joen watched the scouts take off in separate directions and then looked at Tenara. "Don't go far. Ok?"

Tenara smiled. She knew Joen had the greatest fear of being alone. "Not far."

She stopped a moment to check if the others were in sight, and then proceeded to the nearest tree. As soon as she walked up, she heard a humming and saw a sudden blur. She focused her eyes carefully for a hint at whatever it was and then, seeing nothing, she kicked the dirt and mumbled, "Show yourself."

At that same time, the outline of a Camelio leaf flashed for a second before disappearing. "Ahhh," she whispered. She dropped down to her knees and quickly moved her hand over the dirt to push the leaves away.

"There you are," she whispered. Nestled between the joints of the knobby roots was a small hole. She started to lean down when suddenly a blue-striped bird shot out and fluttered its wings. It then puffed up its chest while looking straight at her and pulled the leaf back over its hole.

She immediately ran back to Frondameer to tell him the news, but before she could say anything, Blendefest came up and began his own report. "The birds must cover their tracks well. I found no clue to anything that flies."

Frondameer shook his head. "I too am perplexed."

Tenara looked around and then touched Fron-dameer on his back. "Where is Joen?" she asked. "I saw her earlier but not since I've been here. Blendefest?"

"Only in the beginning, when we first left. She was moving in that direction." He pointed.

"Quickly now, she can't be far!"

But after an hour of calling her name and searching the forest nearby, they gave up. Joen was gone and Tenara was left sitting on the ground in shock.

# 15. MISSING

A SHORT DISTANCE AWAY, JOEN HAD BEEN PRESSED TO THE ground by a demon-eyed skink with a long red spear. His brother grinned at their captive and how they had tracked the four so far into the forest.

Blue Spear observed quietly, "Lookie here what came to us. Now, why would we be a seeing such a sight, brother?"

"Maybe its friends don't like it no more."

"Or perhaps they just ain't as smart as they thought." Red Spear glared down at his prisoner. "There are many things I want to do to you, but we got no time. You seen a Saurian anywhere?" He pushed a spear into her back, breaking the skin. "Well?"

"No," Joen cried out, trying to push the spear away. "I don't even know what that is."

"She IS dumb," said Blue Spear, grumbling. "What do ya know about Keltar?"

She hesitated. There was something she remembered from Moss Rock.

"I don't mess with them and neither should you. They're a lot bigger than me and would have no problem squashing you who are only a little bit taller than me." Joen grimaced.

The other one interrupted, "I see the others walking away beyond them trees. Let's take her back as a trophy. Keltar can use her as a slave."

"Up you go. Move it," Blue Spear ordered, pushing the spear again. "Make a sound and this goes right through you. And don't try to get away, because my tail is faster than you know. And it will sting you into a long sleep."

Joen looked at it and wondered if that was true. Only the senior scouts would know such things. She pulled herself up and gently rested her hand on her dagger tooth.

"And you can forget about that little bitty weapon o' yours!"

She knew by now her friends would be frantically looking for her, but fearfully, she worried for what Tenara would do.

"Which way back to Songentrope Creek?" Blue Spear asked his brother.

"That way I think," said the skink, looking quizzically to his right.

"How 'bout you?" he asked, pointing his spear at Joen. "Which way?"

Right now, all she wanted to do was to run as fast as possible from these two horrible creatures and rejoin her friends, but the danger to them made her change her mind. Instead, she stared back at both of them, wondering if they were born upside down. She had to take the gamble.

"This way," she said, pointing.

"Well, then get along," Blue Spear said, sneering. "We don't got all day."

Joen glared back and walked off. After a few hours of silence her captors noticed the light beginning to fade. Thirst was constantly on their minds, but the one stream they crossed was too small and insignificant to offer any refreshment. Red Spear suddenly felt the sun on his face and looked up to find an opening in the forest canopy. At the same time, he noticed his shadow was behind him.

"Stop!" he growled, running up to the front. "You lied to us! My shadow is behind me, which means you are taking us deeper into this forest. You said you knew the way west to Songentrope Creek! "

"I have no idea what you're talking about," she replied innocently. Puffing her face up, "I've never been here. As far as I know, we were doing well. Course, pushing that stick in my back may have helped mixed me up some. Anyway, serves you right. I'm tired."

She abruptly sat down and quickly noticed most of the trees in the clearing were young. What caught her eye was the one closest, with the lowest limbs. She looked back at the two skinks, who were pacing back and forth nervously, and an idea started forming in her head.

Suddenly, one of them stopped. "Well," said Blue Spear confidently, "since we know which way now, let's turn 'round and go back."

Red Spear walked over and slapped him on the head. "We don't got time for that! It'll be dark soon." Pointing to the sun, he said, "You shouldn't ah asked her opinion in the first place."

His brother grimaced. "You didn't think of a way, so why throw it on me?"

"Because you're always slowing me down," said the other, tightening his grip on his spear while moving toward his brother.

Blue Spear pointed his weapon back. "Yeah? Well, you decided to be leader when we left Grivelridge. And what did it get us?"

"You fool!" exclaimed Red Spear out loud.

While they were arguing, Joen inched herself slowly away until she was just beneath the closest limb. Standing up slowly, she reached up and pulled herself gradually into the canopy. After securing a good foothold, she looked around to ensure she was hidden and found a small peephole from which she could watch the skinks closely. She was now grateful to the scouts for introducing climbing to her.

"What are you going to do? Huh?" said Blue Spear. "Leave me here and face the king by yerself?"

Red Spear just glared at him for a moment. Pulling his spear back, he stabbed at the ground and then looked around for their prisoner.

"You stupid oaf, you let her get away!" he spat.

Blue Spear looked around quickly as well. "She ain't so far," he said in shock, holding his spear tightly. Then, looking around, he said, "You check over there." He pointed to the far edge of the clearing, away from the sun.

They searched the base of every tree and rock within the clearing, but the prisoner was not found. Exhausted, they returned to the center and sat down. Blue Spear looked up. "Perhaps she went up one of them trees."

"Them kind don't climb!" he said, shaking his head. "When was the last time you saw one of 'em climb?"

"Never, but maybe YOU can climb up one and look yerself, since you so smart!" Blue Spear said with a smile. "See that tree there?" Incredibly, he pointed to the very one that Joen was hiding in. "Just you go over there, get yerself up and see what you find."

"I ain't no squirrel."

"You is scared," laughed Blue Spear, who stood up and stabbed his spear in the ground. While looking back at his brother, he walked over and grabbed a lower limb. Then he thought better of it and started to let go. At that instant, he heard the tiniest of noises from the canopy above. Removing his hand from the limb, he motioned his brother over and winked. Pointing up, he said out loud, "Maybe she got away and is running back to her friends."

"Yeah," he said, smiling while tiptoeing away into the forest to hide behind a tree.

For a long while, there was no sound or movement from the tree. Exasperated, Blue Spear yelled, "We know you up there! Give me your spear, brother. I want to toss it and see if anything comes down," he said, smiling.

"Forget it! Use yer own!" he griped. "Cause if it gets stuck, you can just climb up yerself and get it!"

His brother glared at him for a moment, then retrieved his own and aimed it carefully. With a hard throw, he tossed it up. Joen held her breath as it struck a limb and fell back, banging on the lower limbs as it went down. The next throw, however, was much closer and made her yelp when its tip brushed her skin, before falling away.

Red Spear, surprised at his brother's intuition, joined in. "Getting closer, are we?" He giggled.

This time, Blue Spear threw it closer to the trunk, but on the way in, it buried itself in a limb just beneath Joen's feet. She reached down and tried to lift it with her foot, but just when she reached for the weapon, it broke free and fell to the ground.

Blue Spear dashed to his weapon and quickly brought it back. "This is your last chance or you're coming down on the end of my spear!"

Wanting to prove himself the better warrior, he reared back and was ready to throw it when he felt something on his back that was sharp and uncomfortable.

From behind him, a voice said, "I find it puzzling that two of your clan are so far from home."

Blue Spear slowly turned around and faced two giant frogs dressed in armor that shined in the light, making him squint. Underneath the metal were blue and gray frocks attached to their necks by a ring of rounded stones that seemed to glitter in the sunlight. His brother was sitting down on the ground with a massive spear pointed at his head.

The one behind Blue Spear came around and took his weapon, then asked indifferently, "Why are you so interested in the one up there?"

"What do yer mean?" Ignoring him, the other giant moved to the tree and climbed it effortlessly until it was out of sight. Just above, Joen jumped back in fright when this new face appeared within the protected cover of her patch. "All is ok, little one," he said in a soft voice. "You are with friends, so it is time come down, unless you like the comfort of a bird." She shook her head in silence and stared at his large eyes and her glittering reflection in his decorative amour.

She followed him slowly to the ground, where they both landed just in front of the twin skinks. Joen brushed herself off and walked up to Blue Spear. "You don't aim too good, do you?"

The skink frowned at the insolence but was unable to reply with the giant warrior holding his neck tight.

The other observed, "Soon it will be dark and that which prowls the night will have no mercy on any of you. Because of this, you will come with us."

"Where?" Red Spear asked suspiciously.

"Does it matter? Or do you wish to remain here and take your chances? If so, we will look for you again tomorrow, if you have not been eaten by then."

"No. No. We're good!" he said, coughing from the chokehold.

The giant looked at them indifferently. "My people will provide you food and protection. Later you will be released, if that is the decision of our queen, the one we call the Stone Changer. I am Feyorin and my companion is Baldmar."

Turning to Joen, Feyorin smiled slightly. "Young one, you will walk with Baldmar." "You two," he said, unsmiling, "will accompany me."

"What about our weapons?" Red Spear asked insolently.

Feyorin leaned down to retrieve both and said nothing.

"Well? What about us?" Red Spear growled anxiously, desperate to know what future was in store for them.

Feyorin abruptly turned his back and walked off, saying, "As I said, your fate and hers will be decided soon enough."

# 16. The Lighted City

Joen looked up and noticed an unusual rock hanging from Baldmar's neck. It cast an eerie glow that reflected off his armor and onto the ground. "Where did you find a stone that lights your way in the forest?"

Without breaking his stride, Feyorin replied, "They are called mystic stones and are found in the caverns, deep within the foot of our mountain. Each of us is given one at birth to remind us of our origin and purpose."

She looked puzzled. "You sort of look like some friends of mine, who come from a place called Moss Rock. They are clever like you."

"I am not familiar with that place, but there are others of my kind who have traveled beyond the edge of Shadowguard."

"Shadowguard?" Joen asked.

"Where we walk now: what you know as the Eastern Forest."

Joen looked up at him anxiously. "I mention this because I lost my friends in this Shadowguard: the ones I spoke about.

With each step, I fear that I am moving further away and may never see their faces again."

"If they are as wise as you say, then you need not concern yourself."

"I hope so," said Joen in a low voice.

"It is dark now, so we must remain quiet. It is not much further."

Joen looked ahead and followed quietly in the soft light of Baldmar and Feyorin's stones. After a brief time, she looked up in the hope of seeing some stars, but none were found. However, when she looked directly ahead, she saw a dim light flickering in the distance. She squinted in puzzlement and curiosity. With every step, the light became brighter, like a morning sunrise about to make its entrance, yet, strangely, the shadows still clung fast to their backs. Finally, the huge trees gave way to a towering wall whose sides stretched across the bottom of a mountain. On it were evenly spaced stones that threw their light against the shadows that raced back into the forest.

After a few more moments, they were greeted by two sentinels, dressed similarly to Baldmar and Feyorin, that spoke quietly to both while occasionally glancing at Joen and the two skinks in tow. After what seemed a long time, Feyorin turned back to her. "You will be taken to a cottage deep within our village."

"Will I see you again?" asked Joen.

"Yes. We must now return to the forest."

"Will you look for my friends?" she asked anxiously.

They nodded once and were gone.

Their guides then escorted them into the lighted village and up a long hill near the edge of the mountain. One turned to Joen and pointed to a cottage built into the face of a rock and lit by the same odd stones that seemed to cover the city.

They abruptly surrounded the skinks and said bluntly, "You two will come with us to another place. There will be food and drink for you as well and a place to sleep."

The Dither Twins looked at each other and then back, distrustful as ever.

The first guide turned to Joen. "You will leave us now. This is your place of rest. There is another, like you, that lives there. He is very old."

Joen thanked him and remained for a moment, watching her escorts disappear up the long path with the skinks firmly between them. She then looked at the dwelling again. The house was made of smooth rock with a tall slender door on the front and many differently shaped windows scattered around it. In fact, all of them looked as if they had been thrown on the walls by a blind man facing the other direction.

One in particular that caught her eye was tiny. It stood close the ground and next to the front door. Leaning over, she peered inside to ensure there was nothing that would cause her a fright.

But what she saw instead were two eyes looking back. The fright was so bad she screamed and fell back on the grass. Then, just a moment later, the door burst open and a hand reached out. "Oh me, oh my, what have I done? My poor dear, I am so sorry. Please come in," he said, waving her to the door.

Joen just nodded while being pulled to her feet. As soon as she walked in, she saw her host move to a sink with a small stove beside it. He was dressed in an apron that covered a shirt of shiny green material held to his waist by a belt of colored stones. Long pants fell to his feet, partially covering his green and brown shoes that had long passed their prime.

Something was cooking and it smelled wonderful.

"Oh me, where are my manners? Here I go again. Hello, hello," said the stranger, pulling his hands out of the water and tossing a towel to a hook on the wall.

"Hi," said Joen, still confused.

"My name is Fladon and I was told that there would be visitors from the forest. Come in, come in, and tell me all about your adventures while we wait for your friends."

# 17. THE WAY FORWARD

EARLIER THAT DAY, THE SEARCH FOR JOEN CONTINUED THROUGH-
out the morning and most of the afternoon. Her loss had been a
blow to the team's morale. Now it was getting late in the day and
the scouts had become increasing worried that the answer to
her disappearance did not lie nearby. Tenara, however, was still
swept with guilt from the loss of Joen and continued to walk the
forest for clues that might help them find her friend.

Frondameer came up behind her. "We can do no more. Blendefest and I are confident that she is no longer nearby."

"I did this to her. It was my fault," she said quietly.

"She had a choice as well. Do not forget why you left your
home. But right now, we cannot allow ourselves to be lost in
these woods. The only way we can help her is to continue our
search tomorrow. And that will not happen until we know which
way to walk."

He waited for a reply, but she kept staring into the distance.

He walked back. "The ground has little vegetation and these
are the only rocks we have found. You remember. We passed
over and around these stones many times and found no tracks."

Blendefest walked up, looking exasperated. "This forest confounds me! It is like no other I have experienced in the way it hides its secrets."

"Hides its secrets?" Tenara asked.

Blendefest looked down, not sure what to say.

She exclaimed, "Wait. Just before Joen went missing, I was about to tell you something."

They both looked at her curiously. "Yes?"

"The birds…if the leaves hide the ground, they also…."

"Hide the nests," finished Frondameer. "Of course!" he added, clenching his fist. "Well done!"

She continued, "When I was sitting near the bottom of a tree, I brushed my hand against the ground and some Camelio leaves suddenly appeared. Before they floated back down, I saw what looked like a burrow among the roots. Reaching down, I moved a leaf carefully aside to peak at the hole and a bird popped out and gave me a most unpleasant face!"

Frondameer turned to the other scout. "Blendefest, look for the same nearby."

Tenara walked off. "If you find their nest," she said loudly, "be sure to cover it quickly. I think that the birds sort of get quite huffy when they're disturbed."

Frondameer and Blendefest shook their heads and continued forward. She heard one of them mumbling, "Touchy birds, if that's all we have to worry about."

Within a short time, they had indeed discovered several burrows, all of which were on the same side of the tree relative to the rock circle.

"So," Frondameer said happily, "the forest finally gave up one of its secrets. We know the direction we first came to the circle and now we know this. So we continue this way." He pointed.

"But we must wait until tomorrow to continue," said Blendefest, pointing at a darkening sky.

"Yes, of course."

Tenara stared into the dark forest again and then sadly turned to follow the scouts. Once in the clearing, Frondameer pointed and said quietly, "We will rest behind those two stones and use them for protection."

"You are expecting something?" asked Tenara.

"I am not sure. Like Blendefest, I am also uneasy in this forest. Something is wrong about it."

After finishing the few scraps of food left, Tenara sat down beside Frondameer and drifted off to sleep, leaving Blendefest as guard. The darkness that crawled over them now was impenetrable.

After a few hours, Frondameer awakened and exchanged places with his partner. He was about to sit down for his two-hour watch when he heard a sharp whistle.

Then he saw a flash of light in the forest. A moment later, a crashing sound followed, and then another to his left and just beyond his sight. He quickly pulled his sword out and listened closely, trying to sense the location of the threat that was ravaging the ground beyond his vision. But without light, he was defenseless. That meant the attack could come from any direction.

A whisper came from behind. "Why didn't you wake me. You want the beast yourself?" asked Blendefest.

"You can have the second one."

Another explosion to their right was followed by a *whump!* nearby that sprayed dirt into their faces.

From out of the blackness, a light shot through the air and disappeared in an explosion of sparks on the rocks nearby. What followed was the unmistakable sound of a yelp, followed by a thunderous crash that vibrated the ground around them. Another explosion came, then the sound of something thrashing against the rocks, filling the forest with an aura of hate and violence that was more terrifying than anything they had previously experienced.

## 18. HOPE

THE ATTACK RATTLED THE SCOUTS AND TENARA SO MUCH THAT none found any more sleep that night. Each waited patiently for the ghostly glow of early morning to give reason for what happened during the night. Only when first light crept across the ground did they begin to feel safe once more. But it was short lived; a thick mist soon descended and once again blinded them.

Tenara spoke up. "Have you ever experienced anything like that before?"

"Never. It's as if this place wants us to leave or die. Let us hope that Joen is safe," Frondameer replied.

"So you suggest continuing east?" Blendefest asked, walking around and looking for evidence of what they had heard last night.

"I do. And I am also filled with confidence that we will somehow survive this mysterious place."

"You believe that?" he asked, holding up a fist of fur pulled from one of the nearby rocks.

"Hmmm. Think about it, Blend. That beast or whatever

it was could have easily taken us, but something or someone stopped it. And how could they have Fire rocks?!"

"I don't know, Frond. You remember what I said when we first entered this place?"

Frondameer gazed at Blendefest for a moment, ignoring the comment, and then turned to Tenara. "Are you ok?"

"Are you serious?!" She scowled. Inside, she was terrified at what just happened and irritated with the scouts for their lack of experience.

Frondameer turned to face her but no words emerged from his mouth.

Tenara looked away and said, "Can we just find her and leave?"

Frondameer looked at the mist. "Of course."

"The fog will slow our progress," responded Blendefest, hidden in the mist just beyond their sight.

After only a few minutes of walking, they once more stopped to determine what direction they faced. The rolling fog continued to make it difficult to keep on course. They quickly visited several trees nearby, looking for other nests. Again and again, they repeated the pattern until the fog lifted in the morning heat. Soon after that, the trees began to change their shapes. The tall sentinels that reached to the sky before were now a mix of smaller ones much closer together. The nests became fewer and fewer until none could be found.

"Well, that's it!" said Blendefest, disillusioned after finding an empty tree base for the third in a row. "What have we missed?"

"Perhaps if you dug further down, the answer could be found," said a voice in the distance.

The scouts reached for their weapons and pushed their backs to each other, ready to strike at the disembodied voice.

It added, "Further down, you would have stuck a rock that is emblazoned with lines from the great mountains, back when sheets of ice first covered this place. They point east and west. Is not east the direction of your travel? You seek Bulltop, do you not?"

Frondameer squinted his eyes at the mist, trying to discern where the voice was coming from. "If you know so much, then you must know that one of our group is missing."

"We do." A long moment passed before two apparitions emerged from fog with heavy spears at their side. They were slightly taller than the scouts and imposing with their armor and robes.

"There is no further need for you to look for that one. The way forward is with us. I am known as Feyorin, and this is Baldmar. We have been aware of your presence in our forest since shortly after you crossed the Songentrope Creek."

Both scouts were stunned.

Feyorin looked down and then at Baldmar, who in turn replied, "All those who are in this forest, invited or not, are known to us."

"I am dreadfully worried about her. I am Tenara."

"Frondameer," he said, sheathing his sword. My companion Blendefest…."

"Of the village known as Moss Rock," continued Feyorin.

"Yes!" said Frondameer, startled. "How do you know this and have such knowledge of our forest as well? Do you also walk among our woods and swim our rivers?"

"Baldmar and I do not. However, there are those of us who have. But the knowledge of your village was brought to us from one like you," he said, looking directly at the scouts.

"Like us? I don't understand," replied Frondameer

"Someone in your past who, like you, was also a wanderer of places and a collector of things."

The scouts looked at each other. Blendefest replied suspiciously, "There was only one like you describe who did not return to Moss Rock. However, he cannot be the one, since he would be too old to still be in this world."

"Then perhaps I am mistaken." He paused. "I can see from your eyes that you have many questions. Come. We are expected back before the fall of night."

They quietly followed their strange guides until the sun was low once again. After a few hours, both scouts noticed the trees had shifted into giants once again. Frondameer was just getting ready to ask how much further when they burst out into the light of the setting sun. A sigh of relief fell from his lips when the last shadows of the giant trees fell behind him.

Before his eyes stood a magnificent village set upon the foot of the mountain, sweeping far up its base. Inside its walls, they saw many dwellings: some sunk into the side of the mountain while others, like fixtures, hung from the rocks above. Just in front was an entrance gate that framed a single painting of a tree. Looking closer, Tenara saw a pair of eyes staring out between the limbs, as if the tree itself was watching them. And, on each side, stood a wooden tower supporting a single rounded stone marked by strange runes.

Tenara looked in awe and exclaimed, "Who made all of this?"

"The Stone Changers," said Feyomir without hesitation or feeling. "It is Orora, our village. Come."

After passing through the gate, they entered a plaza made up of several stone buildings, each decorated with flowers of every color and kind. In the middle were multiple Ororans busily chipping away at rocks, many of which had been turned into fine works of art. Beyond that, the road began to climb. Almost immediately, they began to pass huge boulders that were shaped into buildings with entrances on the top, sides, and even overhead. Upon reaching the end of the thoroughfare, they turned around and saw the swirling mists riding above the dark forest, lit red by the setting sun.

They turned back and let their eyes travel up the mountain and over crests of snow disappearing and reappearing behind the shifting clouds that framed the deep blue sky.

Feyorin interrupted their thoughts. "We must leave you now. This," he said, nodding at the cottage on their right, "is your home for however long you would like to remain." He then looked directly at the scouts. "You all do our place honor. We will talk more in the days that follow. Until then."

Abruptly, they left, leaving the scouts perplexed and not sure what to do. Frondameer stood still a moment, looking amazed. "How is it that we have not known of this place or its people?

No one said anything. Then Frondameer took the lead and rapped on the door with his fingers. In a moment, they heard a small voice. "I will get it, Fladon." The door opened. There, before Tenara, Frondameer, and Blendefest, stood Joen with eyes as big as saucers.

# 19. ORORA

TENARA RUSHED INTO THE HOUSE, NEARLY CRASHING INTO ITS owner, who was laughing at the cheerful reunion. After everyone embraced, the scouts turned their attention to Fladon.

Blendefest looked, dumbfounded, at the stranger. "Can it be?" he asked in a quiet voice. He walked over and looked deeply into the man's eyes. "I know you."

"You should, my boy. What have you learned since I left?"

A smile spread across his face. "That the world is stranger than I first believed."

"Then you passed, Mr. B.," his gravelly voice growled. "Tell me about Moss Rock now. I so dearly miss the place and wonder sometimes how many new things you have stuffed into that cottage of yours. And tell me too, how is Mrs. Gilgatop and that pompous old husband of hers?"

"They all miss you, sir…as do I. They will be grateful to know that you are well."

He nodded. "And your partner; this must be Frondameer?" He turned to greet him. "Your mother was a great inspiration to me and also a scout at heart. Did you know that she even suggested some of the places I visited? She wanted very much to be a part of every adventure. I see that you have her eyes. She is well?"

"She is," he said, bowing his head. "My father is gone now and she has taken to studying the writings under the Great Tree."

"Indeed now, has she! And what has she learned?"

"That perhaps our village was born from the hands of others, from another place entirely."

Fladon smiled lightly. "And what place would that be?"

Frondameer shook his head. "She does not know."

"It is always good to know one's past. Perhaps you will find some answers before you return."

"That would be most helpful. But I am puzzled by something," Frondameer continued, looking directly at Fladon. "I remember years ago a story about a great scout who left one day and never returned. Many of us wondered what happened. We looked him for a long time, but gave up for lack of clues."

"Perhaps he didn't want to be found. There are many things that have changed since that time, like the sword at your side."

Frondameer grimaced. "Anzenar has become increasing dangerous, Fladon. Alliances within its forests have been created where none existed before. Friends like the chameleons can no longer be trusted and have taken up with the Saurians that have been seen walking the forest."

Fladon sat down in a chair woven from purple vines. "Yes. I've heard such things." He took a deep breath. "It's true that Anzenar has changed. But so too has the danger it faces now.

And, as you said, the great dragon lizards have begun to look south. Have you two been to Gravenbroke?"

Frondameer nodded his head. "Many times. But one thing you may not know. It was the Colonel's orders that sent us east. But we are at a loss at why."

Fladon nodded his head. "Interesting. When did you learn about the Saurians in the North? Eh?"

"Since joining the scouts and I saw a map within our cottage that marks their location."

"Did you know that it was I that created it? Eh?" he asked, looking deeply at the scout.

Frondameer's mouth fell open.

Fladon commanded, "Come with me." Frondameer and the others followed him to the stone terrace outside the small house. In a sweeping gesture, their host continued, "I've lived here a long time. But a few things I know now. The Eastern Forest of giant trees and the Anduin Mountain keeps Orora hidden from Anzenar. Did you know it was built before Moss Rock? In fact, its builders go back to a time before the Saurians arrived."

Everyone began to talk, but Fladon held his hand up. "Hear me out," he said. "Yes, even before," he repeated nodding.

Frondameer and Blendefest looked aghast at Fladon.

"You need to know that the hills of Anduin that shadow this city…are the same that shadow the Saurians, and their king Keltar. The Ororans haven't told me everything, but I believe this village has been here as long as the lizard king ruled Gravenbroke. And they're watching them. Oh yes. And now they know he's turned his eyes south toward Anzenar. You said before that you didn't know why the lizards were seen in the forest?"

Frondameer nodded.

"It is because Keltar's brother left to seek his own throne - an act of treason. So the king sent others to look for him."

"He left alone?"

"No. Two others left with him."

Fladon leaned forward. "If they are not found, Keltar will lead his army into Anzenar, plundering everything until his revenge is complete. But the worry is this," he said, pointing down at the village. "In their search for the three, they must not find Orora."

For a moment, everyone was quiet, and then Tenara spoke. "Those lizards could be anywhere in the forest now."

Frondameer interjected, "Not anywhere. We know they are not east of Moss Rock and not within the forest where Feyorin and Baldmar found us. They would have said so. I suggest we look south along the Songentrope."

Fladon stood up. "Perhaps," he said pensively. "There is a council tomorrow between Jraden, the master of this village, and his immediate staff. You already met two of them: they brought you here. There is also the possibility that you will meet their queen, Miralassen, also known as the Stone Changer. If you do, I suggest that you answer her directly. She will determine your future now."

# 20. THE COUNCIL AND THE STONE CHANGER

TENARA OPENED HER EYES AFTER A LONG SLEEP AND LOOKED around for the others but found no one nearby. Fearful that something horrible had happened, she rushed outside to find Blendefest and Frondameer calmly talking to each other on the terrace, which overlooked the city below. Before they could greet her, she ran back inside and saw Joen casually walking down the stairs, munching on something dark that smelled like sweet bread.

"If you're looking for Fladon, he's not here," she said between bites.

The shock of seeing her ok brought a smile to Tenara's face. "Actually, I was looking for you. Where did Fladon go?"

She shook her head, stepping off the bottom step. "No one knows, but someone left a nice breakfast upstairs."

Tenara strolled out to the terrace to find the two scouts still quietly talking. She walked over to its edge and gazed at the forest canopy below, where splotches of mist drifted quietly in the wind. Closer in, the velvety green trees gave way to smaller seedlings and grass that bordered the village to the west. Peering ever closer, she could see a few of the city's inhabitants walking casually along the forest edge beyond the wall. And still closer, just inside the walls, she heard a buzz of voices mingling in the squares below, where food and supplies were traded by the Ororans.

She looked out over the impressive village. On each side of the entrance gate, a wall extended around the village and up the gray rock of the mountain, where it turned and merged into tall obelisk of green stone. At each corner was another rounded rock that shone brightly in the morning light, just like the ones on the gate towers.

The city center was a mixture of houses of all shapes, each perched beside paths of soft moss and clay that contrasted with the hard stone of the streets. In its center was a fountain that cascaded into a huge pond that shimmered in the sunlight. And from that pond emerged the laughter that permeated the village, giving it a feeling of solitude and peace. She wondered if it would last.

It was truly a beautiful place and beyond anything that Tenara had ever dreamed of. As the old raccoon said, there was so much more to the Great Land of Anzenar than Rippleshy. Nevertheless, it was still not her home, the one she missed so much.

"It's amazing, isn't it?"

Startled, she turned to find Frondameer staring at her.

"Yes. Good morning."

"I agree but I find it disturbing as well," he said, unsmiling.

"How so?"

"The runes on the gate are similar to the ones found under

the willow in Moss Rock, which make no sense. And how has this city remained hidden for so long? Did you notice the balls that sit atop the walls?"

Nodding her head, she said, "They seem to glow."

"Yes. What magic is this? And where is Fladon?"

She shook her head and pointed up the hill. "We have company."

Two Ororans were strolling down the path. They appeared slightly different than the others that they'd encountered. Each was dressed in a green robe that fell from their shoulders to their feet and was fastened around their waist by a belt of woven ropes buckled with a large flat stone. In its center was etched a single rune. Frondameer squinted, noticing it was one of the runes they had seen on the gate when they first came through.

With a grave bow, the closest one approached. "The Stone Changer has ordered you to meet with her."

"I thought we were to meet with Jraden," Frondameer replied, surprised.

"No longer."

"As you wish," replied Blendefest.

The other shifted his eyes across the group. "One of you is missing. Find her."

"Yes," Tenara said, "she is in the cottage."

Joen came out the door and the group began following their escorts up the path. Very soon, they were passing homes and gardens that reminded Tenara of both Moss Rock and Rippleshy. Before long, the houses disappeared and the path itself became a series of markings that pointed to a large entrance carved in the mountain just ahead.

After entering, they descended through a hall lit by hundreds of small glowing rocks lining the walls and floor. Very soon after, they passed into a larger cavern where many of the citizens were quietly facing a female that was adorned in sparkling gems and rich cloths. Her age was impossible to tell.

Joen was shocked to see the Dither Twins there as well, chattering to themselves. She looked closely and saw them making faces at her just before one of their guards whispered something in their ears. Their eyes flew open and they suddenly became quiet and civil.

One of their escorts pointed to the floor. "Please sit." As they did, their guides returned to the tunnel and disappeared.

Tenara looked at the female and was shocked to find Fladon sitting quietly behind and to her right.

The woman raised her hand and paused just before she looked at the visitors. "Why did you come here?"

Her abruptness caught Frondameer off guard. He stared back for a moment and then stood up. "To seek lost friends."

"And what made you think you would find them here?"

"Because there were no clues to be found west of your land.

"And did you find them?"

"No."

"I suspect you have another reason to be here. Speak!"

Tenara saw Frondameer grimace. "We also look for clues as to why the great lizards are roaming the Northern forest. We are concerned they may be a threat to our village and the others who live nearby."

Before answering, she leaned over to Feyorin, who was also at her side, and whispered something. He nodded. She then looked back at Frondameer. "Your village is Moss Rock, is it not?"

"It is."

Miralassen waited a long moment before continuing, "For a long time we have been aware of all the villages within Anzenar. Moss Rock is one of those with which we share a history through our friend Fladon. However," she said, looking directly at Tenara, "I do not know of yours. Where is your home?" she asked.

Tenara stood and blushed. "Joen and I come from a place called Rippleshy. It is a beautiful village at the bottom of a mountain where the water is wonderful and cool to the touch."

"Are there many of you who live in this village?" she inquired.

"Yes. At-at least…there were," she stuttered.

"And what happened to those you speak about?"

"They disappeared. My friend Joen and I left to search for them."

The woman contemplated this.

"And you, the small one beside her. You are her companion?"

Joen was so frightened, she could only nod.

The Stone Changer stood up. She looked solely at Blendefest and Frondameer. "Scouts of Moss Rock," she said, pointing, "Fladon has stated that you have chosen to be with these two in their search?"

"Yes."

"And how have you found them to be?"

"As courageous as anyone we have met." Tenara and Joen blushed at the praise.

"Indeed!" she said, surprised. "Feyorin, Baldmar?" The two

walked up and faced the Stone Changer. "You both will train these visitors in our ways and then accompany them until they find the ones that disappeared."

They nodded. "Yes, my queen."

She looked at the four again. "Be warned, for I sense the loss of your friends is but part of a larger quest." She paused for a moment before continuing. "Since our arrival here, we have worked to build a great village that honors the forest and the mountain it cradles. And like you, we will defend it from those who have no respect for the living things that work and play within the forests or fly above her trees.

"Your observations about the lizards concern you. It should. Like us, they came across the mountain long ago and have been since content with their place under the sun. However, as you have said, we have also learned that some now move among the trees and possibly along the rocks at the base of the mountain as well."

She looked hard at the four guests. "Know this before you leave: there may come a time when I summon each of you back. You must agree to this as the price of my help. Decide now!"

Frondameer turned to the others, who nodded their heads, and then faced her. "We accept."

"Then it is done." Almost at once, her entourage joined her and they disappeared into a tunnel.

Fladon jumped down off the raised platform and quickly joined the scouts. "I could tell she was most impressed with you. Yes, yes, she was."

"Who is she, Fladon, and where did she come from?" Joen asked.

"You know who she is. Where she comes from…well, I'm not sure. What I can say is that she is a descendent of another who traveled here with many of her kind long ago. Some say that place was beyond the Anduin Mountain, where we stand now. But, maybe that's just a story."

"Beyond everything we know?" asked Joen.

"It seems so. But don't look at me. I stopped prowling the woods long ago. If there is, you will have to find it."

Tenara shook her head. "Not me. Maybe those two," she said, pointing to Frondameer and Blendefest. "They seem to enjoy it.

Fladon looked at her closely. "I don't think you know us quite well. Do you fear this place?"

"No. No. The people here are gentle and kind."

"And what about my home, Moss Rock?" he asked.

"Oh yes. It's a lovely place too. And your Colonel and his wife are very kind."

"Then…I do not understand. You chose to leave your village to look for your friends. But now you wish you wouldn't have left?"

She looked back at Blendefest and Frondameer, who had risked themselves coming here. And now the Ororans are offering the same help. Would she trade it all to be back in the secure surroundings of Rippleshy?

"No!" she shook her head emphatically.

Fladon just smiled. "Then perhaps you found the person you are."

She just stared at him, not knowing what to say.

A guard interrupted, "You both have been asked to return

to the surface and join Baldmar and Feyorin. They await you at the entrance."

It was near noon when they emerged from the ceremonial hall and found their two familiar guides standing just outside the entrance. Each was in the same green robes and armor they had been wearing when they first met. However, this time, their spears had been replaced with slender swords made of brown stone held in a scabbard under a wide black belt.

Feyorin was the first to speak. "Joen, you and the two Serveyans will accompany Baldmar to the Hall of Shapers. Tenara, I have been ordered to take you to the home of the Stone Changer. Afterwards, we will reunite at Fladon's cottage, where lunch is being prepared as I speak. Tomorrow, when the sun touches the top of the mountain, we will leave Orora together."

Joen just stood there in shock. Feyorin, seeing her distraught face, bent down, and whispered something in her ear. A second later, she smiled, and waved goodbye, leaving the two alone.

Tenara had to walk fast to keep up with her escort as he moved between several paths that crisscrossed the city. After several minutes, they arrived at a home emblazoned with a large blue rune on an oval door with a silver handle.

Feyorin looked down at Tenara. "This is the house of Miralassen, the Stone Changer who spoke to you earlier. She will see you now."

"You're leaving?" she asked in a slight panic.

"The invitation is for you and you alone. I will return later to bring you back."

Tenara was stunned. "She really wants to see just me?"

"Yes."

"But why?" she asked, perplexed.

"I do not question my queen. Go," he said, walking away.

Tenara climbed the steps and slowly opened the door. Just inside was a large room decorated by several objects on its walls. In a way, it reminded her of the scout's cottage and the fascinating objects that had been retrieved from so many places. But these were different. None of them were things made by the graceful hand of nature and found by the lucky few. Instead, they were sculptures born of the imaginations of fine artisans any museum would envy.

Further in, there were two chairs and a single wooden table where food and drink sat. And standing to its side was the same woman, still dressed in a long blue robe fastened at the neck and waist by two dazzling white stone buttons. She looked down at Tenara and gestured. "You are safe. Sit with me."

Tenara walked over and sat down. "Thank you." She was, in fact, terribly afraid that she had done something wrong.

The Lady of the Rocks sat beside her. "I find it puzzling that someone as small as you was willing to leave your village and venture into the forest blindly. Why did you do it?"

Tenara looked up. "I-I don't know. It seemed right at the time. I didn't want anyone else to get hurt."

"So courage had nothing to do with it?

"I suppose some."

"What have you learned since leaving home?"

"Mostly that the world outside my village is both exciting and frightening."

"Yes, it is but there is something else about this trip of yours I sense. It's your fear of failure."

Tenara looked down at the table.

Miralassen continued, "You listen to the voice inside that says you can't, more often than the one that says you can. Doubt is your real enemy and the enemy of your friends. You will not save them unless you believe in yourself first. Look at me."

Tenara looked up.

Miralassen moved her head closer. "I make no promises other than telling you that your journey ahead will be fraught with danger. What I do know is that before the war within you can end, a great many sacrifices will be made."

Tenara was in shock. "How will I know when that is?"

"You will know…when you are there…"

"But…."

She held her hand up. "No more discussion on this. Now to the other reason I summoned you here."

Miralassen pushed her chair back and walked over to a shelf from which she retrieved a long box and carried it back to the table. After opening it, she lifted out a sword with a silver handle, its glass-like blade a shard of blue stone.

In a flash, she pointed it at the ceiling and whirled it about, sending bolts of fire crashing down around the two, which nearly caused Tenara to fall out of her seat in terror. The Stone Changer quietly sat down again and placed it carefully on the table in front of Tenara. "Take it now. Pull it out when you must. It is made from a special stone that will drive caution into even the most fearless enemy."

Tenara stared at the object as if it was a specter that would consume her if she dared touch it. But for some unknown reason—or was it the presence of the woman beside her? —she reached for its handle and lifted it up. The weapon felt incredibly light and warm to the touch. She looked up at the Stone Changer, who then took the sword from her hand and returned it to its scabbard. Leaning forward, the lady fixed it to Tenara's waist with a gray belt adorned with the same white rock the woman wore.

Miralassen stood up and bowed to Tenara. "We will see each other again." The Stone Changer smiled, placing her hand on Tenara's head. Then, slowly, she walked out of the room.

A moment later, still dazed at what had just happened, Tenara was escorted back to Fladon's cottage with Feyorin at her side.

# 21. THE HALL OF SHAPERS

AFTER WALKING FOR FIFTEEN MINUTES TOWARD THE HALL OF Shapers, Joen yelled, "How much further is it, Baldmar? I have to walk twice as fast as you."

Without losing his stride, he answered, "Soon."

Frondameer leaned down. "We could carry you."

She showed him her fist and then looked behind them at the village below. To her astonishment, everyone she saw was hurriedly walking or working on something. It was as if the whole city was preparing for something.

Looking ahead, she saw a wall containing an oval door come into view. It led to even more steps.

Finally, they arrived on a sweeping terrace that was large enough to hold half the population of the village. There, they looked upon the breathtaking panorama of Shadowguard, Orora, and the Anduin Mountain itself. Joen's escort motioned her over to an enormous opening in the rocks that led to a hall below. She looked up at the high ceiling just as she passed through the entrance.

The sunlight was instantly replaced by the radiance of stones neatly embedded in the walls and ceiling. Further down, the tunnel widened and the noise of tapping and chiseling could be heard. Rounding a corner, they saw several well-dressed artisans in fine robes each sculpting a single stone into different shapes, including animals and other strange figures.

One in particular was being worked on by a small, young worker dressed in a green robe that was fastened at the waist with a blue rope. He had a small, odd-shaped hammer and was busy plucking away when Joen suddenly noticed that the stone looked like a bird. She stopped for a second to gaze at the creation, and he looked up.

"Hi," said the young one, greeting her with a smile.

"Hi. What is that?" she asked, walking over while her group drifted away down the tunnel.

"It's a Jalypso."

"A what?"

He giggled. "You're one of the visitors from beyond Shadowguard."

"Uh huh. Your village is amazing."

"Thanks. This bird is found in Shadowguard. When you see it, you get good luck."

Reflecting back on the skinks, she murmured. "I wish I had seen it. I've had a lot of bad surprises."

"Not all bad I bet."

"No, course not. I met a lot of nice people. Maybe I will see the bird when I go back through Shadowguard."

Smiling, he waved his arms and said, "First, you have to know where to find it. It likes to hide under a dirt leaf."

"A what?"

"It's a leaf that when you look at it, you think you see dirt. But it just tricks you. You have to pick it up and it will then show itself properly."

"Ahhhh! I remember that leaf! The scouts called it a Camelio."

"I like that name," he said, smiling again. "You want to try to help me create the feathers? Oh, sorry, my name is Rilen." He stuck out his dirty hand.

"I'm called Joen," she replied, grabbing it.

While she was starting her private class in sculpturing, the others arrived in a large room decorated with multiple drawings on its walls and strange objects lining the floor.

Frondameer looked up. "Baldmar, it is difficult for me to believe that our kind would ever create such places as this in a mountain. How is it that your people left the water for the rocks? Is it not in your nature as well?"

Baldmar nodded. "It is, but our people came from another place entirely: a place beyond this mountain. I will explain." He sat down. "For generations, we lived near the water. And like you, we were very proud of our village and the beautiful river that meandered through it. But then, a terrible thing happened. A storm came upon us, more fearsome than any before. From it came bolts of fire that struck the forest floor on every side and instantly burned our homes. The destruction was so complete that our survival was at risk. So we sought refuge near the foot of a mountain. By then, the forest was ablaze and all manner of creatures ran in panic, some of whom followed us to the cold water that poured from the snows above.

But there was another clan that came to the mountain as

well: the Chilltails. They were the Saurians, or great lizards, that ruled the edge of the forest on the northern side of the Anduin Mountain."

Blendefest interrupted, "Excuse me. Would these Saurians be the ones that threaten us now?"

"Let me continue. Our people tried to live in peace with them while we waited patiently for the fire to satisfy its hunger. But it was not to be. The Chilltails would not agree to share their territory with us or the others that fled the burning woods. We begged them to give us time to return, but their king just spat and warned us to leave. When we refused, they attacked and many of our kind were lost, including some of our young. We have always been a peaceful race, but this ravaging was too much for our leader to bear. A council was formed and a plan was created to fight the Chilltails in response to this unprovoked attack."

Frondameer pointed to the wall again. "The paintings there. Is that the battle?"

"Yes. They are there to remind us of that day and to symbolize our promise that it would never happen again."

Blendefest's eyes found a sculpture on the floor, a giant lizard three times his size. "I know that one," he said, looking at the beast. "He is the one who rules Gravenbroke."

"Yes, he is Keltar, their king. But the story continues. The Chilltails were too strong and drove our people up the mountain, into the frigid cold, where we nearly perished. It was only the insight of our queen that saved us that day. She led the group underground, where we could hide and rest from the cold. But there was little food, so we had to leave and reenter the battle once again. For many hours, we rolled hundreds of ice rocks at the lizard's army, but it merely slowed them down. We had one choice left: divide ourselves."

"Our leader, Proliptus, taunted Keltar to chase him and his many warriors in a different direction while my father and others fled over the mountain and down the other side, where we live today. Few of the Chilltails followed us, and the ones that did were destroyed," said Baldmar.

"And Proliptus?"

"My ancestors never saw him again. If he survived the battle, he would have left our runes somewhere for us to find.

"This Stone Changer, Miralassen. Is this the same one who led you into the mountain that day?"

"She is her daughter."

Frondameer thought for a moment. "And this lizard king is the same one that drove you over the mountain?"

He nodded. "Yes. We are a long-lived race, but they live longer still. But Keltar knows nothing of this place or that we survived. If it became known to him, the war would begin again."

"Then we will never speak of this place," stated Blendefest.

Baldmar nodded his head once. "I accept your promise, but do not deceive yourself in thinking they will not discover Orora, my friends. We have known of this possibility and are even now preparing for it still. If there is to be a battle, it will not end here. It will consume all of the great land that you know as Anzenar. It is for that reason that the council allowed you safe passage thorough Shadowguard when you first arrived. Our queen sees you as friends, but also as warriors. Even you, Joen," he said, looking back but not seeing her. "We seem to be missing one of you," he observed casually.

After retracing their steps up the tunnel, they found her still engaged in rapt conversation with Rilen. By now, both were covered in dust and dirt. Baldmar walked up behind her.

The boy glanced up with a sheepish grin. "Hello, Baldmar."

"Rilen, she is your guest. You have so little thought to make her work as well?"

Before Rilen could answer, Joen jumped up. "Oh, no, Baldmar! I had a most wonderful time with Rilen. He taught me many things about your people and how to make things from rocks. Look," she said, holding the sculpture in her hand. "I put some feathers on this bird."

"What kind is it?" Frondameer asked.

"A Jalypso - it's found in tiny holes under the dirt leaves in the forest."

Frondameer and Blendefest nearly fell down with shock, recognizing the bird instantly.

"Most impressive," said Blendefest, staring at the sculpture.

"Rilen," interrupted Baldmar, "I must take your guest back to her cottage.

The young boy nodded and reached to touch the bird in Joen's hands. "I want you to have it. It's for you to remember me by."

A big smile spread across her face and her eyes got teary. "Thank you, Rilen. It's beautiful!"

As they were walking away, she turned around and met his eyes. They both waved until she disappeared around a corner. She wondered if she would ever see him again.

## 22. PREPARATION FOR DEPARTURE

FLADON WAS COOKING THE EVENING MEAL WHEN JOEN WALKED in.

"Oh my, oh my, you're back already," he said gaily as he pushed his pots around the stove, making a horrible racket. "What did we learn?" he asked.

"Fladon," said Joen, walking up to him holding the bird sculpture, "what do you think?"

"Where did you get that?" he asked in shock.

"I made it with the help of a new friend. His name is Rilen."

He laughed. "Indeed! You must be their newest shaper. It's wonderful. You know, I tried it myself once but I just couldn't get the feathers right."

"They are a bit tricky."

"So you like caves, do you?"

"I might get used to them," she replied smiling.

"Uh huh. With the right teacher, I'm sure."

"Smells good, Fladon!" said another entering the room.

Joen turned around to see Tenara. Almost immediately, she

noticed the blue sword hanging from her waist. "Oh my," her eyes grew big, "that's amazing. Did the Stone Changer give that to you?"

"Yes. I'm not sure why. I just hope I don't have to use it."

Fladon turned and stood transfixed, looking at the weapon. "My dear, the Lady of the Rocks must see great things in you to grant such a gift."

"I don't know how. Ever since Joen and I left Rippleshy, it was the scouts and Ororans that did everything."

"Not what I heard."

"What?"

"They said the same things about you and Joen. Ororans don't give things lightly unless they expect something in return."

Tenara stared at him and was about to ask a question when Feyorin came through the door with the scouts and Baldmar. "We will leave tomorrow when the sun first crosses the wall. Shadowguard will be quiet, and its darkness and mist will cover us until we come to Darmok's Pond."

Baldmar came up behind him. "The two you know as the Dither Twins will accompany us as well."

"What?!" exclaimed Joen. "Those rotten skinks? They'll do anything to make trouble. Why do they have to come?"

Feyorin interjected, "Our village is not a prison. They are creatures of the forest that deserve their freedom as well. But to soothe your worry, their fear of Shadowguard should control their desire to flee."

Joen puffed up. "Well, just to be sure, I'm going to watch 'em every second."

Feyorin continued, "There is something else. We believe that the Saurians have made allies of more than just the skinks."

"I'm confused," Blendefest grumbled. "If you release the skinks, will they not run immediately to Keltar?"

"We are counting on that. However, to your concern, we have dispatched a chameleon," he paused, "one that is loyal to us, to advise Keltar that they have been lazy and doing little except sleeping by the river. When the 'Twins' arrive, the king should dismiss their report for two reasons. One, they continue to have no clue to his brother's location and two, he will believe their description of this place is a lie to cover themselves. Keltar believes he destroyed us. However, to your point, there is the risk that he may wonder if a place such as this could be built so close to his own land. As a result, we are preparing for both possibilities."

"And you know this chameleon well?"

"Yes. His line stretches beyond the mountain to the time when we first arrived in Anzenar. His village lies on the northern edge of Shadowguard and his family is honorable."

Tenara walked over to Fladon. "And what do you think?"

"I think that dinner is ready."

Tenara grimaced and then giggled. They all sat down and shared many a story about their adventures and family. When it was over, Feyorin requested that Tenara follow him to terrace. "Did you know that the gift that hangs at your side was crafted by Miralassen herself? It was carved from the joining of two different stones found deep within the mountain. Take it out and point it to the floor." She did. "Now look on each side of the blade and tell me what you see."

"It shines on this side but the other is dull."

"Turn it around."

She sucked her breath in. "Ahhh! The side that shines now is dull and the other is bright!"

"It will do this when it faces the mountain that gave it birth. It will forever be your guide to Orora. Even Shadowguard cannot fool the sword."

Joen walked past Tenara and gazed at the blade while yawning. Then she leaned closer and saw a strange rune on its side. "What is that?" she asked, pointing.

Fladon walked over. "I noticed it too. The first time I saw one like that was when I was a young scout. It was after I had crossed the mountain and survived Ildon's swamp. That was some time ago. Hmmm…oh well, I'm forgetting where I was. Oh yes, while trying to figure out how to cross it, I was pricked by one of those dreadful pinecones and fell into the water. Before I knew it, I was being chased down by a vicious snake. Just before it leapt, I felt myself being pulled from the water by someone who had the same mark on his clothes as you have on your sword." He pointed to it. "I have since learned that it means *strength*."

Feyorin nodded. "It is late and we must rest. It will be a long day tomorrow."

"Thank you both." Tenara then walked up to her room and leaned the sword against the wall. As she pulled the covers up, a prickly fear crawled up her back. She looked back at the sword and thought, *What if good company is not enough?* Her intuition suggested there was more to this trip than just rescuing her friends.

# 23. JOURNEY THROUGH THE FOREST

SOMETIMES IT'S JUST DIFFICULT TO GET OUT OF BED. IT WAS ONE of those lazy mornings for Joen as she watched the others completing their final preparations.

"Perhaps we can carry her," suggested Frondameer.

"Oh no, no," replied Fladon as he twitched about the room. "I should like her to stay here and help me. She is very pleasant and I enjoy her company."

Joen glanced over at him. "Wish I could, Fladon, but I have to go and protect them from those stupid Dither Twins. Where are they anyway?"

"Follow me," ordered Feyorin as he walked on the terrace. She grabbed her cloak and dagger tooth and followed him out. He then pointed to the far side of the village wall. "There, waiting for us at forest edge."

"They are alone?! Why don't they run?" asked Joen.

"Do you not see the Ororan warriors who wait in the shadows?"

Joen nodded, understanding now. She turned back to Fladon.

"Now don't go and get hurt or something, or I'll have to come back right away."

Fladon hugged her and then stood stiffly, smiling. "I promise, Ms. Joen. Now, don't you go getting yourself in trouble either or old Fladon will to have to leave his comfortable chair and start prowling the woods again."

She was about to join the others when Rilen walked in.

"Hi, I'm glad I caught you before you left. I wanted to give you something."

Her face turned red. "You already did. Fladon will keep it for me...if I come back."

"It's something else." He reached into a pocket on his robe and brought out a glowing stone. "This is for you. If you get lost at night, it will help you find your way, especially in Shadowguard."

"Oh, it's wonderful," said Joen, looking at it shining in the morning sunlight.

He added, whispering, "Oh yeah, one more thing. Baldmar doesn't talk much, but he's pretty smart. He will take care of you."

"Thanks," she replied, grinning.

He stood there a moment and then turned and left. Her eyes followed him up the walk until he was out of sight.

She turned and ran after the group, which was already halfway to the gate. Once through, the group walked slowly up to the Dither Twins, who sat sullenly on a rock. Beside them were four Ororans with armor and gleaming spears. Feyorin nodded to them and they promptly left, leaving the skinks glaring at the scouts, Joen in particular.

Feyorin walked over and spoke quietly to them. "You are re-leased. From this point on, you are free to travel with us or to return to your land on your own. Should you decide to leave, we will not chase or pursue you. But, should you attempt to do harm to anyone or anything within the forest, then I will permit the one here," he said, referring to Joen, "to do with you as she pleases."

They looked at Joen's hand, tightly held against her dagger tooth. Red Spear snarled back, "Where are our spears?"

"Because you entered our land with intent to do harm, your weapons will remain here."

He barked loudly, "Then how do we defend ourselves?"

"You don't. You hope that we perform that service for you."

Blue Spear nudged his brother and weakly suggested, "Can we talk in private about your offer?"

"As you wish, but we leave now."

The two skinks walked a short way off. Blue Spear whis-pered, "You and your stupid idea to go east got us into this!"

"Yeah? Well, if you didn't like it, then why didn't you stay with the beavers? Besides, it would have worked if the big ones hadn't come along and rescued that big mouth in the tree," he spat, pointing at Joen in the distance.

"Well, when we leave this place, you can forget my help."

"I don't need your help!" said Red Spear and poked at his brother.

The next instant, they were rolling around, brawling on the ground, only to stop when they abruptly hit a tree. Their hands were at each other's necks, but both looked up to see Joen shak-ing her head.

"What a bunch of losers," she said, smiling.

"Where are your big friends?" Blue Spear asked.

"They're around. You want to run away?"

Red Spear jumped up and slapped his brother on the head. "Come on."

Joen walked in the direction she'd last seen the group. Within a few minutes, she noticed Tenara rounding a tree. "You playing with your friends again, Joen?" she asked with a wry grin.

"They don't play too well, even with each other," Joen replied dryly.

In these few moments, the two Ororans had stealthily come up and flanked the Dither Twins. Both skinks took in their size and realized they were no match for them or whatever lived within the forest. It was also getting darker, and the further they walked into Shadowguard, the more nervous they became. Tenara occasionally removed her sword and looked at the glowing side that pointed back to the mountain.

It was just before sundown when they arrived at the same rock circle that the scouts, Joen, and Tenara had slept near the first night. Blendefest stopped and looked around, then motioned to Feyorin to come over.

"It was here that we were attacked the first night by some animal, just before the sky became a blaze of fire. Would you know anything about that?" Blendefest asked suspiciously.

Feyorin sat on one of the rocks while Baldmar strayed out of sight. Tenara, Joen, Frondameer and the Dither Twins found their own resting places around the circle and listened intently to Feyorin's reply.

"The animal you speak about is known as a Razaboar. Its

territory is Shadowguard, where it finds protection as well as its prey. It is ruthless in defense of the forest and our village."

"Then you were aware of the attack?"

"Not only that, we were aware of you shortly after you left the Songentrope Creek. We tracked your group to these stones and saw the Razaboar attack. What you saw were flametes, or special rocks thrown against another that explode in a shower of sparks when they hit the ground. They are forged deep within the mountain by the shapers."

"How did you know we had entered Shadowguard?"

"Because many of the creatures within it give us a sign when something shows up uninvited."

Blendefest interrupted, "The scouts of Moss Rock would be very interested in how you do that."

Frondameer nodded. "So it was these flametes that saved us from the Razaboar." He looked over at Blendefest before replying to Feyorin, "I am curious. Why didn't you join us then and guide us to Orora?"

"We considered that, but Miralassen wanted to know what skills you had first. As I remind you, we are a private race for many reasons, as you have learned. Few outsiders are ever allowed in Orora."

Frondameer shook his head. "I'm not sure your queen was impressed. Direction in this place is confusing. We thought the bird nests under the Camelio leaves were enough to determine our route. Apparently we were wrong."

Feyorin looked at him quizzically. 'Camelio leaves?'

Joen spoke up. "Dirt leaves, Feyorin. Rilen told me what you call them."

Before he could reply, everyone heard a scratching noise in the direction of the skinks. Feyorin looked around and noticed that each of them had found a stick and was using a small rock to whittle the end into a sharp point.

He walked over to one and whispered, "There are many things in these woods that do not like strangers." Pausing to look at their crude weapons, he added, "And none of them are choosy about what they eat. Keep those weapons ready and yourselves vigilant throughout the night."

"You're just saying that to make us scared," Blue Spear blustered. "But we ain't."

"Then it would be ok if the rest of us slept on the other side of the circle of the stones while you watch tonight?" Feyorin asked, smiling.

Red Spear kicked Blue Spear in the leg. "My brother only meant that we can fight too if something happens."

Feyorin nodded and left the Dither Twins glaring at each other.

Joen looked over and shook her head again. She turned to the others. "If you're hungry, Fladon sent some food: one of his special recipes, a loaf of Flencin, and some fruit." She pulled some of the loaf out of her pocket and passed it around. The 'twins' looked over and smacked their lips but refused to ask for any. Joen noticed, tossed two pieces over the rock, and then heard a subsequent scuffle and some mumbled words between the two. She just shook her head again.

Blendefest gazed at the thick trunks of the unusual trees and looked at Feyorin and Baldmar. "I have passed many years in all manner of woods and I have never seen any like these, which keeps its secrets so well."

Frondameer shifted the subject. "Did you ever think about returning to your native land?"

"Yes, we considered it, but Keltar did not. While we remain mortal enemies, we were not going to leave Anzenar to the mercy of Keltar and his followers. What they had done to us and the animals of our forest will never be forgotten. They are cruel and have no love for anything except the barren land they sleep upon. So we planted the seeds of Shadowguard and spread them as far as the eye could see."

"You made this forest?" asked Blendefest incredulously.

"Yes. It contains the essence of what we need to survive. And the animals you fear within it depend on Shadowguard for their way of life. They too fled over the mountain after the fire. We are its protector as it is ours. Neither can survive without the other. The village you left this morning was built as a sentinel, designed to watch the forest and the animals within it."

"Did anything live here before Shadowguard?"

Feyorin nodded. "Another lizard clan equally as cruel. We watched them as they became angry at Shadowguard while it pushed them further and further south toward the Sorrowful Mountain.

"Where did you live during this time?"

"For a short time, we hid under the Anduin Mountain. Soon after, when we found that Keltar had no ambitions to explore, the first stones of Orora were laid."

"Then you are taking a great risk by coming with us," Blendefest said somberly.

Feyorin leaned backed against the rock and replied in a low tone, "We have no choice. It's only a matter of time before the Saurians and our people cross paths again. Our queen has always known this. It's why we prepare now for the war that will eventually come."

# 24. DARMOK'S POND

JUST AS THE MORNING LIGHT WAS BARELY MAKING ITS WAY through the treetops, Tenara woke to the feeling of cool mist drifting across her face and sending rivulets of water running down her arm and to the ground. She blinked and saw the forest appearing and then disappearing between intervals of thick fog that drifted over the ground like ghosts on a midnight prowl. Even the nearby trees were just trunks that sprouted from the ground only to vanish into the mist, as if some magician was casting a spell for an audience of one.

She was the first one up this time and turned her head to listen to the ragged sound of snoring from the two skinks, who had fallen on top of each other during the night. Joen was prone on the ground with her hand tightly around her dagger tooth while the others, except Feyorin, were casually sleeping with their backs against the rocks, as if they were at home and breakfast would be served soon. However, Tenara was already awake. She looked around, worried about the day ahead. Feyorin opened his eyes and slowly stood up. He noticed Tenara watching the forest anxiously and quietly asked, "Do you see the way the fog hides the forest?"

"Yes. So, can we wait until it clears before leaving?"

Shaking his head, he said, "It's typical for it to remain on the forest floor throughout the morning. Unfortunately, we don't have the time for it to clear. It will take us the rest of the day to complete the walk to Songentrope Creek before we can resume looking for your friends.

"How do we get there if we can't see where we're going?"

"Baldmar and I will guide you, but you and I must first find a safe path to avoid the creatures that may be nearby. You have good ears and, as Frondameer described, 'a good sense of the forest.'"

She looked into the swirling mists and then back at the Ororan. "I don't understand. Why are you asking me to do this? Why not Baldmar? He knows these woods better than me."

"This is not for him. It is for you. There will be many things that will test you before you see your village again. And it was the direct order from Miralassen that we would train you. Now follow me."

"What is that I am doing?"

"We're going to walk into the fog and then separate. Your objective is to make it back to where we are standing now, alone."

"Sounds simple," said Tenara.

"There is nothing simple in Shadowguard. Every Ororan your age or under has done this. You must depend on yourself before you can trust others. That's what you did when you chose to leave Rippleshy."

"But…"

"Enough questions. Now come." Tenara watched him get up and slowly disappear into the fog. When she saw him vanish, she immediately got up and ran after him. Once in the mist, she was shocked at how dark it was.

"Feyorin?"

"I'm here. We will separate now," said the ghostly voice in a whisper to her right. "Turn to your left and go for one hundred steps. I will do the same in the opposite direction. Go slow and listen. Draw your sword and extend it with the side that glows behind you. Then return to where we started."

"Feyorin, really, what's the purpose in this?"

There was no answer.

"Feyorin?" she whispered louder. "Are you still there?"

But only silence returned and her heart began to race. She remembered his words and listened quietly, but nothing could be heard except the sound of a few birds claiming their territory high in the canopy. She almost wished she could be up there with them. Gritting her teeth, she turned left and began walking while counting the first few steps. She wanted to get this over as fast as possible.

After a short moment, she stopped when she remembered her sword. "Please work for me." She pulled it out, saw the side that glowed, and made sure that it pointed directly behind her. Then she set off again, trying to keep walking in a straight line. But instead she found herself, after a few more steps, bumping into a large tree, and then another after that. For the third time, she began pacing forward when she heard a noise.

Freezing, she tried in vain to see where it came from, but the fog was too thick in every direction. A terrifying stab of fear coursed through. Where was Feyorin? *Perhaps it is he who made the noise*, she thought.

Then it came again, this time from behind and much closer. She turned and faced the sound while holding her sword out, but then it shifted to footsteps running toward her. She pushed herself back against the tree and listened as the sound grew louder. Peering around the side, she suddenly saw a shape resolve into an animal twice her size with rows of jagged teeth and a back supporting sharp scales from head to tail.

It made a horrible sound, a mixture of snorts and whistles that drove her lower down the trunk of the tree and into a crouch.

Then it passed, leaving the fog swirling around, causing the Camelio leaves beneath her to become visible for a moment. She held her breath, hoping it would continue its run. But then she heard it stop abruptly, followed by what sounded like sand being thrown onto a pile of dry leaves. In a sudden break in the mist, she saw its head move from side to side, sniffing the wind, and suddenly turn backward to stare at the tree it just passed.

Now she could see it plainly. It had three tusks on a dog-like head and a furry body that ended with a small spike on a short, thick tail. It was at least four times her size now and many times her weight. She sensed that it was waiting patiently for a sound that would give its prey away. The fear that penetrated her body screamed at her to run, but what she had experienced since Rippleshy kept her focused and motionless against the roots. Escape was not possible.

To make matters worse, a second sound of something running her way escalated in intensity until a familiar shape shot over the roots past where she hid. She jerked her head around and saw Feyomir bursting out of the fog with his spear in hand, throwing something that sparked in the direction of the creature. But it anticipated the attack and leapt forward at the warrior's head with long claws.

Back at camp, the others had awakened and instantly noted the absence of both Tenara and Feyorin. Fearing that something happened, they started to stand. However, Baldmar reassured them that their absence was expected. They relaxed and prepared themselves for their last day in Shadowguard by eating some of the bread that Fladon had provided. It was then they heard the angry snorts of something that echoed from deep in the fog, beyond their sight. The Dither Twins tried vainly to hide behind each other while the rest grabbed their weapons and readied for an attack.

The sounds of snarling and hissing nearby crashed against their ears and drew fear from their hearts. Sparks shot out of the fog and yelps and anguish cries permeated the air, but the group held their ground and steadied their fear. Screams of torment were suddenly heard and then all was suddenly quiet. Each strained their eyes and waited patiently for what they were sure was an imminent attack, but nothing came. Baldmar motioned them to move forward toward the noise with their weapons ready.

After a few steps, the last of the fog drifted away and a silhouette appeared on the ground, soon resolving into Feyorin. Joen's heart thumped wildly when she noticed that Tenara was not with him. But as they closed the distance, they could see another form coming into focus. This time, it was Tenara who had her foot on the neck of a huge beast and a sword pointing at its head. Joen nearly fainted.

Baldmar walked up to Feyorin and pulled him up casually while looking at the beast. "A Kulumper. You ok?"

"Yes," Feyorin said, brushing himself off. "I suspected there might have been one prowling about. I just didn't think it would be so close." He then turned to Tenara, whose sword was shaking in her hand. "Thank you, Tenara. Remove your foot now and allow it to leave. It has little fight left."

But all she could focus on were its long claws moving back and forth against the ground. Baldmar walked over and replaced her foot with his. Only then did Tenara step away. Once done, he stepped back himself and kicked the beast lightly on its side. With a large snort, it jumped up and glared at Tenara, then ran into the fog, where it hoped its hunger would be satisfied before the day was gone.

Joen was wild with excitement and ran up to hug her best friend, who was still shaking slightly from the adventure. The scouts came up as well and stomped their feet proudly. "Well done," they said. The Dither Twins, however, were speechless and cowered behind a rock. Each assured the other that they would have certainly done the same thing as Tenara but faster.

Sometime later, just before midday, the heat of the morning forced the fog to the tops of the trees, allowing the first rays of sunshine to strike the forest floor. The mood of the Dither Twins instantly improved, since it would not be long before they could leave this wretched forest forever. Nevertheless, Joen kept an eye on them, wary for any signs of mischief. However, the two remained quiet while they stumbled along not far behind.

Every so often, she heard them mumble the name 'Keltar' and something about 'rewards' and 'giants.'

As the afternoon wore on, the colossal trees of Shadowguard were gradually replaced by smaller ones that littered the valley beyond. In its center was the Songentrope Creek, where the sound of rushing water filled the air as it swirled among the mossy rocks that lay beside its banks. Joen looked back at the skinks but they were nowhere in sight "They're gone!" she yelled out.

"Who?" yelled Frondameer.

"The skinks!"

Everyone except the scouts turned at once and began searching around for them. Frondameer and Blendefest, however, traced their path back to the last point they had seen the skinks. Blendefest, who was kneeling on the ground, noticed the two Ororans walking toward him. As they approached, he looked up. "The dirt and leaves are scattered around, which suggests there was a disagreement between the two. Their tracks lead north."

Frondameer came around from behind Feyorin. "You still believe they are heading for Keltar?"

"They have no choice," he said serenely. "They've been absent from their king too long."

"And you have no concern for Orora or your people?"

"If the Chilltail king believes their story, then we made a grave error. But Baldmar and I suspect the skinks will only provide half-truths to Keltar."

"How do you mean?"

"It has been two generations since our kind and the lizards last fought. Our gamble is that Keltar assumed he destroyed us and will reject such descriptions as nonsense. Instead, he will press them for the information he sent them for in the first place: his brother's location. However," he said somberly, "the information they provide may plant a seed of curiosity in the king. Miralassen understood this and accepted the risk." He turned to Tenara. "It is urgent that we begin looking for your lost friends now."

Frondameer walked around to take the lead but paused when he saw something shimmering attached to Blendefest's belt. He looked closely and recognized it at once: a Camelio leaf. Looking at his friend curiously, he asked, "For our wall?"

"It's Fladon's gift to the Colonel," he replied, smiling. "He asked me to bring one back as a present with the following words: 'Top this, my friend.' You remember they were a pair at one time."

He nodded smiling. "And something for our wall?"

"No need," he said, shaking his head. "I have a strong feeling we will see Orora again. Until then, the wall will wait."

Frondameer smiled, but Blendefest did not.

They soon descended a steep embankment and arrived at Songentrope Creek. After looking up and down the river and hearing nothing but the turbulent noise of falling water, Frondameer yelled out loud, "We are north of Darmok's Pond. We must travel downriver. Do you agree, Feyorin?"

The Ororan nodded.

Tenara and Joen brought up the rear as they began threading their way along the bank. When it was nearing sunset, they noticed the water had lost most of its noise, indicating that the headwaters of Darmok was another thirty minutes away.

Tenara spoke up. "The last time we were here, we had to secretly cross his dam at night. They don't like visitors, I guess."

Feyorin replied, "Because it is their home and a part of what they are. Beavers descend from noble families whose histories stretch far back in time. Their lodges are built from the wood of their parents' and are lovingly cared for and expanded by their descendants. And they are fearless in defending them. But they do have friends among other creatures. You must simply know how to knock."

After quietly walking along the lake for several minutes, Feyorin approached the edge of the lodge and watched it for a long moment. Then, turning, he walked quietly into the woods and returned with a long, straight branch. With his spear, he carved the limbs away before handing his weapon to Baldmar. Once done, Feyorin carried the stick to the side of the lodge, where he plunged it into the water and began rubbing one of the stout logs that braced the beaver's home. He did this for a few seconds and then hurled it, like a spear, into the center of the pond. He then kneeled and waited.

Tenara was so fascinated and confused by this unusual display that she started to ask a question but was motioned to silence by Baldmar. Instead, she watched the stick drift on the water quietly. Joen and the scouts slowly moved their hands to their weapons, but Baldmar waved them back. Then, there was the tiniest bit of movement. They almost missed it, but the slightest sound of moving water followed. Then, all at once, the stick disappeared. Feyorin stood up and remained motionless.

For the rest of the group, time appeared to stand still. Tenara was fingering her sword while watching the water closely for anything that could be a threat. But it was Joen who saw it first and whispered loudly, "Look." She pointed. "On the other side of the pond!"

In the twilight, they saw the stick rise above the surface, surrounded by hundreds of bubbles. It began to move slowly at first, then rapidly toward the group, who remained motionless at the edge of the pond. With an explosion of water, a huge beaver erupted out of the pond and landed in front of the Ororan, releasing the stick and dropping it gently to his feet. Everyone, except Baldmar, nearly fell back in shock.

"You received my sign," the beaver said casually to Feyorin in a deep voice. "I am grateful you have come." Baldmar handed the stick back to Feyorin.

"What?!" asked Tenara, shocked and not understanding what had just happened. Then, looking anxiously at Feyorin and Baldmar, she said, "I don't understand." But the two seemed indifferent to what had just happened. "He was expecting you?!"

The scouts and Joen were equally puzzled. As if reading their minds, the beaver turned to the group. "Feyorin and I go back many years. All of you who stand with Orora will be welcome as well. Baldmar, it is good to see you."

"And you as well, Darmok." The Ororan bowed.

Feyorin faced Darmok. "Many things have occurred that delayed our response to the message you sent. Our apologizes," said Feyorin. "Your warning about the skinks was acted on immediately; however, they are a minor problem. They escaped upstream today, where they will surely make their way to Keltar. I present their weapons as a contribution to your lodge." Feyorin pulled the skinks' spears from a quiver on his back and gave them to the beaver.

"I remember them well," the beaver said menacingly, breaking the spears with his hands.

Tenara interrupted, "Feyorin? I'm sorry. Darmok knew we were coming?"

Looking back, he replied, "While you slept the first night in Orora, one of our warriors saw his sign and reported it." Feyorin looked back at the beaver. "The note said the skinks warned you about Keltar. But you also mentioned something about a renegade from his group?"

"His name is Scalar."

"Yes! We are aware of him," Feyorin said with disgust.

"Good. The skinks said that two other Saurians joined him. They are powerful and dangerous, Feyorin, even for you." He looked over at the four others standing near Baldmar. "And those that joined you are few."

"Perhaps, but I have found them wise and to have the souls of warriors!"

The beaver nodded. "I know where Scalar hides."

Feyorin was taken aback. "That was not in the message."

"Even so, I only learned of it recently. One of my clan, Brondanur, who built a fine lodge on the same water that we stand beside now, came to me three days ago in the middle of the night.

"He said three Saurians commandeered a group to build a fortress below his dam. He was most upset about the removal of the trees, but the lizards forced his family to clear them. Brondanur took a great risk to his family and those imprisoned there to deliver this information. He believes the forest is being eliminated at its southern edge for a reason."

Continuing in a lower voice, he said, "We believe they are trying to make another Gravenbroke, Feyorin. That must not happen! Brondanur asked for my help and I intend to offer it, whatever's required. As you know, the Sorrowful Mountains of the South are just beyond his lodge. He believes these three intend to join with the southern dons. You understand now where this is going. Your sign to him is the same you have for me."

Tenara interrupted. "Darmok? Did he say anything else about this group of prisoners?"

"I apologize, Darmok," Feyorin said, looking back at the beaver. "This one and the other beside her live in a village called Rippleshy in the Southern Forest beyond the western hills. Many of her friends have disappeared and we seek them now."

Darmok looked over, stared at Joen, and then darted his eyes toward Tenara. "Yes. He said they were small like her," he glanced at Tenara, "and their leader was a brave one called, I believe, Tealick."

Tenara's eyes popped open. "Tealick! But how could he have…" Sensing she had interrupted again and looking up, she said quietly, "Sorry."

Darmok and Feyorin smiled. "There is no need," rumbled Darmok, returning his eyes to Feyorin. "For now, you are welcome to camp at the side of my lodge. If my family has further information, I will return before you leave."

Joen didn't wait a second before she ran up to Feyorin and blurted, "You mean that you just wiggle a stick and the beavers come?"

Feyorin was jolted out of his thoughts and then laughed out loud. "It was not the movement but the markings I put upon the stick that opened his home to us. Before this journey is over, Joen, you and Tenara will have your own sign and your own rune."

Darmok stared directly at Tenara and grumbled in a serious tone, "You have been this way before. Have you not?"

She gulped and then glanced at the scouts. Turning back, she replied somberly, "Yes, at night. How did you know?"

"Do not make the mistake of thinking that beavers sleep only when the sun is gone. You were seen and heard."

Blendefest walked in front of Tenara and bowed. "It was I that led them here. We apologize for our carelessness and disturbing your family. If there is punishment to be had, I will accept it."

"It is not important. To remain hidden from a beaver, you must cross the water upstream from his dam."

Frondameer laughed. "Why didn't you think of that Blendefest?"

His friend returned a deadpan face.

Darmok turned back to Feyorin. "Be prepared. Brondanur will soon smuggle one of the prisoners out at night and place him on the trail south of me. It is imperative that he survive this trip. Look for him where the Songentrope makes war against the rocks. He will be alone and, I am sure, terribly frightened."

At that, the beaver nodded to Baldmar, reached down, grasped the spear in Feyorin's hand, and shook it twice. Once done, he released it and plunged into the water, leaving a shower of droplets that fell around their feet.

## 25. KELTAR'S PURSUIT

As soon as the Dither Twins saw their opportunity to escape from the others, they made for the creek to hide in the foliage nearby. Red Spear was horrified at what Keltar might do to them for being so late. He looked back, expecting his brother to be just behind, but instead saw him aimlessly walking around a tree. "What are you doing?" he growled.

"Looking for a new spear," his brother said petulantly.

"Fine! I'll tell Keltar that someone took yours."

"Took yours too! You will be sorry if the giants come back!" whined Blue Spear, looking on the ground.

Red Spear could partly see the logic in that. However, his intuition told him no number of weapons would help them if that happened. On the other hand… "Ok. Well, get me one as well."

"Get yer own," barked Blue Spear as he walked further away.

His brother grimaced and then looked up at the sky. It was growing darker, so finding a weapon would not be easy. However, after a few minutes, Blue Spear spotted a bush along the side of the river that would be perfect. He reached for one of its straight limbs and pulled hard, but it refused to break. Again and again he tried, but still no sign of a crack. Angrily, he picked up a stick on the ground and began beating the limb senselessly, as if it would just give up and fall off.

Red Spear looked over and put his hand to his head. He watched his brother for a moment as he engaged in a fight to the death with the tree. "Need help?" he asked sarcastically. His brother just glared at him and threw his beating stick on the ground. Together, they grabbed the limb and pushed and pulled until, at last, it snapped, sending Blue Spear back on his tail, down the bank, and into the water below. His brother laughed until he saw him grab a rock and start to fashion a sharp end to his stick.

Not wanting to be left out, he marched down to the water and knocked his brother in the head. Then, pointing to a limb hanging over the river, he ordered, "Get over here!" Together, they jerked it back and forth until it broke away sending them both this time into the creek.

"Mother must have plucked you from a bird's nest!" growled Red Spear, walking out of the water.

Blue Spear raised his voice over the water and echoed back, "You were just as much…."

"Shhhhh, it's dark now. You wanna attract attention?" He looked around to ensure they were alone and said quietly, "Them giants might still be around."

After a quick survey of the woods, the two found a cluster of bushes that could be used as a hide-out during the night. Blue Spear jabbed his weapon into the ground and soon fell asleep. The two slept together and were soon on top of each other, where they remained until morning.

Red Spear woke first, finding his head being pressed into the ground by the weight of his brother. His mouth was contorted and he could barely get out a word. "Get off me," he mumbled, but there was no response. Then, reaching for his spear, he pulled it close, turned it slightly, and rammed it up.

"Yeoowwwwwwwww!" went his brother, leaping up and jumping around. "Why did you do that!?"

Red Spear stood up and moved his mouth back and forth, making sure it still worked. "Get your spear and let's go."

His brother walked over and grabbed his weapon, which was still stuck in the ground, and started to pull. Nothing happened. He pulled again. Nothing. Grunting and groaning, he tried again and again. Frothing at the mouth, he started slapping and kicking it, which caught the eye of Red Spear, who watched the pathetic spectacle.

"Problems?" he asked casually, leaning on his own weapon.

"I can get it," he said, snorting and growling.

Red Spear stalked over to his brother, pulled the top of the spear back, and let it smack into his brother's head. He then stuck his foot against the spear, close to the ground. "Pull it now."

Dazed, Blue Spear pulled it out.

By noon, they arrived in a small clearing where the sun warmed the ground, ready to rest. They had just about fallen asleep when they heard the snap of a limb nearby. Startled, they opened their eyes to see two monstrous lizards looking down at them, one holding a huge club.

"Well, look at what we found here, Roozen," said Korzen,

waving his weapon back and forth. "Two little skinks that must have gotten lost in the forest."

"Maybe we ought to show them the way back to Keltar, huh?" growled Roozen. "Been over a week since we seen you two and the king ain't happy with you being late—figured you skipped out on him."

"We're going now, if it's any business of yours," Red Spear growled back. Then, standing up and reaching for his weapon, he said, "We have a good report for him, more'n the likes of you."

Blue Spear grabbed for his own spear, but Korzen knocked it away with his club. "You want to play that game?" he asked menacingly. The skink stared at him for a moment and got ready to jump when Red Spear kicked him in the leg.

"We don't have time for these two. Forget em. We know they got nothin'."

Both lizards took a single step toward them but then hesitated. If it was true what the skinks said, then Keltar would feel even less favorable toward them if they delayed the skinks' news. Korzen thought about this for a moment and asked, "So you found Scalar?"

They said nothing.

Korzen lowered his head and smiled. "Thought so. You got nothin' too."

Red Spear puffed up. "You sure?"

"Only thing he wants from anybody is his brother and those idiots: Borgjump and Barkchew. Come on, Roozen. Let em go to Keltar with nothing! We'll see them later as his personal slaves." The two lizards turned away and walked off.

After the skinks made several faces at the backs of the lizards, they left for the northern desert of Keltar's kingdom. By mid-afternoon, the trees ended abruptly, as if the forest wanted nothing to do with the ground that lay beyond. This was the southern boundary of Gravenbroke. They both took a deep breath and then walked out under a brutally hot sun. Giant boulders were scattered across the dirt from some cataclysm long ago. Within the enormous clearing, they saw dozens of horned lizards, dinosaurs to them, asleep on the mighty rocks, soaking up the remaining heat of the day.

Several glowered at them while they made their way up the short trail. Blue Spear looked behind them to find three of them following closely in their tracks. After a few more steps, the skinks stopped in the shadow of an enormous boulder.

Keltar lifted his heavy head.

"My king," said Red Spear shakily.

At that moment, one of the other lizards behind Blue Spear mumbled, "They look tasty."

Red Spear stood frozen to the ground while Keltar ravaged his eyes across them both. But it was not this movement that struck fear in their hearts: it was his tail crashing down in a vicious stroke. "Did you get lost?"

They shook while the other beasts around them guffawed at the remark.

With a flash, the giant lizard whipped its head down and growled, "It was a simple task that anyone here could have done. All you had to do was search for my brother for two days and then come back. Yet, you dare to show yourself after several more have come and gone. Speak!" he thundered.

Red Spear trembled. "Sire, yes, you are right to be angry,

but we have learned much that will please you." He felt Blue Spear clawing his back, trying to get away from the other lizards just behind him. Annoyed at the pain, Red Spear kicked him backwards, causing his brother to fall under the mouth of one. It looked down, smacked its lips, and then anxiously looked at Keltar.

Annoyed at the interruption, Keltar said in a low voice to his general, "Leave him, Gradig. He would only cause you indigestion!"

The lizard sulkily retreated.

Red Spear steadied himself. "After the first day, we found the Beaver. Very soon, we had him on the ground and telling us everything."

"And what was that?!"

"That we would find Scalar in the Eastern Forest."

"There is nothing there!" bellowed the king.

"Begging your pardon, sire, but there is," said Red Spear weakly. "We discovered some frogs that live in that woods that are twice our size!"

"You stand there and waste my time telling me this?" He looked up at the huge lizard standing behind the skinks. "Gradig, I may change my mind."

The general smiled and looked hungrily at the two.

Red Spear stammered, "B-but the beaver said to look there."

The king just glared at them.

Red Spear continued, "We followed 'em in case they knew something." Then he quickly added, "We followed 'em until they disappeared inside a village of rocks and then we hid and waited until they came out a few days later."

"You have said nothing about my brother," grumbled the king again.

"Sire, they live in rock houses, and at night, they got rocks that glow," Red Spear blurted.

Keltar began moving toward them.

Suddenly seeing the king's loss of patience, he quickly added, "Wait! We followed 'em back to the beaver pond where they went south. That's where we think your brother is."

The king paused. "What proof do you have of that?"

"Well, none, sire. But we know he ain't hiding in the Eastern land now. To the west is Ildon. Nothing crosses that accursed swamp. If north, you would have found him. That leaves south. So, you see, while we could have safely hidden away near the beaver's pond, we risked our lives to find your brother."

Keltar paused a moment, reflecting back on an ancient memory. He looked up and motioned his hand to another Saurian nearby. Very soon, a large chameleon ambled up next to Red Spear, where it remained, staring at the two skinks.

The king said soothingly, "This one says you did nothing but sleep the entire time."

Shocked, the two skinks shouted, "That's a lie!"

"Then I'm supposed to believe you?" demanded Keltar.

"Y-yes," stammered Red Spear.

"So then one of you is lying." Keltar looked down at Red Spear. "Tell me what you saw in the Eastern Forest again."

"A huge village inhabited by giant frogs."

Again, Keltar shook his head. Squinting, he murmured, "Not possible."

"I tell ye, Mr. Keltar," cried the chameleon, "dem skinks a been sleepin' the entire time. They just makin' this stuff up."

"I think so as well. But to be sure, all three of you will remain here. And later, when I find the one that lied, he will personally be my lunch."

Blue Spear nearly fainted.

Keltar recounted, "You said you left the beaver pond and went east?"

"Y-yes… We swear it."

"But you never saw my brother."

"No!"

Keltar shifted his glance to the lizard just behind Blue Spear. "Has there been any news from Korzen or Roozen?"

"Nothing," Gradig growled. "But knowing them, they've probably lost their way back by now."

The king returned his gaze to the skinks. "Then it is on your lives that we go south. "Gradig: assemble a force and tell the others to remain behind. I will lead."

The lizard nodded once and left the group, moving swiftly over the rocks.

"All three of you will sleep beneath my rock tonight. Tomorrow, we march south together." Then, leaning down to within inches of Red Spear, he smiled with malice. "Hope you're right, for if not, I will take both your lives and your families'."

"Wh-what about him?" stuttered Blue Spear, pointing at the chameleon.

Keltar casually replied, "There are things worse than being eaten."

Red Spear gulped and stared at the changeling beside him, who met his eyes with just the barest hint of a smile.

# 26. PARSNIPPY'S CHOICE

IT HAD BEEN SEVERAL DAYS SINCE BRONDANUR LEFT FOR Darmok. Since then, Tealick had feared that he had been lost in some terrible accident or caught by one of the many spies that roamed the woods nearby.

During his absence, Scalar had ordered the beaver's family to clear the trees downstream so he could view the mountain to the south. For what reason, Tealick had no idea. As it slowly came into view and he saw the ugly swirls of dark clouds and tendrils of fog that clung to its peak, his heart raced. But what was most interesting was that Scalar's minions had also become increasingly agitated as they watched the mountain. Why? And where was Brondanur?

Meanwhile, a plan of escape at night had been devised among the captives, but none of them were sure it would work without the beaver's help. And leaving by day was not possible while the skinks and chameleons watched.

So instead they bided their time and continued to watch for his return.

Finally, on the third night, they heard the familiar taps coming from the darkness and a deep voice echoing in the chamber. "Tealick?" The beaver stepped forward under the silvery light of the glow worms.

"Where have you been, Brondanur?" Tealick replied.

"I was delayed."

"Unfortunately the skinks noticed your absence on the second day and demanded to know where you were. They told Scalar as well."

For a moment, the beaver started to panic. He was not sure what they would do to his family if he knew he had left.

Tealick noticed his apprehension. "Scalar threatened to tear down your lodge."

"My family?!!!" he cried out.

He shook his head. "I don't know... I'm sorry," replied Tealick, looking down.

"You took a risk. Were you harmed because of this?!" Brondanur asked quickly.

"No. But when you didn't appear, I told him you were gathering food for your family and that you would be back soon."

"If I didn't return?"

"He would kill one of my people tomorrow."

"Dear Tealick, I'm the one who is sorry.

"Thank you for taking the risk! I regret not being here sooner, but I traveled at night. By day was not possible, since the paths along the river north are patrolled by the skinks and the chameleons. Even then, I was nearly discovered but fled into the Eastern Forest. They didn't follow. Perhaps," he smiled, "they feared the demons that hunt within it."

"Demons?"

The beaver saw some near the wall jump up. "I apologize. I should not have said that."

Tealick ignored the remark. "Did you see Darmok?"

"Yes. I gave him your name and where to find us. He agreed to help us, but we must have patience."

"I'm afraid we have little of that," Tealick replied with a sigh. "We are tired and have become weary. Many have lost their will to continue unless someone can offer us some hope."

"Perhaps I can provide that. But first," he said in a low voice, "Darmok said that two skinks had come to him demanding information about the location of three giant lizards."

Tealick interrupted, "Could it be the same ones that hold us here?"

"Yes. We both agree and believe that more of their kind are coming as well. As a result, any plan of escape should be delayed."

Parsnippy jumped up. "How can this be good news? It makes it worse!"

"Yes. But what you do not know is that others of your kind are looking for you now."

"Others?"

Brondanur nodded. "Many nights prior, Darmok spotted two similar to you crossing his dam."

One voice from the back spoke up. "Well, it can't be Millard Dew. She couldn't find her way out of the pond without some help!"

Tealick ignored the giggling. "Brondanur, while you were gone, we decided that the way you came to us is the best way to escape."

"You forget that this is my home." He shook his head and replied somberly, "The path that runs beside the river and above is patrolled constantly. If you are caught, I can offer you no help."

"Then there has to be another way."

Brondanur shook his head. "There is one more thing. Darmok wants one of you to come to his lodge…alone."

"What?!…Why?" exclaimed Parsnippy. "Why would that be helpful?"

"He did not say but insisted it must be done. The one you choose will go upstream to a place where water beats against a giant boulder. Beyond that begins his territory. He would not ask this unless he thought it important. You must choose the one who takes this risk. I will return tomorrow night, after the moon goes into hiding, and set the chosen one upon the trail."

Brondanur backed away into the darkness.

Tealick looked around at the group. "I will go."

Parsnippy abruptly walked up and faced him. "You cannot! You are the only one among us who has stood up to the lizards. Whether you meant to or not, your place is to lead us now." Then, even quieter, he uttered, "I have to be the one."

Tealick was stunned. "No!"

"It's the only way," he said quietly.

"But Parsnippy, the risk…"

"Is mine to take."

Tealick just stared at him sadly.

The next morning, the guards arrived and pushed them out immediately to work. Before Parsnippy started digging, he took a moment to gaze at the beaver's dam and saw Brondanur casually looking back.

Tealick walked over to him and whispered, "I should be doing this."

"Quiet!" yelled a guard nearby. "You there, get ta work!"

Tealick's eyes lit up like fire. He immediately dropped his shovel and took a step toward his tormentors but was yanked back by Parsnippy, who yelled out, "We are!" Then, in a frustrated voice, he turned to Tealick. "This is the reason it must be me. Your strength binds the others, but you can't risk them by angering Scalar. Look at him! He watches us even now. He wants you to provoke him!"

Tealick looked at the evil pouring out of the lizard's eyes. "You're right."

That evening, after the prisoners had been counted again and prodded back to the cave, Tealick found the beaver waiting again in the shadows. He stood up. "The choice is made. This one," he said, pointing to Parsnippy, "will make the journey."

"And if he is missed?"

"Then we will tell the skinks to search the cave. As you said, there are many ways to lose yourself in here."

The beaver laughed. "Indeed. I've been here long and its secrets still evade me." He looked down at Parsnippy. "You're ready?"

"I am."

Tealick watched Parsnippy wave to the group and disappear into the darkness with Brondanur just in front. He then heard a sound outside and looked out through one of the cracks in the guarded entrance. He saw that it was just starting to rain, and a feeling of dread washed over him at the terrible omen.

# 27. A Fearful Trip

"A little further now, Parsnippy," said Brondanur, "and you will feel water under your feet. It originates from the same stream that flows beneath my lodge."

"It's so dark in here and I do not like swimming at night," he replied in a fearful voice.

"Let your hands be your eyes." The beaver moved into the water just behind him. "Now stop and use your hands to follow the smooth rocks. They will guide you to the outside."

He held tightly to the beaver's right hand and blindly reached out to feel the rocks with his other while the beaver drove them deeper into the water. Within moments, they had passed through the exit and surfaced a short distance downstream from the dam. Looking around to ensure that no one was nearby, Brondanur motioned him to dive again.

From there, the beaver pulled him through a short tunnel, where they emerged from a hole into a grand room decorated with elaborate wood carvings that hung from the walls. "Ha-ha! So, what do you think of a beaver's home, Master Parsnippy?!"

"It's amazing!"

Brondanur saw him looking down at three framed runes emblazoned in the center of the floor. "Ah, my friend, you see the mark of my colony. Each is unique and known to all the others. But come now, and meet my family," he said with a jolly demeanor. "And share a hearty meal, where you will learn more about the beavers!"

Parsnippy followed him into the next room. He wondered how Brondanur could be so happy when so many terrible things were happening around them.

All at once, he was surrounded with the smell of freshly baked bread, which drifted from the kitchen. Just after Brondanur stepped into the room, he noticed another beaver standing to the side, dressed in a red apron and with two small beavers to her side. One was dressed in a vest like his father and the other with an apron like her mother.

Brondanur's wife looked down at Parsnippy and exclaimed, "We are so happy to have you as our guest. Please, share our table and tell us stories of better times!"

One of the two smaller beavers interrupted, "Can we give him his gift now?"

"We haven't even sat down yet," Brondanur declared.

"Oh please, father," said the one with the vest.

"Well, if you must."

He quickly darted out to the other room and returned with a black rock, sharp on one side and dull on the other. He gave it to his sister, who handed it Parsnippy.

"We call it Beavertooth," said the small beaver with the vest.

"We found it in the same cave where you are," said his sister beside him.

Parsnippy looked quizzically at the stone.

"Everyone around here thinks we use our own teeth to gnaw on wood. But," he winked, "when they're not looking, especially those dumb ole lizards, we use these stones. We grab it here and cut the wood. We want you to have one! Now you're a beaver too!" They laughed.

Parsnippy's mouth almost fell on the floor. "Thank you!" Then, looking at the stone in his hand, he held it up. "Thank you very much!"

For Parsnippy, who had never left home and had no idea of the forest beyond his own pond, this was truly an amazing experience. He had almost forgotten the evil that lay just beyond the wood that surrounded them. The beavers at Rippleshy had never invited anyone to their home. And now to be their guest made him almost emotional.

Brondanur remained standing while the others took a seat at the table and declared, "We are honored to have such a brave warrior and a friend to share our home, for tonight, before he embarks on a perilous journey."

Parsnippy heard them all slap their tales on the soft carpet several times. "You are very kind, but I am not as brave you think."

"Nonsense!" Brondanur said, looking down and smiling. "You are a beaver, my friend! Courage is given, never taken, never loaned, and never stolen. It is a treasure that sits within each of us that comes from our friends and our families. Before this journey of yours ends, you will find yours as well."

Before he could respond, the young female to his right spoke up. "Tell us about your pond and where you come from."

"Yes," said the one with the vest. "What is the name of the colony where you live?"

"Well, my colony, uh, village, is called Rippleshy. The beavers there are called Packard and Mulsey." He quickly added, "And they are very friendly."

"What good names! Do you know any other ones?" asked the mother, passing some bread to her children.

"I am afraid not. However, tonight, I leave to find Darmok."

"Darmok!" exclaimed Brondanur's wife. She looked over at Brondanur. "Husband, you did not say that Parsnippy was to make such a long trip! It will take him at least two nights!"

"He requested this, dear. He said it must be done. What was I to say? I am to guide him to the trail and provide directions."

Parsnippy looked from one to the other during this talk.

"And how will he have protection during the night?" she demanded.

"From Nimdoor: I sought her out before I returned."

"That old eagle? You sure she can still see in the dark?"

"She found me before I began the journey back. And she has friends among the owls."

"Hrummphhh. Well, you should be with him."

"We have already been through this. I cannot. You yourself said the great lizard asked for me while I was gone the first time. The risk is too great!"

"He's right," whispered Parsnippy. "All of you have been wonderful. I don't want to put any of you at further risk. May I ask a question?"

"Of course," replied Brondanur.

"The bird you speak of. Will it stay with me?"

"No. But it will always be near," Brondanur replied in a soothing deep voice. "Now, let us enjoy a glass of maple cider!"

Parsnippy's hand was shaking as he lifted the mug.

Throughout the rest of the dinner, he described Rippleshy and the cool pond that hugged its banks. He talked of friends and family there and learned the story of the beavers and how they helped the forest. But most amazing was the story of Brondanur and how he had descended from the family of Darmok, which was one of the noble families of ancient Anzenar.

After dinner, Brondanur's wife came around the table and knelt down in front of him. "Good journey to you, Parsnippy." She then handed him some bread wrapped in leaves. "When you get hungry, here is something to remember us by. Go well into the night."

"Thank you. I so hope to see you all again." The kids waved and he followed Brondanur into the next room. "How do I greet a beaver? I mean, how will Darmok know me Brondanur?"

"From this," He reached up on the wall and took down a small piece of wood. On it were carved the same runes he'd seen on Brondanur's floor. "This is the symbol of my den. Show this to him and all others of my kind that declare themselves to you. If he doesn't see you once you arrive, then tap his lodge and toss it in the water."

Parsnippy wasn't sure he understood, but he pushed the wood deep in his pocket anyway.

"We must leave now," said Brondanur.

Parsnippy turned back and waved, then dropped down through the hole and followed the beaver into the tunnel. After a moment, they emerged at the front of the dam and felt heavy rain drops strike their faces. The beaver motioned him to remain quiet, but Parsnippy ignored his request. "The rain is a bad sign to me, Brondanur."

"No. It's bad for the lizards and skinks," said the beaver, leaning down. Then, in a lower voice still, he continued, "I've watched them. Unlike you and I, they run and hide when the rain hits them. They won't be looking for us now. Keep close. We must make for the eastern side of the pond."

For Parsnippy, it was difficult to navigate without a moon to guide him. His fate rested entirely on the beaver. After a short time, he looked up and saw the bank in sight. Brondanur was the first out after looking for any danger nearby.

He turned to Parsnippy. "I must leave you now. Continue upstream and keep to this side of the water. When you come to where the river bends around a giant tree, you will be halfway to Darmok. If you must leave the stream for any reason, go east. Few will follow you there."

"Why east?" he asked in a worried voice.

"It's safer. A dangerous swamp exists to the west."

"So east is better?"

"I must be honest with you, Parsnippy. Some say it's haunted by terrible beasts, but I have seen none, and I have lived here for a long time. Now, remain on this path and move through the bushes as much as you can. Darkness is your friend. This water will take you to Darmok. His lodge is mighty and more impressive than mine. Do you have any questions before I leave you?"

Parsnippy looked up and could hardly see the beaver. "When will I see Nimdoor?"

"You will not unless she so chooses. But I have no doubt that she has already seen both of us."

Parsnippy looked into the night, hoping for a sign.

The big beaver gently smiled. "You carry with you the hope and courage of your friends. When you return to this spot, do this." The beaver took two rocks and banged them twice under water. "I will know it is you. Have faith. We will see each other again soon." With that, the beaver moved back into the water and was gone.

Parsnippy stared at the rippling surface and then took a moment to look up and feel the rain against his face. He then felt the Beavertooth in his pocket, gave it a squeeze, and thought about Nimdoor watching him from somewhere above. He looked back at the small lake one last time and took a step, and then another. Within a moment, he too disappeared into the rainy night.

# 28. KELTAR'S MARCH SOUTH

RED SPEAR LOOKED UP AT THE MORNING SUNRISE AND SHIVERED. He looked over balefully at the chameleon to his right and was about to say something when he felt a foot on his back. He immediately kicked it off.

Blue Spear grunted in pain and rolled to the side. "What was that fer?"

"Shhhhh," his brother hissed, looking up at the Saurian king. "Keep yer voice down!" he whispered.

Blue Spear massaged his side and then looked back at the sleeping chameleon. Like his brother, he also despised the creature seeming to rest so peacefully nearby. He looked at it closer. For an instant, he saw one of its eyes fluttering and a smile drift across its face.

It knew something, and he was going find out what.

A voice rumbled from above. "The last creature that lied to me was torn apart. Remember that while you walk," threatened Keltar.

"We ain't lyin'," stuttered Red Spear, looking up.

Keltar ignored him. "And you, chameleon. You have something to say!?"

Stretching his arms and smiling, he casually replied, "I have had a most restful sleep, sire. And you?"

The king glared down at him for several seconds before turning away. "Gradig!"

His general hoped off his rock and moved quickly to the king's side. "Yes, my Lord?"

"Have two guards take them to the forest's edge and let them feed upon whatever they can find. We need them fresh in case we come up short on food. Then assemble a force and wait for me at the forest's edge!"

Gradig nodded once, then immediately signaled to two others nearby, who began prodding the prisoners down the path. The chameleon glanced at the guards and immediately ran to the front, leaving Red and Blue Spear following behind. One of the lizards, just behind Red Spear, suddenly kicked him in the back. "You still tired? You wanna be carried?"

The skink nearly fell down at the pain. "I can walk!" he growled back loudly.

"Hee hee. I'm looking forward to seeing ya at the end of me stick roasting over a fire."

The other lizard added, "You can't have 'em to ya self. We gonna share."

Red Spear turned around and suddenly realized that both his brother and the chameleon had intentionally moved further ahead, leaving him at the mercy of the two guards. With a loud hiss, he grabbed his brother and threw him back.

The other guard laughed and replied, "We don't mind which one we eat first."

But Blue Spear wasn't having it. He quickly pushed himself back, only to trip over his brother's leg, causing both to fall to the ground. Red Spear immediately lashed back at him, but it lasted only a moment before one of the guards kicked them both forward.

At the same time, Keltar began walking in the opposite direction toward a giant rock outcropping that towered behind his army. After ensuring he was not followed, he disappeared behind it and began clawing at the base of one of the stones. As the dirt was pushed away, the etchings of deep runes began to appear at its base. This was the Remembrance stone that described the great battles Keltar had won and the territories he had conquered. It alone determined who led the Chilltails.

The Saurian king moved one of its claws across a rune, written in the language of the Chilltails long ago, and whispered out loud.

"*Not even their king, or the lighting he wielded, could save the frogs of stature from their mortal end.*

"*For it was the hand of the Chilltails, when their citadel fell, that smote the army that could not defend.*"

"None survived," he said to himself. He was sure of it.

But the skinks description of what they saw in the Eastern Forest still nagged at him.

"My lord," intruded Corot, the lead guard, "the force is ready and awaits you at the forest's edge."

Keltar, startled, looked up. "Very good. You will remain with the others here. If we do not return after ten suns, you will lead the remaining force south. Destroy everything! Do you understand?"

"Yes, my lord."

Keltar covered the runes once more. He instinctively felt that more victories would be added to the stone when he returned. "Make sure everyone is aware of my command after we leave. I will join Gradig now."

"Yes, my lord!"

As the chameleon and skinks were prodded into the shade of the first trees, they sighed in relief at the cool forest that surrounded them. But it was not so for the lizards.

"Only good thing about this place is finding something to eat," said one.

"Yeah, lucky for us, we don't have to go too fer to git it," replied another, snickering at the three prisoners.

Blue Spear noticed that the chameleon appeared to be smiling, indifferent to the taunts.

Red Spear noticed it as well and said loudly, "Don't think about leaving or turning a different color, because we're both watching ya."

"And they're watching you," it replied with its thumb pointing backwards.

"No matter, we're important to the king—you ain't nothin'."

The chameleon just laughed.

"Silence!" Keltar hollered back. "You two will lead and the chameleon will follow just behind. Should anything attack, you'll be the first it eats."

"Yes, of course. We were gonna suggest that! Just watch him," Red Spear said, pointing to the chameleon.

"Ain't no worry. If he starts a changing color," said one of the guards, "I'll jest step on em."

It was Red Spear's turn now to smile at the chameleon. But try as his best, he could not get it to turn around. So he just jostled it out of the way. "You heard em—us first!"

With a sullen stride, the two skinks quietly marched under the green canopy while listening to the heavy footsteps of the lizards and the rushing waters of Songentrope Creek on their left.

After a few hours, Keltar growled out loud, "We'll rest there and eat." He pointed to a bright clearing just ahead. "You three will sit beside me."

The army slowly shoved their way forward toward a sunlit space. Since leaving Gravenbroke, they had all been miserable and complained constantly.

"Move it," cried one.

"Move it yerself," grumbled the other.

The two skinks and chameleon were pushed to the center of the crowd. Just in front of them, the king pulled something from his bag that had a terrible odor and tossed it toward them. But none of them touched it.

"Not hungry?" he asked.

"I, uh, don't think so," said Red Spear, stumbling to move away from it. "We ate a lot before we left."

The chameleon turned his eyes to the forest beyond the stream. He squinted and noticed some movement, and then a rock splashed into the water. Keltar quickly turned around but saw nothing.

"What are you looking at, chameleon?"

"Nothing, sire," he said plainly. "I was just enjoying the forest once again."

Keltar glared back. "We leave now!" He got up, tossed what was left of his lunch into the woods, and then prodded the skinks back to the front. "You two will continue to lead. The chameleon will follow. If it disappears, I'll take it out on you!"

Upon hearing that, Red Spear stopped and shifted his eyes to the chameleon and then to the king.

"Surely it would be better to have him in front, sire."

"You said you knew where my brother is. The chameleon did not."

Both skinks nodded sullenly and started back on the trail. Red Spear took the lead and concentrated on ensuring that his original path to the beaver's dam was correct. However, Blue Spear often glanced back to make sure the chameleon was still there. And each time, it just smiled back, irritating him even more. Nothing was going the way they had hoped.

As Keltar's army marched into the afternoon, they had become increasingly agitated at the number of trees they had to dodge. In the desert, he could see his enemies far off. Here, however, it was another story. He stopped walking at one point, near the edge of Songentrope Creek and stared across its waters toward the Eastern Forest, remembering what the skinks had said.

Then, all of a sudden, he felt a violent impact from behind that nearly sent him falling down the embankment. He recovered to find another of his kind splayed on the ground, looking up.

"I apologize, sire!" the soldier gushed. "I did not hear the halt."

"Get up, you fool," Keltar snarled.

"Sire," Red Spear interrupted. "*We*," he said, while glancing at his brother, "would like to suggest an excellent spot for to-night's rest: a clearing just ahead. We should be near the beaver's lodge tomorrow."

Blue Spear made a face at the chameleon. However, it had turned and was staring at the king.

"Then go!" He turned to look back and shouted, "Gradig!"

His general rushed to the front while purposely knocking the same soldier down.

Keltar, ignoring the hapless soldier, pointed to Red Spear. "Follow that one to a clearing ahead. Then post guards to watch the skinks and chameleon all night. If any move, eat them."

Red Spear was shocked that the king found him no more valuable than the chameleon. His face turned purple with rage, but he hid it by looking away.

Upon arriving, the three moved to the center as ordered. Their guards quickly surrounded them, effectively eliminating any pathway to freedom. Before long, the still of the night de-scended, broken only by the sound of insects and the soft light from the moon above.

The twins, however, had become too anxious to sleep—but not the chameleon.

"Don't think we can't see ya move," came the sinister voice of a guard. "We never let a meal get away. We gonna be lookin' at you tasty things all night."

"Ignore him," Red Spear whispered to his brother. "They need us." Then, looking at the chameleon close by, he added "But we don't need *him*," he replied, showing his teeth.

Just above, the moon slowly clawed its way across the night sky, finally disappearing into some heavy clouds. The three guards did their job and carefully watched the skinks and chameleon. But, as the hours passed, something seemed to be odd about one of them. As more time passed, they became agitated and finally poked at the creature. With relief, one said, "I see 'em."

"Yeah," replied another, rubbing his eyes to make sure.

But only a few minutes later, when the moon had disappeared, the lead guard poked at the creature again – but there was nothing there. Somehow, the ground had swallowed it up.

In a panic, he yelled, "It's gone!"

# 29. A Frightful Journey

IT HAD BEEN MORE THAN TWO HOURS SINCE PARSNIPPY HAD BEEN left alone in the darkness and rain. Already, he was having second thoughts about his choice to leave. Again and again, he tried to focus on his friends and their hopes in him, but thoughts of his own failure intruded. The rain had now become merciless and was pelting him harder, slowing his pace even more. Worse still were the puddles in his path that turned into small streams that swirled around his feet. He glanced at Songentrope Creek, which had now grown into a roaring lion with its cascades and white water, making it all but impossible to hear any threat nearby. He wondered if he could make it to the bend in the river before day fall.

He muttered to himself, "Maybe Tealick should have gone. Oh, Nimdoor, if I could only know you are there," he said forlornly, looking up.

He took a few more steps and stopped. "No!" he whispered, shaking his head. "If the two from Rippleshy can risk so much and leave, so can I."

With a new determination, he strained for any sound above

the noisy river and took another step. But the darkness was so intense that he had to feel his way forward in order to avoid the trees and obstacles that lined his path. Suddenly, he felt his foot strike a stick that was resting in one of the large puddles that flooded the trail. Frustrated, he was about to kick it away when it occurred to him that perhaps it could be useful. Reaching down, he felt rounded knobs on one end and discovered it straight. He then picked it up and jabbed it in the ground just ahead.

After several more hours, it had become even more difficult. Many of the puddles had become so deep, he felt he had to swim across them. And it was only getting worse. The rain had increased, which forced him to move even closer to the edge of the stream. But the closer he got, the greater the chance that a sudden runoff would carry him into the current.

Using the stick, he began measuring the depth of the rivulets that crossed his path before entering each. He was about to test the next one when the rain abruptly slowed. In this short time, he could now see the fast-moving water as it thrashed across the rocks to his left. Realizing that he was dangerously close to the bank, he quickly moved to his right and was starting to walk forward when he heard a small hissing sound.

"Well, looksss a here, brotherssssss, what we's ah seeing."

With a start, Parsnippy jerked his head to the right, where he saw two sets of glowing eyes peering at him from the darkness. Snakes! He immediately pointed the stick at them. "You leave me alone! I'm not bothering you!" he cried out.

The serpents moved a few feet closer. One was twice the size of the other and both were wound tightly in a circle. He stepped back. "I'm not scared of you."

"Well, you should be," hissed the larger one, twice his size.

The smaller one slowly slithered to Parsnippy's right. "All alones, is ya? Where you off too that's soooo important?"

"If it's any business of yours, I'm helping some friends. Now, may I please pass?"

"You know, we likes the rain. You see, the air in our cold cave is not near as refreshing as a warm rain. And what a ssssurprise! Imagine finding something tasty just outside our hole."

"That will be enough of that!" said Parsnippy nervously. "Good night. I will be on my way."

"Why don't youse come back with us to our nice dry home? The entrance isss behind us. Not very fars at all."

"Thank you, but no. I have to be somewhere else."

The smaller snake on his right began moving closer, causing Parsnippy to wave his stick at it. It stopped abruptly. "That's no way to be a friend, isss it, brother?" asked the smaller one.

"No," the larger one hissed. "I guessss it needsss some mannersss. Maybe it would rather be your dinner."

Emboldened at the remark, the smaller snake started advancing, causing Parsnippy to immediately back away. Looking back, Parsnippy saw the raging stream just behind him now. There was no escape. The snake reared back to strike when a huge feather drifted down to land just in front of it. Parsnippy looked down at the object. At first, he didn't recognize it, but within a short moment, a smile formed on his face. He reached down and scooped it off the ground. Then, standing up, he looked at the serpent. "Look what I found," he said, holding up the feather that was twice his height.

The larger serpent looked up. "What's it got in its hand?"

Then a terrible feeling came to it. Something about the object made it pause. It strained its memory for an answer while it watched its prey dangle it in its hand, as if it were taunting him.

"I'm leaving now," Parsnippy said, waving it at them both. "Enjoy the rain. Goodbye." With an abrupt turn, he started back on his path.

The larger snake saw his brother coil for the kill. Then he remembered. "Stop! Stop!" he yelled.

But before the shorter serpent could respond, there was a huge flash of something in the air. Parsnippy and the larger snake were blown back across the ground, as if a tornado had fallen upon them, and then it was gone. Both slowly looked up in a daze. But where there had been two snakes, only one remained.

"You! You!" the snake hissed loudly. "Where isss my brother?!!!"

Parsnippy vaguely sensed what had happened and could only weakly reply, "I'm sorry. I think he's gone. Perhaps he went home."

The one remaining snake just glared at him for a moment. Then it hissed loudly, "My brother is lost because of you!!! Ssss-sorry you say!!! You will paysssssss!!!!!" With that, the snake coiled and struck at him with malice. But before it could pass half the distance, a huge gust of wind came again and blew the frog ten feet back, where he landed in a large puddle.

Recovering from the second shock, he opened his eyes to see a mighty eagle standing near him that was, at least, ten times his size. In its fearsome talons was the larger snake. Pulling himself to his feet, he looked up and asked in a shaken voice, "Are-are you Nimdoor?"

"I am," came a sonorous voice. "This one will not bother you again. You must be on your way now, as the night is old."

"What will happen to him?" he asked shakily.

It turned its head slowly toward the snake and then back to Parsnippy. In a slow and serious tone, it replied, "He and I will have a short talk after you go. There is no need for you to worry."

Parsnippy just stared at the huge creature and said limply, "Thank you."

"Go now and complete your journey."

He simply nodded.

Nimdoor's sudden presence was the confidence Parsnippy needed. All the fear that had stalked him since leaving the beaver now drained away. For the first time, he felt optimism and hope for the friends he left behind.

After finding his stick, he glanced back at the huge bird once more before walking away. He never knew what Nimdoor said to the snake; he just knew it wasn't pleasant.

However, two other serpents that hid in the shadows did. Both had watched in horror as one of their own disappeared. Terrified, they just stared blankly at Parsnippy as he ambled by, just inches away from their fangs. They slithered down the trails and listened to the words of the sky demon as it held their companion beneath its claw, and then they fled, hoping to never again be in the presence of the creature that commanded it.

More than half the night remained for Parsnippy, and he was nowhere close to his destination. He blinked the water away from his eyes and listened quietly to the occasional rumbling of thunder in the distance. Deep down, he sensed the storm was not finished with him yet.

After several more hours, most of the rain and thunder had finally disappeared. But the small streams of water that crossed his path had not. At one point, they suddenly shifted direction. Curiously, he followed one of the flows until he heard a gushing sound coming from the other side of a tree that lay in his path. As he stepped over its roots, he found himself standing on a small cliff overlooking an angry tributary to Songentrope Creek.

He immediately dismissed the thought of swimming, as the danger of being swept downstream was too great. Besides, there were too many holes on the far bank that could harbor a snake. And he had no interest in repeating *that* experience. After a few minutes, he found a log that had fallen across the stream a short way up.

After carefully balancing, he began walking across. But about half-way, a tremendous clap of thunder stuck, instantly causing him to lose balance. In a desperate attempt to save himself, he flailed his hands overhead and grabbed a branch. Fearfully hoping the limb would hold, he tried again to get footing. But it was not to be. The limb cracked and he felt himself falling forward.

"There you go. I gotcha," said a voice slowly next to him. "Yes siree, I gotcha. You ok there, mah friend?"

"I don't know."

"Name's Boxel. Live down there in the big hole on the right. Yup! Great place for a home."

The turtle noticed Parsnippy staring at the water below.

"Whoa now," said Boxel. "Guess ah better pull ya up."

With a swift jerk, Parsnippy felt himself flung up on the log, where he stood, staring at the face of an old terrapin.

"Now, that ain't half bad. Got ya on the first try. Guess I got some stories to tell the family tonight!"

Parsnippy smiled crookedly at the warm stranger. "Thank you. I thought I was all done."

"No siree, got my family and friends nearby. See dem holes there?"

"Uh huh, but I thought they were snake holes!"

"Yeah, used to be until we run the varmints out," he replied, laughing. "Don't go and worry yerself about dem crazy things. They can't ever agree on nothin'. Now, why are you a walkin' by yerself here in the middle o' the night?"

"I have to get to a giant tree that sits in the middle of Son-gentrope Creek before morning."

"Well now, I ain't so much heard of that place, but your kind gets a round more 'n us. Morning say? Well, you best be a crossing then. Stay left o' the big rocks. Hear tell there are some bad varmints that live near 'em. But if'n the creeks on ya left, they won't get near ya."

"Thank you, Boxel!"

"You come back when you can stay a while longer!"

"I will," Parsnippy said, stepping off the limb. He turned to see Boxel swing down under the log, bounce off the water, and slide into the bank, waving to him the entire time.

Parsnippy followed Boxel's directions and stayed to the left. However, he found that the path at one point had washed out. His only choice now was to move further east into the forest with each additional step.

After an hour of walking, he noticed the faintest hints of light begin to appear in the canopy overhead. The sun was coming up and he was lost. How could this have happened? Frantically, he continued forward, hoping there would be an opening that would offer a way back to Songentrope Creek, but all he saw were the dim silhouettes of huge trees that towered above him. He noticed a stick beneath one and took it for protection. But it was crooked, unlike the one he lost, and of little use. Nevertheless, it felt good to hold onto something.

He scouted the perimeter of the bushes, taking care to look for any passageway that would lead to the other side, but there was none. After a few minutes, he had become exhausted and found a place to rest. But before he could lay his head down, he heard a loud snort.

He looked out from under a bush and saw a gigantic head with a long horn slowly moving up and down the clearing, munching on some bushes nearby. It was even more hideous than the giant lizards that imprisoned his friends. Even Nimdoor with her mighty wings would swoon in the presence of such a beast.

He watched it closely while at the same time backing deeper into the bush. But the thorns were already pressing into his back and he winced in pain. He stood as still as possible, but it was too late. He watched it stomp furiously and abruptly turn around.

Parsnippy jumped at the sound, forcing a sharp thorn in his back. "Ahhhh," he cried, whimpering.

This enraged the animal even further. It pointed its eyes immediately in his direction. Parsnippy, sensing the attack, darted out from his hiding place to a large tree nearby, missing the beast's horn by inches. No time to look back.

Looking deeper into the forest, he spotted a bird chipping away at the base of a large boulder. It glanced at him and suddenly flew away. For a moment, he was curious. He squinted carefully and saw a large burrow just beside the stone where the bird perched, dimly lit by the rising sun that filtered beneath the trees. With a quick breath, he shot for the opening and plunged in just before the beast crashed into the stone behind him.

# 30. THE REUNION

SHORTLY AFTER LEAVING DARMOK, BALDMAR NOTICED THAT
Feyorin had become unusually quiet. After a few minutes, he
looked back to ensure the others were following and then sped
up beside him. "What is bothering you?"

"Scalar," he replied matter-of-factly.

"He is no match for us."

"True, if it's just him and his two friends," said Feyorin quietly.

Baldmar moved closer. "You're speaking of the kingdom of
the Dons?"

Feyorin nodded. "As Darmok reminded us, we cannot allow
him to make an agreement with the Southern lounge, even if it
means that we sacrifice Orora. Otherwise, we risk all of Anzenar," he said, nodding to the others.

Baldmar was transfixed at those words and walked in silence
for several moments. "But surely they know their history and
would not choose this."

"I'm not so sure," he replied, shaking his head. "Why would
Scalar choose a location so close to them?"

"But to take such a risk, considering the hatred between Keltar and the Sargon?"

"Think about it. So close to the southern edge *and* Scalar's hatred for Keltar as well?"

"I see your point. To make an agreement with the southern dragons that does NOT include Keltar suggests how naïve Scalar is," Baldmar replied flatly, looking ahead.

"Exactly—but it will be a false one. Scalar, like all the Chilltails, is easily swayed by opportunities to extend his power. And yet, time and again, they have demonstrated no honor in truces or agreements. They are traitorous to their own kind as well as others. You remember the stories before the crossing. Our people saw it all too often."

"But wouldn't some of the others who do not side with Keltar attempt the same?"

He shook his head. "No, Scalar's the key to all of it. His proximity to the Dons of the south cannot be an accident. He must have discovered Sargon's army somehow. We need to find the ones from Rippleshy quickly. Even now, I believe the forces of Keltar's army approach."

Baldmar looked perplexed. "But there is one question left to answer. Surely Sargon would be shocked to find others of his kind so close to him."

Feyorin replied slowly, "I am sure he would. However, it would be in the interest of Scalar not to mention his relationship with Keltar. By leaving Gravenbroke, he burned any hope of returning to his brother."

"But if Sargon's emissary from the South is present when Keltar arrives…"

"Miralassen ordered that under no circumstances can that be allowed to happen. Not now. Not before we are ready. She also knows that Shadowguard cannot keep the two kingdoms apart forever. They are both threats to Anzenar. War is coming soon, my friend. We can only delay it."

"What do we say to them?" asked Baldmar, glancing at the others.

"Nothing for the moment."

"And if Keltar does not find Scalar?"

Feyorin narrowed his eyes. "We must ensure that he does."

"Baldmar!" Tenara yelled.

Startled, both Ororans turned around sharply.

"Look!" She pointed.

Far off to their left, they could see several large Toadans standing in the morning light that filtered down from the tree-tops. One of them stood in front of the others.

Feyorin scowled and walked over. "You are out of your territory."

"I can say the same for you," growled the one in front.

"You cannot. This is ALL Ororan. You know this to be true, Darga."

"You know them, Baldmar?" asked Joen quietly from behind.

"Yes," he replied quietly, motioning her to be quiet. "They inhabit the extreme southern portion of Shadowguard. And they need to explain why they are here. We have had a truce with them since we arrived."

"Forget it, Darga! They're not interested!" said one of the Toadans to his right.

Feyorin ignored him. "You have something to say?"

Darga scowled and waved the other Toadans back. "You are aware of the ones that make their home beyond the southern forest."

A few seconds passed. "Of course!" said Feyorin. "Tell us what we don't know."

Darga eyes squinted. He said slowly, "The one you look for and two others."

Baldmar was shocked that they knew so much. Feyorin, however, remained impassive while staring at the toads.

"Continue."

Darga grimaced. "Do not let the things of the past cloud your eyes, Feyorin. We can help you with this threat. We know where they make their home. We have known since they arrived."

"And for this little information, I am to trust you?"

"Only if you think you have a choice. Set aside the past and listen to me."

Feyorin pondered the request. He had trusted him once before and it cost him dearly. "Then say all that you know."

"Three of them make their home in the place you call Glen of the Rock, where the trees have been forcibly cleared."

Feyorin was stunned. "Brondanur's home? That is only a short distance from the southern edge!"

"Yes. They are attempting to create a liaison with the Southern Dons. Sargon has sent one of his own to meet with them.

"I suspected that."

"Then you know what this means. Like you, we have no use for those that despise the forest." Darga abruptly turned to the others and waved them back. "We are on the same side, Feyorin!"

With a swift movement, Darga pulled an arrow from his quiver and fired it into the ground. "What was once friendship between us can be again." Then, abruptly, he moved backward and retreated into the mists.

Most of the others were in a mild shock as they stared at the now empty forest.

After a moment, Frondameer walked over to Feyorin. "Some of our own scouts brought back stories of terrible acts committed by the lizards that live beyond the southern border. Some say that even the Northern dragons fear them."

Feyorin just gazed silently at the arrow stuck fast in the ground and then grimly faced him. Tenara and Joen moved closer to listen.

"They had every reason to believe these stories, because both of these clans were once part of the same lounge long ago. But as we know, lizards are never satisfied until one king rules them all. At that time, secret allegiances and promises were offered to the members of Sargon's army for their loyalty to Keltar, which ultimately led to the War of the Dragons and Sargon's defeat.

"Soon after, he and many of his warriors escaped to the Anduin Mountain, leaving Keltar, in his moment of victory, to strike Sargon's name from the runes of Melinar, the first and greatest of all lizard kings that ruled before Sargon. Unfortunately, like Keltar, we had presumed Sargon was lost, along with his remaining army, in the snows of the Anduin Mountain. It was not until the great fire consumed our land and forced us to flee over same Mountain that we realized our mistake."

CHIP SIMMONS

"So he wasn't lost," Frondameer said.

"No. We discovered Sargon's new home among the Southern hills and then immediately extended Shadowguard so that the two Chilltails would never meet again."

"Then the stories we hear are true," Blendefest commented dejectedly.

"I'm afraid so. Sargon's lounge must have crossed the snow and ice later than we thought and taken a different path to the foot of Sorrowful Mountain."

Frondameer and Blendefest looked vacantly at the rest, who stood nearby.

Feyorin added mournfully, "Our problem is young Scalar. He knows nothing of this battle or the loathing that Sargon has for Keltar. If the Southern lounge should find out that he is his brother, he would be killed instantly."

No one said anything for a long while. Frondameer suddenly looked back at Feyorin. "Then this quest of ours is only partially about helping Tenara and Joen find their friends!"

Feyorin was quiet.

Tenara looked at Feyorin. "Is that true?"

"Yes," he replied simply. "The journey we share is larger than any one of us. Our success here will not only determine the future of Rippleshy, but possibly Anzenar itself."

"Why didn't you tell us this before we left Orora?" demanded Tenara.

"You weren't ready," he replied softly.

"I don't understand."

Feyorin looked down at her. "When we first met, I saw a young female who did not believe in herself and what she was capable of. But the more I observed, the more I saw someone who found the courage to leave her home and venture into the unknown to save others." He turned his eyes to Frondameer and Blendefest. "And I believe that Blendefest and Frondameer saw this in you as well."

Feyorin faced the scouts. "Fladon taught us the courage of the Serveyans that risk their life for Moss Rock. But we needed proof that can only be demonstrated." He shifted his eyes to all of them. "Later, Miralassen saw this as well at the council meeting where you were questioned. It is for this reason that I tell you now that you are part of something larger. However, if your choice is to rescue only those of Rippleshy, I will understand and release you now from any further danger."

No one talked for a moment, and then Joen perked up. "I can't leave. Who's going to take care of Baldmar?"

Feyorin turned to stare at his partner, who could only grin sheepishly. "Indeed!" he said. "I see your point."

Tenara looked up at Feyorin. "Joen and I would never have made it this far without both of you. We will continue to walk and fight by your side."

"The Scouts of Moss Rock are honored to serve as well," stated Frondameer.

"I'm hungry," said Joen, breaking up the camaraderie.

Baldmar pulled some sweet bread from his pack and passed it around. Its fine aroma reminded them all of what they left behind and what was at stake.

Frondameer saw some sudden movement on the ground. "Look at that," he causally observed.

Feyorin turned his head and noticed a small bird standing

completely still, not far from where he sat, just staring at them intently. He smiled. "You have good eyes, my friend. Few have seen a caven beyond its home."

"I was unaware that they lived nearby," Blendefest said.

Feyorin frowned. "In fact, they do not." He puzzled the question. "Baldmar."

His companion pulled himself up, walked slowly toward the bird, and knelt a few feet from it. The bird took off at once and landed again further south. He followed it and the same thing happened again. Then he stood up, drew a circle in the air with his hand, and walked out of sight.

"What was that he just did?" asked Joen.

"He will follow it and meet us later. For now, we must return to the creek. The land is wet from the rain last night. We must move quickly if we are to meet the one from Rippleshy that Brondanur sent."

They quickly finished the bread and left. As they approached the swollen stream, they noticed some heavy foot prints in the soft mud. Frondameer spoke up. "Saurians."

Feyorin nodded. "Yes. The tracks run downstream, but we cannot be sure if they turned back. Quickly, we must return back to the protection of Shadowguard."

Tenara stopped. "But Feyorin, we could miss the one we're looking for. What if he follows the same path? He could be on the trail as we speak."

Blendefest touched Feyorin's back. "Look!" he said while pointing.

Two huge shapes broke the reflection of the early morning sun off the river.

Feyorin waved his hand low. "Back quickly into the mist!"

When they passed into the ground fog, Feyorin whispered, "Frondameer, can you track them without being seen?"

"I believe so, if I stay at the edge of the fog."

"Then do it now. Return when you can."

Frondameer immediately left.

"Do you think it wise, Feyorin, to split us up with Baldmar gone as well?" Blendefest asked somberly.

"We must know where the Saurians go before we know if the trail south is safe. It's why I sent Frondameer. Baldmar will instead keep to Shadowguard. For now, we must wait."

***

By now, Baldmar was already a good distance to the South. He had noticed in the last few minutes that the bird was flying shorter intervals before landing to allow him to follow. Its last flight was into a thicket of thorns. The Ororan thought it was odd that it would choose a place like that to live. He squinted and started to say something when he heard some heaving breathing nearby. Turning to his left, he saw the strangest scene: an enormous Klumper sleeping just in front of a tree with a small opening near its roots.

"I see your problem, little one," he whispered. "But I cannot defend every home in Shadowguard. You must wait him out."

The bird instead ruffled his feathers and then flew silently above the beast and into its hole. Baldmar chastened himself for taking the time and was about to leave when the caven flew back and landed at his feet again. This time, it hopped around in distress.

He looked again at the dark hole and the beast before it. Tangling with a Klumper was extremely dangerous and certainly not worth the lost time it would incur. He looked again at the hole, but this time, he saw a faint outline of a face looking back. The shock drove him back against a thorn and he stifled a moan.

Parsnippy began waving his hand outside the entrance, but the motion caught the Klumper's eye. It immediately stood up and roared furiously at its meal, which was still out of reach.

Baldmar realized the bird's problem at once and pulled a short spear from his back. Aiming just above its head, he threw it so that it nicked the ear of the animal, causing it to squeal in pain. Immediately, it dropped down, shoved its head across the ground for several feet, and then looked back at the hole, wondering how its prey could have done that. At once, it rushed at Parsnippy, stopping short of the opening.

It was about to charge again when the small bird drove a thorn into its other ear. The Klumper instantly collapsed into a spasm of pain and dragged its face again around the ground. After stamping its hooves several times, it took off into the forest, where it was quickly lost beneath the dense canopy and rolling fog.

Baldmar looked at the bird as it landed on a limb nearby. "I'm impressed," the Ororan said to himself. The bird instead turned its back and squawked at the one who invaded its home.

Baldmar grimaced at the thankless caven while walking over to the hole. "Come out. It's safe now."

Parsnippy emerged and looked up in shock. "Thank you!"

The bird flew by Parsnippy and landed at the door of its hole. It then turned its back on both of them while scraping Parsnippy's footprints away.

He looked back. "Hmmm - I guess it doesn't like guests."

Baldmar laughed. "Caven are solitary. Like many creatures, they only want you when they need something. May I ask you a question?"

Parsnippy nodded.

"Are you the one that Brondanur sent, the one we were to meet near the Songentrope?"

The weight of a mountain collapsed from Parsnippy's shoulders, causing him to slump to the ground. "The forest pushed me away from the river. I had given hope of finding my way again."

"What is your name?"

"Parsnippy. Brondanur sent me to meet Darmok. Are you here to help rescue my friends?"

"Your questions must wait. Walk fast with me now and keep to the mists."

*** 

Further north, Frondameer had still not returned. It had been more than an hour since he had left. Blendefest had repeatedly begged Feyorin to search for him but he would not allow it.

"As you said yourself," Feyorin said quietly, "I am short Frondameer and Baldmar. I cannot risk you as well. Even with all of us, it's not possible to take on a single Saurian, much less two. You must have patience, my friend."

Blendefest just nodded.

On the other hand, Frondameer was well aware of the time he had spent tracking the two lizards. By now, they had moved far enough up the path to avoid any chance of their discovery. Anyway, he was out of time. His shadow was growing longer by the moment. Then, one of them suddenly turned around and looked in his direction. Frondameer jumped behind a tree and froze.

"I saw something!" it growled.

"What?"

"I'm not sure. One of the prisoners I think," the other rumbled back.

"We have them all locked up. Besides, you want to go in those woods and chase it?" Borgjump asked, looking at the mists swirling within the forest of Shadowguard.

Barkchew thought a moment while feeling the wet mud beneath his feet. He flexed one of his enormous claws, digging it deep into the ground, and then grumbled, "No." They began to walk forward again.

Frondameer carefully looked around and watched them amble off down the path. He was irritated at the mistake he had just made. Furthermore, he had been gone too long.

After waiting several more minutes, he moved back toward the river, which was still engorged from the rain last night. Logs and branches quickly swept down its banks only to be beaten up in the frothing white water that churned its way south.

After an hour walking back south, Frondameer spotted a ghostly figure seeming to appear and then disappear within the forest to his left. He ducked quickly behind a bush and watched the two silhouettes.

\*\*\*

By now, Feyorin knew something must have happened to Baldmar and Frondameer. He turned to Blendefest. "I did not anticipate they would be gone so long. Perhaps you were right." He was about to say more when a strange whistle was heard. He motioned them quickly back toward the mists.

Blendefest shook his head. "No, it's ok. It's a warning from Frondameer. We need to remain here!"

Within a minute, they saw three figures emerging from the rolling fog. Feyorin relaxed when he saw Baldmar and the scout but was curious about the other that walked between the two.

"Parsnippy!" yelled Tenara and Joen. With laughter, the three from Rippleshy fell into a crushing embrace.

"So it was the two of you that Brondanur said were looking for us!" Parsnippy exclaimed in astonishment. "I don't believe it!"

Feyorin suddenly saw a shadow cross the ground and looked up. All at once, a great bird twice his size landed nearby, blowing them all back in a wash of wind.

Tenara and the others looked up in shock but Parsnippy smiled.

The creature turned toward him. "It is good to see you safe."

"I would not be here without you, Nimdoor."

Tenara's struggled to her feet. "You know her?"

"She's Brondanur's friend," said Parsnippy, standing up.

Feyorin looked astonished. "You are a friend of the beaver?"

"I am. Do you have a message for him before I return?"

Feyorin glanced at Baldmar and then back. "Since when do the great eagles of the North make friends with those who walk the ground?"

"There are many creatures in Anzenar who are friends of us, including the beavers. There is much you do not know, Ororan."

"Neither Brondanur or Darmok ever spoke of you. And neither has our queen, Miralassen. I would know."

Nimdoor moved her head closer to Feyorin. "Perhaps there is a reason for that. Again, is there a message for the beaver?" It started to lift its wings.

"Tell him that Parsnippy will be returning soon." He took a step closer. "Please. Wait. Before you leave, tell me how is it that you have come to know the beaver so well?"

"I did not say I did. I said I was a friend. But that's not really your question, is it?"

He paused long before answering. "No. It's not."

"Then ask it."

Feyorin blanched at the directness of the bird. "How…how have I—we," he began, glancing over at Baldmar, "not known of you before?"

"But you have. You knew me through Proliptus."

Feyorin nearly fainted hearing the name. "That's not possible. He was lost on the mountain when my people first crossed, destroyed by the Chilltails. "

"Was he?"

"I don't understand."

She echoed, "You do not understand because you do not know the entire story."

"Perhaps you are mistaken, Nimdoor," Baldmar interrupted. "There is no history written in the old runes in our village that describe what you say."

She turned and looked at the two scouts. "Not in yours, but in theirs."

Feyorin looked at the Blendefest and Frondameer blankly.

The eagle looked back at Feyorin. "They are your kindred. They are the ones who descended from others like you, before your arrival in Anzenar. But they don't know this because they lost their ability to read the old runes. She moved her claw across the ground. "Inscribed in the first stone is the mark" |\-. "Do you know it?"

"The mark of Proliptus," replied Feyorin.

Nimdoor nodded once. "He was not destroyed as you believe. He survived the Chilltails that chased him deep into the forest on that fateful day. He was the one that wrote the history of the battle in the stones of Moss Rock," she said, looking at Frondameer and Blendefest.

The two scouts exchanged glances with each other with their mouths agape. Frondameer blurted out, "How did he know to make for Moss Rock?"

"Because he had come to Anzenar before the great fire that drove the Ororans across the mountain," the eagle replied. "Like you, he had a curiosity to know the world beyond his village. But, more importantly, he also realized there would come a time when his people would once again have to face the Chilltails in battle. So he brought other Ororans with him and founded Moss Rock as a place to begin again."

Feyorin shook his head in disbelief. "But it was written that he sacrificed himself and others to lead the Chilltails away. So if he knew we survived, why didn't he return to us?"

"Return where? He and the few that remained fled to Moss Rock to join the other Ororans that were living there. And of course, Shadowguard did not exist. But you know that, don't you?"

Feyorin looked away. "I only knew that he would never have given up."

"It was his legacy and his curiosity of the world that later became the tradition of scouting. He named his descendants the Serveyans. He could not take the chance that the name Orora would again be known to the Chilltails, so he swore them to secrecy."

Blendefest looked at Feyorin and Baldmar as if for the first time. "Then our meeting with the Ororans was not a chance event."

"No," explained Nimdoor. "In fact, it would not have happened at all except for the one who stands among you now," she said, pointing a claw at Tenara.

"I think you are mistaken," Tenara replied, confused.

Frondameer turned to Tenara. "No. She's right. You and Joen must have been an excuse for the Colonel to send us there in the beginning."

Blendefest nodded. "I agree. He must have finally understood the Willow Runes that suggested Moss Rock was founded from another place entirely. But he didn't know where to look until Fladon brought back an arrow from Shadowguard. The Colonel must have then suspected that the clues to the origins of Moss Rock would be found there. So he sent Fladon, who, according to the stories, was lost. But in fact, he is living a more comfortable life than us. Apparently, there is more to Fladon and the Colonel than the stories tell."

The eagle looked over to Feyorin. "We watched you when you fled over the Anduin Mountain. And we saw the Chilltails that followed. Some of my kind suggested we assist."

"Why didn't you?" interrupted Tenara.

"Because the Ororan is correct," she said, referring to Feyorin. "It is not the nature of us to trust the ones that live on the ground. However, many things have changed since then. The Chilltails have grown in numbers and now have the power to destroy Anzenar. I am one of the last of the great eagles of Anduin. I will do what I can to convince the others to save your home," she said, looking at all of them.

Nimdoor stretched out her wings and then looked at Feyorin. "I will deliver your message. If there is a reply, I will return. But know this: the Chilltails are coming. I make no promises that the others of my kind will help. Prepare yourselves."

Then she was gone.

# 31. THE LIZARD MARCH

**"THE CHAMELEON'S GONE!" THE GUARDS YELLED AGAIN.**

In a fit of anger, Keltar thrust his way into the clearing and looked angrily around for the traitor. But after a moment, convinced that the chameleon was gone, he drilled his eyes into the guards, whose faces screamed of terror. In a flash, he swung his spiked tail, sending both into a tree, which cracked on impact. Each dropped to the ground and rolled to the side. Neither of them moved.

Red and Blue Spear immediately began moving out of his sight, but Keltar's glistening eyes found them before they could take two steps.

"You had a part in this, didn't you?"

Both looked at the guards lying broken at the foot of the tree. "No. We didn't!" Blue Spear was climbing up his brother's back again. "You remember sire, we tried to tell ya that he was lying. He's the traitor, not us. We're loyal!"

Keltar began moving toward them, but then abruptly stopped. Something hit his head. He looked up at the dark sky and felt it again. Rain! More rain!

With a thunderous bellow, he growled, "Gradig!"

"I'm here at your side, my king."

Keltar flipped a claw around and grabbed him. "You are now responsible for these two," he said, pointing to the skinks, "and you will remain with them until morning."

Before his general could answer, Red Spear jumped up. "There is no need to worry. We have no intention of leaving."

"Oh, but there is."

"What do you mean?" Red Spear blanched.

"You reported that you talked to the beaver Darmok about my brother?"

"Yes...?"

"Korzen and Roozen said you didn't."

"They LIE!" screamed Red Spear.

"Perhaps you can tell them yourself."

Both skinks turned around and saw the two lizards glowering down at them.

"Yeah, tell us," Korzen replied menacingly while flexing a single claw.

Roozen added an evil smile. "And tell the king more about them big frogs." He looked at Keltar. "Sire, you know dem skinks lie. They just been lyin' around."

"If we were lying, why did we come back? Say!" Red Spear said, glaring at the two accusers. "Because you were probably working for Scalar."

Red Spear visibly shook at the accusation. "Borgjump works for Scalar. How do we know that you're not his spy?"

"Because I didn't abandon my king like you did!"

"You say that but...."

"Enough!" shouted Keltar. "I'll decide soon enough which of you is loyal."

Blue Spear suddenly blurted out, "But, Sire? Sire?"

Keltar looked at the skink with disdain.

Blue Spear, still hiding behind his brother, continued in a shaky voice, "Why not let the beaver decide who tells the truth? They will remember us!"

Red Spear, stunned at the remark, turned around in astonishment. For once in his life, his brother had said something intelligent!

No one said anything for a moment or two. Korzen and Roozen just looked at each other in shock.

"Agreed," the king said slowly.

Red Spear, still looking at his brother, blanched when he saw him make a face at the two accusers. He shot out his hand to stop him but not before the two lizards rushed forward.

"Stay your place!" Keltar thundered.

"But they insult us!" Roozen exclaimed loudly.

"If you said the truth, then you can have them…later."

"You know our loyalty!" he said, facing Keltar. "We've been with you since the time before. We don't have to prove nothin'!"

"Except your continuing allegiance - might I remind you that you were once in Sargon's army."

"What!!?" cried out Korzen. "That was before the crossing! You've been our king since. We accepted that!"

"As did Barkchew, Borgjump, and my brother."

Korzen and Roozen stood in stunned silence.

"So you should have no concern," growled Keltar, "with

whatever the beaver says, unless of course, you want to change your story now?"

Korzen and Roozen grimaced at each other and then looked back. "No."

"Then leave me."

The giant lizards glared at the skinks and then waddled off into the darkness.

Keltar turned to his general. "Gradig, if these two attempt to escape like the chameleon, eat them. When the light returns, we leave."

The skinks had never felt such a sadistic presence before. They looked up and saw the general staring down at them and promptly turned away. Betrayed and in fear of their lives now they both sat down while the rain began pounding them harder.

Blue Spear whispered under the noise of the shower, "Wait till I get my claws on that treacherous chameleon!"

His brother leaned close and replied quietly, "Forget him! We just have to hope the beaver doesn't lie. You remember how we poked his kid." Blue Spear looked at him with his mouth agape.

Red Spear was brutally awakened the next morning when he felt a sudden pain in his side. He looked up and saw Gradig lifting his foot off his back. "What was that for!? We're trying to sleep!" he spat out.

"Get up! We leave now."

"What?"

Gradig ignored the question.

Red Spear rubbed his eyes and saw soft light pouring down through the trees. He started to rise but then felt the weight of a leg pressing down on his foot. Using his other, he kicked his brother in his face.

Blue Spear immediately jumped up and started running. "They are going to eat us! They are going to eat us! Run. Run!"

Aghast at the sight and fearful it would be interpreted as an escape, Red Spear tried to grab him. But before he could jump up, he saw Gradig holding Blue Spear up by his head while watching his legs move back and forth. He then unceremoniously dropped him on his tail.

"Go!" he growled, pointing in a direction with his claw out.

Keltar walked up and stood in front of Red Spear. "You will lead us to Darmok. Gradig will be just behind."

Roozen looked at Korzen as the two skinks approached the path. "You think that beaver will know anything?"

Before Korzen could reply, he heard a voice from behind. "Get on!" said one of the lizards behind them, noticing that neither had moved.

They ignored him and started forward.

Behind them, standing in the numerous puddles, was the rest of Keltar's army. Most had no interest in Scalar or his compatriots. But neither did they want to bring down the wrath of the king as they passed by the two broken lizards that still lay beside the tree. The only thing they were sure of was that many things would be different before they saw Gravenbroke again.

Keltar followed silently behind Gradig, who was himself trying to avoid the mud and countless puddles that lined the side of their way, many of which extended into the forest as far as the eye could see. It was a miserable place for a desert lizard to be. He burned from the inside with each step while loathing Scalar all the more.

Gradig felt a flake of mud stick to his face. Startled, he looked down at the two skinks that plodded along in front of him, each whispering to the other as they walked. In a fit of exasperation, he slammed one of his front feet down, causing a shower of mud to spray over the two.

"Hey!" yelled Blue Spear, holding his hands above his head.

With a menacing voice, Gradig replied, "Perhaps you would like to be washed off in the creek!"

Red Spear jerked his brother back and mumbled something, causing both the skinks to laugh, which made the general seethe even more.

Soon after, Gradig noticed the path becoming more difficult to follow with the numerous puddles that had formed from the rain. Keltar noticed it as well and moved behind the skinks.

"Stop! There is no path here, only water!" he growled.

Red Spear turned around. "I-I'm afraid there is not, sire. But we know this is the way. My brother and I swear to you that we walked this way before and found the beaver."

Gradig took a step toward them with his arm raised and shouted, "Liar!"

The king, seeing what was about to happen, said in a low voice, "You move that claw any further, General, and it will be left here on the trail." Gradig shrank back. Keltar then glared at Red Spear. "On your lives, this is true?"

"Y-Yes sire!"

Keltar slammed his foot down, sending the water flying over the skinks. "And the ground was this way then?"

Red Spear flinched. "N-No. Not as much. The rain made it worse. Because of this, I suggest we cross the creek soon."

"Why would I agree to that? The water that moves within it is both deep and fast."

The skink looked at the stream as well and then returned his eyes to Keltar. "Yes, of course. But going forward on this side can be even more dangerous. This is the beginning of Ildon's swamp, a place of evil, like no other."

He looked down at the two pitiful creatures with fear on their faces. "And why is that?" he asked, barely tolerating their presence.

Red Spear took a deep breath. "Few who crossed it lived to tell about it. Everything avoids it. I beg you, sire! You and your army are powerful. But all those that live within this land respect its boundaries. We humbly ask you again to cross the creek now."

"We will not. You and that idiot brother of yours will continue to lead on this side! There is nothing here that can challenge me." Keltar turned away, dismissing them completely.

Red and Blue Spear stood frozen as the black water swirled around their feet. Though it was nearly noon, they began to notice the world becoming darker from the dense foliage overhead. For the two skinks, the situation was even more unfortunate, as neither had the stature of the lizards and the water was rising fast.

"As you wish," mumbled Red Spear to the king's back.

After another hour of walking, the ground rose up on their left into small hummocks, allowing Keltar and a few others to retreat from the watery ground. The king suddenly stopped and turned to Gradig. "Go back and make sure everyone is still with us."

"Surely that's not necessary. I'm sure they are fine," he countered, looking at the water around them.

"I'm not asking...." But before Keltar could finish, a loud cry was heard, followed by a huge splash. Both whipped their heads around and saw one of their soldiers being pulled across the water on his back until he disappeared deep into the swamp.

No one said anything for several moments. They just stared at the waves, which slowly dissipated after the attack. Keltar looked over at Gradig, whose mouth had fallen open. "General. Why have you not left as I ordered?"

Gradig's eyes bulged at the question. "Surely, Keltar, these two," he said, pointing to the skinks, "are better suited for that."

Keltar tilted his head. "You fear this place, don't you?"

"Of course not," he said quickly. "I will return shortly."

Keltar moved his eyes to the skinks, who watched the general disappear down the trail. "Find us a way to cross—now! I'm growing impatient with you and we are losing time."

Red Spear nodded. "One moment, sire." Then he turned to his brother and they talked quietly until both nodded their heads. Red Spear turned back. "If you and Gradig can push those two dead trees into the creek, then we can use them as a bridge."

Keltar walked up to one and began pressing. At the same time, a snake fell from its limbs to land just in front of him. It had risen up with its fangs ready to attack the giant lizard when Keltar moved his other claw around its neck and tossed it into the swamp. He then swung around and glared, daring it to make another move. However, the serpent lowered its head and disappeared beneath the brown water.

Gradig, having seen what had happened, looked down at the skinks and smiled. "Apparently, it lost a good meal in you two." Keltar turned around at the voice. The general raised his head. "We are missing just the one soldier."

Keltar ignored the remark. "Move to this tree and push." All of a sudden, under the pressure of the giant lizards, the tree trunk exploded and crashed into the opposite bank, creating an instant bridge to the other side. The same was done to another tree beside it.

"You," ordered the king, pointing to Red Spear. "Move to the other side!"

The skink turned, walked quickly over the fast-moving water, and dropped to the bank, relieved to be first. He waited for his brother, but before Blue Spear could reach the bridge, the king shouted, "Not you. You will be last in case your brother has any ideas of leaving!"

Blue Spear about died at those words and looked longingly at his brother for help. Red Spear's mouth fell open at the threat.

"Sire, I have no wish to leave," he said in a fearful voice.

Keltar ignored him. "I will go next."

"I will be behind you, sire," Gradig said fawningly.

The king turned his eyes to his general. "No, you will not. You will wait with that one," he spat, "until all my army has crossed."

Gradig clenched his teeth and looked disdainfully at the skink, wanting nothing more than to swat the irritant into the river and be done with him, once and for all. Blue Spear, sensing his fear, moved his mouth into a slight smile behind the general's back. But the expression did not remain for long. He gazed behind at the swamp and began to shake, as if something terrible would rise from its dark water at any moment and pull him in before he could cross.

He felt the general's hot breath blowing across his neck. "You go last and hope that I don't smash the bridge when I cross," he ordered with dripping contempt.

The skink tried to ignore the threat while keeping his eyes fixed on the swamp. Soon came his army, one after another, making their way across. And with every step, more of the makeshift bridge cracked and fell into the river, quickly disappearing in the frothing currents.

When the second to last soldier began to cross, Gradig jumped when he heard a loud pop. Looking down, he saw the soldier freeze. Just in front of him, a small fissure opened up in the center of the tree, causing it to sag against the water. Gradig bellowed out, "Move or jump. You will not leave me with this creature!" he cried, pointing to Blue Spear.

The soldier stared at the water apprehensively and looked to the other side for help, but none came. He took a deep breath and placed a foot out. No sound. After several more steps, he was across and, with relief, stepped down safely on the other side. Almost immediately, everyone heard another loud *CRACK*. In an instant, the two trees slid down the bank near Red Spear to stop just above the frothing water.

Gradig's eyes swelled up like basketballs at the sight. He

stared into the standing waves of white water and watched the trees begin to creep slowly down the bank and into the current.

"General!" shouted Keltar. "In your words, cross or swim!"

Gradig glanced at the few limbs remaining above the water and gingerly stepped up on the last part of the two trunks that remained on the bank. As soon as he stepped on one of the trees, both began to slide faster into the water, making it increasingly difficult for the lizard to see where to go. After two more steps, the general heard another *POP*, and one of the trees began to break apart.

Blue Spear blanched at the sight and instantly darted across it before jumping to the other bank. Red Spear, grinning at his brother's gall, pulled him up. Gradig, having seen the despicable creature run through his legs, panicked and quickly bounded over to the bank as well. But as soon as he stepped on the muddy bank, he felt himself sliding down its face.

Keltar stared at him for a long moment before growling to some other soldiers nearby, "Get him up."

However, as soon as he climbed out, Gradig reached for Blue Spear, whose smile instantly disappeared. Just before his claws touched the skink, Keltar quietly warned him out loud, "They still have use, General. You may yet have your opportunity, but not now."

"I look forward to it," he whispered before pulling his hand back.

Both skinks quickly ran around Keltar's army to assume the lead once again. But before they started down the trail, they noticed some familiar tracks in the mud, ones they would never forget.

# 32. JERON

THE CHAMELEON HAD MADE FOR DARMOK. AT THE FIRST OP-
portunity, he looked for a spot to cross the river but failed to find
a suitable bridge. Further south, the ground began disappearing,
leaving large dark puddles that extended into the forest to the
right and front. He was now approaching the most dangerous
part of Ildon swamp, and he had no interest in testing whether
the stories were true or not.

The decision was made. He had to cross but where?

After walking for several more minutes, he noticed the dark
water and saw a small ripple moving across the surface toward
him. A snake! In a fright, he jumped to the nearest tree and
carefully made his way up to the first limb, nearly falling in the
process.

"Are you going swimming?" a voice asked

Startled, the chameleon looked up. "What!?"

"Over here," said a small squirrel. "You won't make it on that
limb."

Recognizing it, he calmly smiled. "Really? And how would
you know?"

"Because I do it all the time, and you're not a squirrel."

"Ok. So why don't you be a friend and help me?"

"Because, I'm not interested!"

The chameleon grinned wider. "Perhaps you're just saying that because you don't know how to do it either!"

The squirrel giggled. "I know," he said forcefully, "but I still won't help you."

Thinking to himself, he said, "That's ok. I'll get to the other side myself, and do it faster than you. See that rock on the other side?" he asked, pointing.

The squirrel looked in the direction, giving the chameleon the time to blend into the background.

The squirrel looked back and his eyes got big. It frantically ran over and looked around, but the creature was nowhere to be found. Then, in an instant, it bounded to another limb and crossed to the other side.

The chameleon dropped his camouflage. When the squirrel turned back, his mouth was agape. "How?!"

"Thanks for showing me the way!"

"You tricked me!" it growled.

The chameleon dropped down next to him with a smirk. "Just because you live in a tree does not make you smarter."

The squirrel glowered at the intruder. Then, after a few seconds, it laughed out loud. "I like you. So I've decided to help you find your way back."

"Thank you, but I'm in a hurry. However, I'll remember your offer should I return."

After a several minutes of running down the trail, the chameleon noticed a large animal up ahead gnawing on a fallen tree. Being careful not to give away his position, he crept up slowly and blended in with the background. As he got closer, he saw it was a young beaver.

With a sigh of relief, he called out, "Hello." The creature turned away from what it was doing and squinted. "Who said that?"

At first, the chameleon was confused by the question. He was standing close to the animal, so it had to see him. But then he looked down and saw his legs missing and apologized. "Oh, sorry." But the sight of the transition back into visibility so shocked the beaver that it nearly fell into the raging creek.

Catching a limb at the last moment, it stared at the unusual thing. "What are you? Where did you come from?"

"I'm a chameleon of the Eastern clan and a friend of Darmok," it said in a serious tone while brushing the dust off.

"He's my father! Can you do that again?"

He shook his head. "I would like to, but I have to find your father now. It's very urgent. Can you take me to him?"

"Can you teach me to do that?"

The chameleon laughed out loud. "One day I will teach you many ways to hide in the forest. I promise."

"Ok then."

The beaver scampered down the path beside the creek until the water widened into a huge pond. "We can jump in here and swim to him now."

"Ahhh, that's not so good for me. I don't really swim too well."

"Uh, ok then."

The beaver suddenly flung itself into the water and began

slapping its tail haphazardly against the surface. Within moments, an enormous wall of water exploded out in front of the chameleon's eyes. Nearly in shock, he saw a huge beaver walk straight out of the water, claws extended and ready for a fight. But seeing no threat, it turned to his son.

"I'm ok, Father," he said as the water poured from his face. "I met a new friend. He's right…I don't understand…he was, right there."

Darmok looked around. "Where?"

"I don't know. He can just disappear."

Darmok, puzzled for a moment, turned away and walked over to a tree. Using his claws, he proceeded to scratch off some bark. After grinding it to a powder, he threw it up in the air and watched it float slowly down. There, at his feet, lay a lizard-like creature covered by the dusty mixture. His son grinned.

The chameleon, relieved to be out of danger and to have found the one he searched for, stood up immediately. "Mr. Darmok. Excuse me, sir! It's I, Jeron of the Eastern clan."

Darmok stared at the animal suspiciously for a moment before replying, "Eastern clan? If what you say is true, then tell me who also lives within the same forest."

"Feyorin."

Darmok was taken aback. "How is that you know…"

"That he is an Ororan?" Jeron interrupted.

"He never mentioned you," the beaver said, stepping back.

"He would not have. He respected the privacy of my people. We rarely venture far from where we live."

"And where is that?"

"From the northernmost part of Shadowguard."

Darmok surveyed the small lizard for a moment. "You say that Feyorin sent you to me?"

"Not immediately—only after I left Keltar."

"Why do you come to me now?"

"My mission was to pose as a spy to confuse the Saurian king. But I was found out by the two skinks who spy for Keltar."

Darmok said darkly, "Two skinks, you say?"

"Yes. Do you know them?"

He grimaced and nodded. "How did you escape?"

Jeron winked at Darmok's son just before he shimmered and disappeared.

The normally serious Darmok burst out laughing while glancing at the smaller beaver.

"There he goes again, Father!" shouted his son.

The chameleon reappeared with a crooked smile. "By now, Keltar knows that I've broken my word, so I must leave you quickly with a warning. They're less than a day from us now."

Darmok was visibly shocked. "From which side of the water do they approach?"

"West."

Darmok smiled. "Then they must face Ildon or cross."

Jeron shivered. "Stories of that evil place have even drifted to my own village." Jeron looked across the immense water to where the swamp met the other side. "Yet you live beside it. Why?"

"There exists an agreement between us. Ildon needs the beavers to maintain its home and we need them for our protection. Each respects the other."

Jeron opened his mouth to reply when he suddenly caught

movement of something huge descending overhead. Instinctively he backed up and yelled, "Up!"

The older beaver whipped his head around just as a giant bird landed by his side. At the same time, his son vanished beneath the water in terror, only to reappear with his eyes just above the surface. He could only stare at the huge claws that slowly etched the ground beneath its body.

Darmok recovered and recognized it immediately, but it dwarfed every bird he had ever seen. He watched it closely as it drilled its eyes into him, giving no indication of submissiveness or attack. Instinctively, he flexed his paws and showed his teeth.

The eagle, seeing the movement, said in a deep feminine voice, "There is no need to fear me, beaver. I come as a messenger of Feyorin. You are Darmok?"

"I am," he said, relaxing and trying to remember the stories, handed down over the generations, about the giant eagles that lived within the forest long ago.

"I am Nimdoor. Again, I wish you no harm. The Ororan requested I deliver the following message - the one sent by Brondanur arrived."

Darmok absently replied, "He is safe then?"

"Yes."

The eagle was about to continue when Jeron suddenly re-appeared in front of her. Nimdoor, startled, stepped back and stared at the creature for a moment before speaking. "You are a changling! I have heard about your magic from Brondanur, but I have never met one of your kind."

Darmok's son crawled out of the water and interrupted, "Jeron is my friend. I wish I could do that!"

"Indeed!" said the great bird sincerely. "To have such magic would make one powerful."

Darmok interrupted, "You have known Feyorin long?"

Nimdoor, still looking at the chameleon, replied, "Yes."

"And his people?" he asked quickly.

"Longer."

"Twice now I am surprised. Feyorin did not share his knowledge of Jeron or you."

The eagle looked at him. "He would not have, since he only recently met me."

A pause. "And Brondanur?"

"Not as long."

The beaver stared at the enigmatic bird. Before he could ask another question, the chameleon interrupted, "Excuse me, Mr. Darmok! I apologize, but I must leave for my village soon."

"And why is that?" asked Nimdoor.

"Keltar and his army approaches. I cannot be here when he arrives or my life is forfeit."

The eagle's claws visibly vibrated at the name while staring at the chameleon. "That will not happen. I will take you to your village."

Jeron looked up, confused.

Darmok stared at the eagle while his mind drifted back to a time long ago, when he was trapped on the ground in the presence of a terrible creature. Then he looked up and saw something in the sky that frightened it away.

Nimdoor interrupted his thoughts. "Is there any message you have for me before I leave?"

Shocked out of his memory, he replied quickly, "Yes." The

beaver looked away sadly. "Tell Feyorin to make haste for Bron-danur, and say the following: *Remember the story of Garanthur. Look for my sign, on the second day, when the shadow is short.*"

The eagle looked at him blankly. "I will deliver it when the first rays of dawn strike the ground." Then it raised its wings and, to the terror of Jeron, swiftly clasped the chameleon within its talons and disappeared in the sky.

# 33. DARMOK AND KELTAR

RED SPEAR STARED AT THE TRACKS AND WHISPERED QUIETLY, "Not as clever as you thought, chameleon."

"What?"

"The spy! Those are his tracks!" he exclaimed quietly in his brother's ear.

Blue Spear's loathing of the chameleon burst out. "That no good, sorry…" But before he could finish his rant, he felt Red Spear's hand over his mouth.

"You've found something!?" thundered Keltar from behind.

"Nothing, sire," Red Spear replied quickly. "We were talking about the beaver." Behind him, he heard the king muttering to the general.

"What about it?" Gradig demanded.

Red Spear went quiet for a moment. He then looked up and faced the general. With a serious face, he stated, "My brother said he was quite large and that you must be careful with him."

The two just stared at the skink with their mouths open and began laughing out loud.

Red Spear lowered his head to be out of Keltar's sight and,

in a low voice, whispered to his brother, "Say nothing about this, you understand?"

He nodded quickly. "Why?"

"If we find the spy, he'll just lie to the king again and get Roozen and Korzen on his side. We've gotta hope he didn't survive to cross the river…."

In a flash, Red Spear felt his brother catapulted off the ground and into a puddle further down the trail. "Move!" boomed a fearsome voice from behind him.

Red Spear looked up and saw the general's eyes boring into him. He looked for Keltar to intervene but instead found him staring back indifferently. It was all he could do not to say something back. But that was what they wanted.

Blue Spear pulled himself out of the muddy water and started to walk while rubbing his head. Unlike his brother, he had no intention of looking around. Instead, he just continued forward, feeling their eyes drilling into to his back. His brother quickly ran up beside him and grimaced, then took the lead again.

By now it was late afternoon and little could be heard other than soft whispers and grunts as the lizards stepped over the few remaining puddles. It had become obvious to the skinks that none of them had been prepared for the forest, much less the swamp and rain.

"Sire!" cried a voice from behind.

Before Red Spear stopped, he smeared the next two tracks away.

One of the guards was pointing to the creek. "The water appears be slowing."

Keltar stopped abruptly. However, an unfortunate soldier

stumbled into him. With lighting speed, the king whipped around and crashed his fist into the innocent creature, nearly sending him over the bank.

The king growled back, looking down at the slowing current, "This must be the mouth of the river." He glared back at the skink "If so, we are near the beaver's home, are we not?"

"Yes." Red Spear bowed humbly.

"How far?"

"Less than an hour, my king."

Gradig interrupted, "How do you know the stream don't turn right or split? Maybe we crossed for nothing." He snorted.

Keltar stared at the twisted remains of trees that shadowed the black water on the other side of the river. He remembered the cry of one of his own as it was dragged screaming into that place. "You really want to find out, Gradig?"

The general's eyes were also fixed on the swamp. The skinks smiled when they heard him mumble, "Perhaps later."

Red Spear, seeing an opportunity, bowed humbly and, in a voice loud enough for Gradig to hear, said, "Sire, the general don't know the path as we do. While I'm sure he means well, I can tell you that there is none better."

He noticed Gradig's face contort with rage out of the corner of his eye.

Red Spear continued in a flamboyant manner, "If you would please follow us, we will take you to the beaver's dam. As your faithful servants, our only objective is to assist."

Keltar stared at the skink blankly. He had seen this type of behavior before, but chose for the moment to ignore it. Like all the others who cowed at his feet, they would eventually be removed, permanently.

"Then move!" commanded the king in a cold voice.

Red Spear bowed again. He turned around and saw his brother take the lead. Pushing him aside, he assumed the point again and began to scan for the chameleon's tracks. After a moment, he sped up ahead and carefully erased each one with his foot as he walked along. But then they ended. Shocked, he slowed his gait a bit and looked left and right.

"Is there a problem?" warned the king menacingly.

"No. No problem, sire. I was just making sure that there were no beaver traps."

Red Spear abandoned the search and quickly sped off with the king close behind. When the last of the army had passed, a small creature crept out from behind a bush and slid into the pond quietly. In the blink of an eye, it disappeared and within moments, entered the beaver's lodge.

"I did as you asked, Father. They're coming now!"

Darmok leaned down and stroked his son's head. "Excellent," he said, smiling. "Did you see the two skinks as well?"

"Yes. And I removed Jeron's tracks as you asked."

"Do you still fear them?" he asked, straightening up.

"I don't think so."

"I'm pleased. Now go to the roof of our home and allow yourself to be seen. Signal me when they're nearly upon you and I will come."

The small beaver nodded and disappeared beneath the water. While he was making his way to the top, Red Spear walked the last of the trail and was nearly upon the dam himself when he heard a shout.

"Look there!" Gradig pointed.

Red Spear, startled for a moment, moved his eyes up and saw a small beaver standing on a stout log atop the dam.

"Perhaps our guide has a problem with his eyes, since he didn't see it first," he hissed.

Red Spear ignored the insult and ran to the foot of the dam. "You remember me?" he said, flipping his spear up.

When the young beaver saw the foul creature behind the skink, its courage melted. Never had he seen something so huge and sinister in every way. With rows of teeth and claws like daggers, it stood silently staring back. Terrified, he fell down between some logs.

Red Spear grinned. "Do not hide from me! Answer, or you will have my spear again."

The king roared, "This is the great Darmok, the one you spoke about!?"

Red Spear turned and saw the glowering face of the king.

"NO, NO! The one you seek is another!"

The skink watched the giant horned lizard reach for a log. For the first time, Red Spear saw something in the king's eye beside power: an evil that spread to a wicked grin. "Then you have failed me!"

Keltar was about the swing the weapon at the skink when the water beside him exploded into a geyser. Keltar swung his head but was too slow and the beaver smashed into his arm, forcing the log to go wild, nearly colliding with Red Spear. The concussion blasted each to the ground, where they both lay dazed for a moment.

Darmok, however, was the first to stand up. "Dragon!" In a deep voice, it bellowed, "Why have you left your desert - for this place?! What business do you have with me!? Speak!"

Gradig, stunned at the gall of the beaver, started to lurch forward, but Keltar held his claw up. No one spoke for several moments. The king just kept his eyes on his opponent while he slowly pulled himself off the ground. Once up, he raised his head until it was a foot taller than Darmok and replied in a low growl, "The only reason I don't kill you now is for the information I need."

Before Darmok could reply, Red Spear jumped between them in the hopes of showing his value. "You remember us, do you not?"

"I remember," the beaver spit. Then, speaking over the skink's head to Keltar, he said, "What makes you think I would know anything of interest to you?"

Keltar ignored the remark and instead focused his attention on the skink. He thought back when it first said, 'I remember.' It was a truth laid bare that suggested the skinks had not lied. He flashed his eyes back at Korzen and Roozen, who looked away immediately. As fate would have it, both lizards now realized their futures were unclear; *they* had lied to their king.

Red Spear, feeling the vindication, smiled at the two lizards until they turned their backs to them.

Darmok interrupted his thoughts. "This one speaks for you, dragon?" he growled, looking down at the skink.

Keltar looked at Red Spear indifferently. In a chilling voice, he rumbled slowly, "Leave us." Red Spear immediately slunk back to the side of the pond.

The king looked at the beaver closely and realized that threatening it would have little effect. He then eyed Darmok's son, who lay quietly on the dam. "I speak for everyone here, including you. Do not push me, beaver. I'll ask you once. Has any of my kind passed this way before?"

"I've seen none," he replied indifferently.

"If you lie," Keltar replied, pointing his claw at the beaver.

"As I said, I have seen none. And why would that concern me?"

Keltar was becoming increasingly agitated. "Perhaps you have made an alliance."

Darmok laughed out loud. "Now you insult me."

Keltar slammed his tail to the ground. "I have no time for this! Perhaps I can ask that one," he growled, pointing at Darmok's son.

The beaver dropped his smile. "You think he would keep such a thing from his father?"

"If you offer me nothing, then I have no use for either of you." Keltar turned and motioned the general to his side.

Before Gradig took two steps, Darmok raised his voice. "You're forgetting to ask the others."

Keltar held his hand up. "Others?"

"Do you know what lies on the other side of this water?"

Keltar did indeed - the black waters of Ildon. "What is your point, beaver!?"

Darmok noticed the long shadows and looked at the sun. Night was approaching. "Then perhaps you would know that the answers you seek may be found on the opposite side," he declared, pointing east to Shadowguard. "You've little light remaining. Decide what you want, or be done with it."

Keltar thought a minute and then thundered, "Roozen, Korzen. Get over here."

Both rushed up to his side and tilted their heads.

"You will attend the beaver while he searches for clues of Scalar there." He pointed to the Eastern Forest. "If at any time you suspect that he's playing you, then bring me his head and I will plant it next to the smaller one."

"It will be our pleasure," they said in an acid voice. They both turned and smiled viciously at Red Spear, whose mouth had fallen open.

"Then it's agreed," the beaver said. "We leave now." He instantly swung around and began walking into the darkened forest with the two lizards close behind. When his son watched him pass the first of the giant trees, the young beaver silently dropped into the water, leaving only small ripples that chased each other across the pond.

"Sire," said Red Spear, looking up, "how do you know he ain't leading them into a trap? It's dangerous there!"

"Then perhaps you should join Roozen and Korzen as their personal guard," he replied with the slightest smile.

Red Spear stuttered, "I-I'm sure they'll be fine."

"Fine? So you know something of that forest?" growled Keltar.

Red Spear shivered as he watched Roozen and Korzen disappear into Shadowguard and then looked at his brother, whose face was a mask of terror.

"Only what I've heard, my king."

Keltar was getting curious. "From whom?"

Red Spear thought quickly. "The beaver."

"And what was that?"

In a shaking voice, he said, "There are monsters that live in there."

"Monsters," he roared, laughing. "Since you've been there, then you can go and sit at its edge until the beaver returns. Your brother, however, will remain here, with me."

Both skinks' eyes got as large as saucers. "But sire…"

"I only need one of you. Now GO!"

Red Spear stared at his brother for a moment, noticing his eyes pleading him to stay. He nodded twice and then turned and walked past Keltar into the shadows. Gradig watched and then turned to smile broadly at Blue Spear.

Soon, the last rays of sunlight fell behind the gnarled trees of Ildon and everything went dark. Keltar took advantage of it by ordering his soldiers to make camp beside the huge dam while he waited for the beaver's return.

"Gradig, go and post two sentries to watch the beaver's home. Bring me anything that leaves or enters it." He turned to Blue Spear, who was several feet away. "You'll sleep at my side until your brother returns; if he returns."

Blue Spear made no attempt to move. His mind was consumed by the forest that had swallowed his brother.

Keltar turned to Gradig. "Bring him to me!"

The general smiled and grasped him by the neck. After a few steps, he threw him unceremoniously to the ground beside the king. It took a full minute before the skink stopped coughing.

Keltar looked at him. "Know this: if your brother does not return before I see the sun again, we will leave without him. Do you know the way?"

He didn't and promptly fainted. Keltar just stared at him incredulously.

Red Spear was not so lucky. He was alone now in the darkness with only a few patches of moonlight dotting the ground around him. For the past hour, he had listened to several horrible sounds echoing from the inky darkness. He wondered about Korzen and Roozen and mouthed the word 'fools.'

An hour later, Darmok returned to face Keltar alone.

"Where are my two soldiers?" the king demanded.

"I regret they were lost to one of the many beasts that live within those woods."

Red Spear ran out from under his bush and pointed his spear at the beaver.

"LOST?" roared the king.

Darmok blasted back, "There are many creatures there larger than you that you know nothing about. I cannot explain its dangers to a denizen of the desert. But understand that the beasts that dwell among those giant trees are to be respected and not trifled with." The beaver then lowered his voice. "However, I suspect you already experienced this when you walked along the still water of Ildon!"

Keltar blinked his eyes several times while thinking back to that moment.

"However," the beaver continued, "I have found the information you seek. Others like you did pass this way before. They were seen following the direction of the water south."

"How do you know this?"

"From the ones that live there," he replied. pointing east, "that chose to remain unknown. Now, I've done as you wish. Return me to my family."

Keltar was seething. "I will decide your fate when the light returns again. For now, you may run and hide."

Darmok turned around and walked upstream until he was out of sight, then slid beneath the water and returned to his lodge. The next morning, before the sun rose, he swam through the dark water and peaked above the surface. There was no sight of Keltar, his army, or the skinks.

# 34. FEYORIN'S MARCH SOUTH

TENARA WOKE UP TO A DISTANT GROWL AND LISTENED UNTIL THE sound faded into the night. Normally such a thing would have evoked a terrible fear, but at the moment, she was more focused on her imprisoned friends than what was prowling nearby. She thought of Parsnippy and shivered at the thought of him being so alone in the dark.

"You worry," said a familiar voice, interrupting her thoughts.

Startled, she turned her head. "What?"

"Sleep escapes me for the same reason. We both think about what lies before us."

She turned toward the voice. "How did you know I was awake?!"

Feyorin laughed quietly. "I saw your hand moving along your sword."

Tenara looked down. "Oh right, it glows. Maybe that's not so good."

Feyorin replied softly, "It only glows when your hand is upon it."

She released it immediately and watched the light slowly

disappear. Not to be embarrassed, she changed the subject. "Do you believe there's a chance for my friends to be freed before the Saurians arrive?"

"I'm afraid not."

"Then our only choice is to fight?!"

"Unless another sees different, yes."

"But you and the other Ororans will be there. Right?"

"No."

"No!? Why? We're alone?"

"Tenara, you have never been alone! Remember what I said. The battle we face is for all of Anzenar. Its outcome will determine the lives of many, including your friends. Don't make the mistake of thinking we will not there as well."

"You say you won't be there but you will. How can both be true? We have no chance alone against those foul creatures!"

"When Keltar arrives, he'll see you and Joen as one of the prisoners. However, if the Ororans are seen by the lizard king, then the battle will spread and continue until it consumes all of the villages, including Moss Rock and Rippleshy. We're not willing to risk that."

Tenara suddenly felt like she was suffocating. "What about Blendefest and Frondameer? What if they think they're Ororan?"

"That very question was discussed within the Council of Elders before we left. Miralassen suggested that was a possibility. But we are gambling that their faces and dress are unknown to the dragon lizards. In any event, we will keep them at a distance, if possible."

"Feyorin," interrupted Frondameer, "Blendefest and I agree.

While on a trip to the North, we were seen by two of them. But neither made any attempt to follow."

"I apologize for waking you."

"It's not important. We've trained ourselves to sleep light. Tenara, you will have our swords at your side. Do you have a plan yet, Feyorin?

"I hope to hear something from my people soon."

The next morning, Tenara woke to a red sunrise and feared that it was an omen of something terrible to come. She turned away from the light to see Feyorin and Baldmar talking with each other. To their right, she was shocked to see Joen in a sword fight with Frondameer.

She jumped up and immediately ran over to them. "What are you doing?" she said loudly to both.

Joen stepped out of the range of Frondameer's weapon and held her hand up while grasping her dagger with her other hand. "He's teaching me how to fight. It's sort of fun!"

"Fun!? This is no game!"

Joen looked at her for a moment, puzzled. "No, it's not. But we both knew the risk when we left Rippleshy. It's too late to worry now." She smiled and touched her hand. "Besides, we're gonna kick their tails!"

Tenara stared at her for a long moment. "I guess we both changed since Rippleshy."

Joen just looked at her. "You're right. We're better."

Tenara looked at Joen quizzically and then smiled. At that moment, she noticed Parsnippy looking up and grinning.

She followed his eyes and saw something descending fast

and coming right at her. In a sudden fear, she backed up and nearly fell on top of Baldmar when the great eagle settled in a gust of wind.

Nimdoor nodded at Parsnippy and then turned to Feyorin. "So, Ororan, did you believe I would return?"

Feyorin stood up and looked at the eagle. "To speak the truth, I wasn't sure."

"And why was that?" she asked, gazing back, unblinking.

"Perhaps it was because you were not present when my people were attacked on the mountain by the very same lizards that seek us now."

"Your queen thought different. You were young when I first saw you scrambling up the slopes of the Anduin Mountains of the North, angry and full of fight."

"And why not," he angrily retorted. "The dragons had nearly wiped us out! If you were there, you could have saved many! But you said yourself that your clan didn't want to have any part of those who walk the ground."

"That is correct. But I also said there were some of us who disagreed. It was those who wanted to help, but your king forbade us to interfere."

"Proliptus said that?" Baldmar interrupted, stunned.

The eagle leaned down within inches of Feyorin and said quietly, "Your queen knows this. Why did she not tell you?"

Feyorin stepped back a few inches. "I do not know. Are you free to speak about it?"

The bird pulled back. "I will say only this. Your king needed an ally in this land that would be unknown to Keltar: an ally that would one day be at your side."

Baldmar blanched in astonishment.

Tenara interrupted, "Then you'll help us now with the danger we face?"

Nimdoor turned and hung her head slightly. "Unfortunately, small one, this is not the time for the great eagles to enter the fight with the dragons."

Nimdoor turned back to Feyorin. "I am here only to deliver a message from Darmok. It says, 'The desert beasts of the north are upon my doorstep. It is critical that you find Brondanur and say the following: *Remember the story of Garanthur. Look for my sign on the second day, when the shadows are short.*'"

"The second day—that would be tomorrow!" the Ororan replied.

"What does it mean?" asked Blendefest.

"I cannot help you with that," Nimdoor replied. "I delivered it to you as it was given to me. The army of the lizard king is swiftly making their way south as I speak. Brondanur awaits Parsnippy at his home, the place you call Glen of the Rock. You must arrive before the army of Keltar joins his brother."

Nimdoor then extended her mighty wings and disappeared in another great breath of wind.

Feyorin looked at the others. "Prepare yourselves. We've delayed too long. Baldmar, see that both Parsnippy and the message are delivered to Brondanur before morning. Leave now."

"Must I return to that dreadful place?" Parsnippy was wide-eyed.

"I'm sorry, but it must be," replied Feyorin. "Your absence risks your friends and possibly Brondanur as well. Trust in the courage that brought you here."

Parsnippy looked at the others with sorrowful eyes. Tenara came over and hugged him.

Joen held his hand. "I taught Baldmar everything he knows." She winked at the tall Ororan standing next to him. "He'll take good care of you."

Parsnippy looked up at Baldmar, who smiled slightly and then waved to the others. Within a few moments, they disappeared south.

Feyorin turned back. "Frondameer and Blendefest, I need you to locate Keltar now and return to me with haste."

Frondameer nodded. "We'll follow the path near the stream north."

"No," Feyorin said shaking his head. "Too dangerous. You must keep to the protection of Shadowguard. The Saurians are creatures of the sun and will look for the open spots near the river to keep warm. When you find the king, return south. Do not search for us. My people will find you.

"How?"

"Shadowguard will tell them."

Frondameer looked up at the immense trees with an uneasy expression. "And if Keltar sent his own scouts ahead?"

"Then it will be upon you to slow them down."

"That may not be possible!"

"No, only difficult. Find the snakes. They will be sunning themselves on the rocks after the rain. Promise them a meal for all their family on what comes down the trail."

"Snakes are no match for dragons."

"Not the ones you know about: the ones from Ildon that lie on the opposite bank. They often come out after a rain. All serpents share two things in common. They're arrogant and foolishly courageous."

Frondameer nodded. "Indeed. Within our lodge hangs the skin of one so bold. It made the mistake of entering our village."

"Good luck and good hunting," Feyorin replied.

The scouts gathered their weapons, but before walking off, Frondameer smiled at Tenara and Joen. He grasped the handle of his sword and shook it fiercely. Joen, in turn, shook her dagger tooth and smiled back. Tenara grinned widely and mouthed the word 'thank you'."

After the scouts left, she looked back at Feyorin and Joen. "And now there's just five of us."

Feyorin stared at her. "Five?"

Tenara added, "Yes. We are five now."

He shook his head. "You must have clover in your ears and moss on your eyes. Look around you."

She looked quizzically at Feyorin and then noticed four shapes emerging from the fog: three tall Ororans and one smaller.

Joen squinted. "Rilen!" They ran to each other and shared a warm embrace.

Then together they walked off, talking animatedly with each other.

The adult Ororans were decoratively dressed in shades of green and brown. Hanging to the side of each was a stone sword that was black as night, smooth and curved with flecks of red decorating its tip. And their feet were covered in shoes that seemed to disappear into the earth. The only camouflage she'd seen to rival it was the Camelio leaf.

One of the adults turned to Feyorin. "Jeron has a message for you. He said that the dragons became suspicious of him so he had to escape, but the skinks continue at Keltar's side."

"No matter; he did well."

"We understood there would be more of you here," said one of the Ororan warriors.

"Two from the village of Moss Rock are north of us searching for Keltar. Find them and bring them to me." They nodded and then left.

The other Ororan, dressed in a more regal coat, looked at Feyorin. "The Lady asks if you know of a creature named Nimdoor."

Feyorin was visibly shaken. "I've recently become aware of it, yes."

The Ororan paused while looking hard at him. "It is curious that I, the keeper of the runes of old, have never heard that name before. However, she said that you were to take its words to heart."

"Indeed! Apparently, there are many things she has yet to share about the 'before time'."

"Apparently."

"For now, we have much to discuss." The four of Ororans drifted off while Tenara walked over to Joen and Rilen, who were still gleefully exchanging stories.

"Oh, it's so good to see you again," said Rilen. "Tell me all that has happened since you left."

Joen filled him in for several minutes about the trip and the meeting with Darmok. As she talked, Tenara noticed in her friend a confidence she had never heard before. When Joen spoke of the upcoming confrontation with the lizards, she wondered if it was bravado or hope.

Rilen interrupted her thoughts. "I wish I could join you, but the elders have forbidden it. So I bring you both a gift. To you, Joen, I give you a Camelio robe."

"What is that?"

"Lay down on the soft ground."

Joen was curious but obeyed. Rilen then covered her with it and watched Tenara grin when she saw her friend disappear. "How wonderful!" she cried.

"What?" exclaimed Joen in a muffled voice.

"You're gone!"

"No, I'm not." She stuck her face out and all that could be seen was her head.

Rilen and Tenara laughed.

"To you, Tenara, I give my sword as well. It's not as grand as the one the Lady has loaned you, but it will serve you well if more than one dragon dares to fight you."

"Thank you, Rilen!"

One of the adult Ororans walked up. "It is time, Rilen."

The young Ororan frowned and then turned back. "I know you'll return one day. I made a sculpture of you both, so you have to come back and see it. You will, won't you?"

Tenara and Joen just looked at him for a moment, trying to hold themselves together. "Yes, we promise."

Rilen tried to smile before disappearing with the other Ororans into Shadowguard.

Feyorin noticed the two gifts. "Impressive. Rilen has gone to great lengths to give you something some of our own warriors do not have. Did you know that every gift has a rune inscribed upon it?"

Both Joen and Tenara looked closely at each gift but saw nothing. Feyorin smiled. "It's not a mark so easy to see. It's only in the shadow of each that it reveals itself upon the ground. Hold your sword high, Tenara, so that it sees the sun."

Both saw what appeared to be a silhouette at their feet that was broken up into three parts. Feyorin looked down. "It says '*dragon grinder.*' A fitting weapon for what lies ahead."

Joen did the same with the cloth. As she held up the Camelio robe, she saw five runes on the ground. Feyorin laughed out loud. "It says, '*Your doom lies hidden beneath.*' This time I fear for Keltar," he said, smiling broadly.

Tenara looked at Joen, and for a moment they both forgot the danger that faced them.

Feyorin motioned them forward. "Now follow me south until we reach the edge of Brondanur's home."

Feyorin started walking but suddenly stopped, to the surprise of Tenara and Joen. They watched him look into the empty forest and then yell, "I know you are there. Do not attempt to hide yourself!"

"Who are you talking to, Feyorin?" asked Tenara.

He ignored her and stood still. "Do not make me come to you!"

"I meant no disrespect," said a Toadan as it came around a tree while pointing to its trunk. "It is unfortunate that they do not talk to me as they do to you."

***

Feyorin pulled an arrow from his quiver and fired it into the ground. "I'm ready to talk." He noticed two other Toadans coming up behind their leader.

Darga looked over at Feyorin's two small companions. "Those are all you have to face tomorrow?"

In a flash, both Tenara and Joen held their weapons out.

"They have teeth." Darga grinned. "Good. They will need them." The other Toadans started to move forward, but Darga raised his hand.

"Is there a purpose for this meeting?" demanded Feyorin

"Sargon."

"He knows of Scalar?!" Feyorin fearfully blurted out.

"No. Not yet. But my spies tell me that he sent one of his own to meet with him. But I think he wants no part of Keltar's brother. I think he sees him as a threat."

Feyorin just stood staring at Darga. "You're sure of this?"

"We continue to watch them," he replied, ignoring the question.

"I need to know if Scalar plans to personally meet with Sargon's emissary."

"I'll see what we can do."

"I still don't trust you, Darga, but your help with this erases some of the past. Do you intend to fight tomorrow?

"We've not decided," he replied with a smile. He walked over and pulled Feyorin's arrow from the ground. "There are some that say this fight belongs to the Ororans. But perhaps I'm wrong.

The Toadan turned to Tenara and Joen. "What interest do you have in this?"

Tenara replied, "To get our friends back from Scalar and perhaps, help you as well."

Darga laughed once. "I've already seen you cower among the beasts. You two are not ready for what faces you."

Tenara stood her ground. "You confuse cowardice with good acting. Feel sorry for the lizards!"

Darga blanched. He looked at her for a long moment and glanced at Feyorin. "We know that you cannot show yourselves to the Saurians. We also know that Shadowguard is our home as well. We will do what we can."

Feyorin bowed slightly. When he rose, the Toadans had disappeared.

"This is good, right?" Tenara interrupted.

"We will see," he replied slowly, looking at the empty forest. "For now," he said, turning back to face her, "we must hurry south before the first shadows of night come."

## 35. GLEN OF THE ROCK

AFTER WALKING FOR SEVERAL HOURS AND SEEING NOTHING BUT the towering trees of Shadowguard, Parsnippy had become exhausted and started to fall further behind.

"Baldmar?"

"Yes?" replied the tall Ororan, keeping his stride.

"Are you sure this is the way? I followed the creek."

"Scalar or his guards may be walking that path."

Parsnippy grimaced, realizing he was right. He struggled to catch up, still several yards behind. "Are we close?"

Realizing his friend's fatigue, Baldmar turned his head to the side. In a lower voice, he said, "Yes. We are much closer. Follow me now and keep silent."

Parsnippy tried his best to close the distance between the two, but he was fast becoming weary of walking so quickly. It was only the anticipation of seeing his friends again that gave him the energy to continue. He looked up and noticed that Baldmar was now threading his way through a collection of thorny bushes. He winced when one stuck his side. "Not again," he muttered, remembering when he last huddled under a similar one.

He fought to catch up, but by now, the Ororan had increased the distance again, forcing Parsnippy to push even harder through the devilshrubs. Each step brought a new sting to his skin, making him that much more irritated. Even though he was careful, it seemed that each branch tried to lash out at him intentionally as he walked by.

"Why do you harm me so?" he growled to himself while pulling another spike from his arm. "Do I need to show you my knife!?"

After several more minutes of fighting the menacing plants, he suddenly found himself facing an altogether different foe: an almost impenetrable hedge whose branches seemed to be at war with the thorny plants that were still trying to threaten Parsnippy. He looked around desperately for Baldmar but he was nowhere in sight.

He then pulled out his knife and was just about to yell when, without warning, the hedge opened up and a hole appeared. His jaw dropped from shock and, without thinking, he rushed through to find a clearing just ahead. Sighing with relief, he stopped to pull the last thorn from his side when he heard a noise just behind him. He jerked around to see the opening instantly close, followed by the sound of thrashing again on the other side. He shook his head at the strange plants.

"What kind of forest is this?" he thought out loud. Stunned and confused, he turned around and heard the faint sounds of the Songentrope Creek ahead. After a few more steps, he squinted, looking for the tall Ororan again.

There, just ahead. Baldmar was barely in sight. Realizing this was perhaps a respite from the fast walk, he rushed forward and saw the Ororan's hand raised. Slowing down, he saw why; three huge snakes were coiled on each side of him. The largest one, bulbous and black as night, moved its head close to his friend.

"What is thissss?" it hissed out loud for the others to hear.

The serpent on his right with yellow diamonds along its back echoed, "A tasty meal it issss."

The third, streaked with muddy brown across its head, chided, "It'sss long. We can shares itss."

Baldmar looked at them indifferently. "I have business that does not concern you. Let me pass."

The black serpent moved its tail close to Baldmar's feet. "And why would we let that happen?" it said, smiling ever so slightly.

The Ororan took a moment to look at each and realized he couldn't take them all. Nevertheless, he placed a hand on his sword. "It would be the wiser thing to do."

"You think that black stick of yoursss will make difference?" the brown snake asked slowly.

"It will for the first one that tries," he replied with a deadpan expression.

Parsnippy was transfixed by the scene before him. Numbed with fear, he remembered all too well his last encounter with the long ones. But this time, there was no Nimdoor. He saw the other two beginning to move closer to Baldmar with their tails vibrating in anticipation. His mind screamed at him to run, but the choice to abandon his friend was no choice at all. Not after all they had been through. But then a thought came to him.

He dropped down behind a bush.

As the snakes closed the distance to Baldmar, they all heard a small voice several feet away. "Leave him be."

Whipping around, expecting to see something significant, instead they glared at the pitiful creature that walked into the clearing with no weapons.

The brown one spotted it first and raised its head. "We have not eaten so well for long timesss!"

The other two also jerked their eyes to look at the intruder.

"I will not ask again," Parsnippy said calmly. "Leave him be if you want to live."

The larger bulbous headed serpent turned away from Baldmar and began moving toward Parsnippy. "You threaten us?"

"No. Only to tell you that the last time I faced two of your kind, one of them disappeared, permanently."

The snake stopped. Now curious, its tongue flicked out rapidly as it turned its full eyes upon the newcomer and slithered closer. Baldmar, still holding his hand to his sword, was stunned at the audacity of Parsnippy's bluster. He knew they were no match for one huge reptile, much less three of them.

"Disappeared you sssay?" it asked slowly while cocking its head to the side.

Parsnippy stared back. "Since two nights ago in the rain. It too was like you: confident that I was only a meal. But, when I left, only one returned to its hole."

The snake bore its eyes deeper into Parsnippy and beat its tongue against the air repeatedly. It snarled in a dangerous voice, "You are foolish and stupid. A meal you shall be."

Parsnippy didn't respond.

The serpent continued to eye him with contempt while noting its small size. It looked greedily for fear in its eyes but saw only calm and resolve, as if to challenge it on. Not in all the time since it first left its family had its prey so boldly threatened it. But this one did. It must be bluffing.

"You lie," it hissed loudly.

"Do I?"

It pondered the question.

"Why do you listen?" hissed the serpent with yellow diamonds down its back. "If you will not take it, I WILL!" it spat. With his fangs gleaming, he leapt fiercely at Parsnippy, but before he could reach his mark, he felt a crushing blow to his head. Instantly he whipped around and saw it had come from the black snake.

"You dare interfere with my kill!?" shrieked the serpent, holding the neck of the other with its tail. "I decide!" he hissed. "I decide!" he thundered back with his fangs showing. "You will do as I saysss!" The other snake pulled back, just inches from Parsnippy, while boring his eyes into the black one who struck him.

By now, Baldmar was becoming increasingly anxious and bewildered at the scene. He had lived a long time and had been witness to many things, but such hesitation among the long kind when they clearly had the advantage was more than a shock. He could only stare in amazement at Parsnippy's gall as he held his ground, not knowing what would come next.

"I'm not your enemy unless you choose it," said the small voice again. "But for your own life, I warn you one last time to let us pass."

The bulbous eyes of the snake squinted at the creature while it poured through its memories again, looking for something that would explain the prey's reaction toward it. And then it came: something recently shared by another of its kind, something unnatural. A tale of fear told when something terrifying had dropped down from the sky and took another. And then when it came again in a mighty wind and left a warning and a name. "Parsnipssseee," is what it said, whispering that night into the terrified eyes of another serpent.

"Parsnipssseee," the snake muttered quietly to himself.

Parsnippy nearly stumbled when he heard his name said quietly. He had no idea what Nimdoor had said that night.

The snake flinched at the sudden movement and then stared at him.

Parsnippy pushed his chest out while still rigid with fear and said slowly, "Yesssssss…"

The serpent stared at him for another moment and then abruptly said, "We leave."

"What?! Leave?!" exclaimed the others, hissing loudly. "You don't speak for ussss!!!"

"Now!" thundered the black one.

Livid, the two other snakes followed the larger one out, but not before each looked back with a deadly stare at the two meals that remained behind.

Moments after, the Ororan looked down at his friend and commented quietly, "I have never met someone who can command a snake. I shall look forward to hearing more about this later, but Brondanur and your friends await us now."

Parsnippy, still shaking, followed him out of the clearing.

Within a minute, Baldmar had Parsnippy following close behind as they walked quickly down the path. With every step, they tried to stay close to the creek while taking advantage of as much cover as possible in case one of Scalar's companions came prowling nearby.

Just before the last of the sun rays began to disappear, they arrived at the upper portion of Brondanur's pond.

Parsnippy broke the silence. "This is where Brondanur left me that night to begin my journey to you. I have to call him now."

Baldmar watched Parsnippy retrieve two rocks from the ground and then immerse them into the water. Just beneath the surface, he crashed the stones together several times.

"I see you have learned much about beavers," the Ororan commented.

"Yes. He told me what to do if I returned."

"Then we will wait for him behind the ferns there." He pointed.

In less than a minute, they saw a small ripple moving across the surface rapidly in their direction. Parsnippy was visibly excited at seeing the beaver again. But then, the ripple stopped. He squinted again, hoping it would reappear, but it did not. Instead, a stick slowly emerged from the water and began moving in a circle.

"I do not understand," Parsnippy said dejectedly. "He said this would be my sign for him."

Baldmar was confused for a moment and then smiled. "It is. But he sends a different message now. Come. We must enter the water and join him."

The Ororan scanned both directions, crossed the path, and slipped below the surface with Parsnippy just behind him. Before long, he spotted Brondanur in the dim light. Brondanur motioned for both to grab his tail, where they were then swiftly pulled toward the dam just below the beavers' lodge.

Safely out of sight, the three emerged into the spacious den where Brondanur's family was waiting.

"Oh Parsnippy!" exclaimed the beaver's wife, leaning over. "You made it back! That old bird must have been some help after all," she added, shaking her head at her husband. "And my, you brought a friend, and he is soooo tall!"

The two kits ran over and hugged Parsnippy while Baldmar bowed deeply to the matron of the lodge. "You honor me with your greeting."

Brondanur stared at the strange visitor, who was slightly shorter than he. "You are from the Eastern Forest?"

He nodded once. "My name is Baldmar." And in a somber voice, he added, "Unfortunately there is little time for a more pleasurable visit. I come to you to deliver a warning. A terrible battle will soon be upon this place that will affect all who live here."

The beaver's wife stiffened at the news. "Brondanur?"

Her husband shifted his gaze to his wife. "Do you remember when I left for Darmok?"

She nodded.

"He told me the Northern lizards are coming for the three here who have threatened us. These are the outcasts who fled south after deserting their king and are now hunted for their treachery. I'm sorry for not sharing it sooner, but I knew it would give you worry."

"It does not, husband. In fact, it pleasures me!" she said, smiling slightly.

Brondanur flinched at the reply.

"I hope they drag them back by their heads so that Parsnippy's friends can return home."

Her husband stared at her for a second before turning to Baldmar. "Are you aware that the Southern Lounge knows of Scalar and his guards?"

He nodded once. "The Toadans that live in our forest said the same. What is not known to you is the loathing the southern lizard king has for the one who now approaches: a hatred born before our time in Anzenar. The king of those …."

"You're speaking of Keltar," interrupted the beaver. "His brother Scalar commands the other two lizards that oversee us here. Baldmar, he intends to join with those in the South."

The Ororan's shock was obvious. "You're sure?"

"I've heard them discuss it among themselves."

"That is enough!" blurted Brondanur's wife. "This visit is a time of celebration, not depression. We now honor Parsnippy's return. Join us, Baldmar, for dinner and let us remember happier times."

"Thank you," Baldmar replied bowing slightly.

A small voice came from the side of the room. "You forgot your beaver's teeth," said one of the young kits to Parsnippy.

"I did!" Parsnippy said, smiling broadly. "Thank you for saving it for me!"

"Tell us about Nimdoor and your journey!" they both exclaimed.

Very soon, they all sat around the table, where story after story was told. In the end, the matron held a glass up. "To Parsnippy and his friends—so brave in the face of darkness!"

Each of the beaver tails slapped the floor as they drank the maple cider that had been poured around.

Brondanur motioned Baldmar to the den. The Ororan glanced down at the wood beneath his feet and immediately noticed the heavy runes carved across the floor. He looked up and stared at the beaver. "You're the son of Darmok!"

"Yes," he said simply.

"He has been a friend of Shadowguard for many years. I was chosen to deliver his message to you. '*Remember the story of Garanthur. Look for my sign, on the second day, when the shadows are short.*'"

The beaver staggered back and nearly fell against the wall. "No!" he said, shaking his head. "The second day? That is tomorrow!"

"I'm sorry, but I do not know the meaning of the words."

"Then I will tell you."

They talked quietly together. Then, all of a sudden, Brondanur's wife interrupted. "Husband? Are you ok?"

He quickly smiled. "It's joyous news, my dear. Baldmar has invited us to join his people for a visit within the great Eastern Forest!"

"That is indeed wonderful. When is this to be?" She stepped aside for Parsnippy and the children to come up beside her.

"Tomorrow morning."

"So soon?"

"Yes. I told Baldmar that it has been too long since the kits have played among the trees, since the great lizards arrived."

"Indeed!" She nodded.

Parsnippy smiled at the young beavers. "I've got a friend named Tenara who's been there as well. She said they have rocks like 'Beaver's Teeth' but in many amazing shapes."

"How wonderful," one exclaimed slapping its tail on the floor.

Brondanur leaned over to Parsnippy. "I must return you to your friends now."

"So soon?"

The beaver replied, "Tealick was threatened by one the skinks when they couldn't find you. He claimed you were ill. When they asked what it was, he said you had tooth-drop disease."

"What?!"

"He invited them to look in the cave but warned them if they did, all of their teeth would fall out."

Everyone laughed.

"Ok. I'm ready now," Parsnippy replied, still grinning.

Brondanur walked over to the door in the floor. Just before dropping through, he looked at Baldmar. "You will stay in my lodge for the night?"

He shook his head. "I cannot. I must leave now to join others and prepare."

"You will be here tomorrow?"

"Before the sun rises, I will escort your family to my village."

Brondanur dropped down with Parsnippy just behind. Baldmar looked back at the beaver's wife. "You have a strong family.

Be ready when I return." Then he disappeared too, leaving the woman staring at the empty door, wondering what was left unspoken.

# 36. PREPARATIONS

PARSNIPPY KEPT CLOSE TO BRONDANUR AS HE MADE HIS WAY carefully out of the lodge. Within a few minutes they arrived at the bank, where the last colors of sunset were fading away.

The beaver motioned him forward into a deep trench where some of the water flowed directly into the side of the hill. After a few more steps, Brondanur disappeared between some thick bushes that grew down from the cliff above. Parsnippy stared at the shrubs and froze. All he could think of was the last time he had to push his way through some. The cuts on his arms and legs still hurt.

Then a hand jumped out of the vines and jerked him in.

"Ahhh!" he cried.

"Sorry," Brondanur whispered casually. "We will wait here for a moment."

Parsnippy's eyes slowly adjusted to a soft green light that shined from thousands of glow worms that held fast to the walls. He started to reach for one when the beaver whispered, "Don't touch! They're not friendly."

He shook his head and mumbled, "I'm not surprised!" thinking about his most recent experiences.

After another moment, the beaver motioned him to follow. Slowly, they both retraced the steps made just two nights ago, when he first started his trip to Darmok. Being ever so careful, the beaver kept to the center of the flow before abruptly turning left and pulling Parsnippy out. The beaver then felt a tap on his back.

"Why did we leave the stream?"

"Look at the water closely," whispered the beaver, looking back.

Parsnippy followed it with his eyes and noticed that it suddenly disappeared into a deep chasm. The unexpected realization of how close he had come to falling in it made his legs wobbly. He looked back and saw that Brondanur had stopped again further up the trail.

"Stay here," he whispered, "and be silent. I will greet them first. When you see my tail move back and forth, come forward."

Parsnippy watched his ghostly image fade until only a silhouette was in view.

Within a moment, Parsnippy heard a huge gasp from a crowd and then a single voice. He moved closer.

"It's so good to see you, Brondanur," said Tealick. "And what of Parsnippy - have you have come to tell us the fate of our friend?"

"I have," he replied slowly, watching their eyes if some miracle would free them soon. He knew they were out of time. For the past two days, he had watched the lizard spies come and go after fearfully reporting their findings to Scalar. Many of the skinks and chameleons he recognized, but others not.

"Brondanur?" asked Tealick again, trying to understand why he didn't reply.

But the beaver was stunned at how wretched they all looked. By now, the entire area below his dam had been cleared, leaving a miniature desert that extended up the high bank to the edge of Shadowguard. The lizards had pushed his family relentlessly to gnaw further into it, but the tall trees fought them back. If this evil continued, the land he knew and loved would soon be barren, leaving only emptiness between his home and the Sorofall Mountains of the South. A wave of dreadful despair swept over him.

"Brondanur?" The voice came again.

The beaver woke up and signaled Parsnippy.

Tealick gazed up, waiting for an answer. "I must know," he said in a voice that began to crack. "Is he lost from us?"

From behind the beaver, bathed in the same green light, a silhouette appeared. It moved forward in a deathly silence, until everyone stood up and roared with joy, "Parsnippy!"

But it was only a moment before a dangerous voice growled and the door crashed open. They turned and saw a huge lizard push its head in. Everyone gasped and fell back. Brondanur lowered himself instantly behind a large rock that rose up from the floor.

Borgjump glared at them menacingly, a monstrous dragon with spikes that pointed both forward and backwards from his head. With a swift movement of his claw, he grabbed one of the prisoners, who immediately screamed. "Maybe we don't work you hard enough to be tired! Perhaps I should carry this one out to continue!"

The two skink guards pushed their way around the lizard and pointed their spears at the group. Borgjump looked down at them contemptuously. He despised the miserable creatures and wondered why Scalar had ever recruited them.

Tealick composed himself and was about to speak when Parsnippy ran forward. "Put him down!"

Borgjump was so stunned at the display of bravado that he just stared at the creature for several seconds. Then an evil grin climbed across his face. "Put him down?" he mimicked. "Like this?" he asked with his arm back to throw the poor thing deep into the cave.

Tealick looked on, wide-eyed. Parsnippy took a step toward the lizard. "You don't want to do that!" he said quietly.

Borgjump sneered. "And why is that?"

"As you said, you need us to rest. If we don't, we don't work. And then Scalar will ask why."

Tealick joined in. "And we'll have no problem telling him why."

Borgjump squeezed the creature in his claw gently while listening to its pained cries. "Soon, we will need you no longer." He dropped the helpless prisoner and watched it flee immediately behind some others. Tealick, in a fit of fury, ran at the skinks, but the door was slammed before he could grab either.

He turned to Parsnippy in astonishment. "You changed!"

"If true, why are my legs shaking so much?"

Tealick laughed. "Perhaps because you can't hear them for mine!"

Brondanur walked around the rock. "Quickly, we must talk. There are many things you must know. Come."

Parsnippy and Tealick followed the beaver back into the darkness, where he sat down and faced them both. "All of us will be leaving this place tomorrow. It's not a choice," he said bluntly.

"What?!" Tealick interrupted, shocked.

Brondanur ignored him. "First I must tell you why you were brought here. These dragons that imprison you now, Scalar, Barkchew, and Borgjump, come from a clan that lives far to the north, ruled by a ferocious king called Keltar. Scalar, his brother, disagreed with his rule, left without permission, and fled south along the Songentrope creek, where he found my lodge. It wasn't an accident that he chose it for a place to hide. You and the others were brought here to build defensive walls that would protect them by night from the other creatures in the forest while my family removed the trees that blocked the sun by day."

Tealick looked up. "If we attempt an escape, they will see us!"

The beaver shook his head. "Nevertheless, we must try. Keltar is coming with his army to bring the three back. They will be here tomorrow."

"More of those things!?" yelped Tealick.

He nodded. "Many more, which is why it's important that you and the rest be ready to leave."

"How can we stand against them?"

"You will not stand by yourselves," Brondanur counseled. "There are others who are coming as well. They are the giants among your kind that live in the dark forest of the East."

"Giants? Why would they help us?"

"Why? Because of the courage of two great warriors from

your village, who risked everything to search for you. They've made many friends within Anzenar," he replied with a sweeping gesture of his hand.

Tealick's brain was swimming in astonishment while his mouth was agape. With barely a whisper, he asked, "From Rippleshy. Who?"

"Their names are Tenara and Joen."

Tealick threw his head back in astonishment. "I know them!" Then his voice went to sarcasm. "But they are careless and carefree!"

Parsnippy interrupted, "Not anymore, Tealick. They're different now. Not the same. I met them myself in the forest during my journey back. They've changed.

Tealick just stared at Parsnippy.

"She asked about you."

Tealick eyes went wide. "Tenara?"

"Yes. She believed that you would keep us safe until she came."

"She said that?" Tealick asked in a facetious voice.

"She did."

"Tealick," interrupted the deep voice of the beaver, "you must focus now. When Keltar finds his brother, and he will find him, he will also discover that you and the others helped build his lounge. When that happens, he will destroy every one of you and everything you have built. And then Scalar will be dragged back to the North along with the other two. We have no more time. We must act now, while they are unaware." Brondanur leaned down and looked directly into Tealick's eyes. "For that reason, everyone here must be prepared to leave before sunrise."

A small voice came out of the darkness. "Papa? Papa?" it cried.

Brondanur whipped around and disappeared into the shadows. After several moments, he returned with a small beaver at his side.

"Parsnippy!" It smiled.

"Why are you here," his father interrupted sternly. "You were told to stay with your mother in the den."

"I know. I'm sorry, Father. But Baldmar came back and told us that two skinks walk the trail beside our water. He says their names are Red and Blue Spear."

He shook his head. "I don't know them."

"He said they were spies for Keltar. Who is he?"

Brondanur grimaced. "It's not important. Where are they now?"

"Near the brambles."

Brondanur looked over at Parsnippy. "Those are the thorning bushes …"

Parsnippy interrupted. "Yeah. I remember them!" he said, rubbing his leg. "It's where Baldmar and I left the river trail: the same place we met the snakes." Parsnippy saw the young beaver tremble when it heard the word snakes.

"Indeed? Then I regret asking, but I must lean upon your courage once again. Come with me now." He looked back at Tealick. "I will return him soon; you have my word. See to the others now. It's on you to keep them safe until we return."

Brondanur and Parsnippy retraced their steps to the water and carefully escorted the young beaver to the lodge. After taking a few breaths, the beaver zoomed up the pond with Parsnippy just behind, until they reached its headwaters. Taking care to make as little noise as possible, they stepped out and began slowly looking for the two skinks. It didn't take long.

"Stop scratching yourself!" whispered Red Spear. "It was your fault trying to hide in those bushes!"

"But it was you who broke its limb off. How was I to know they would attack us?"

"Shhhhh. This is our last chance with Keltar. We need to find his brother first and point him out. Now follow me down the trail and quit griping."

Brondanur and Parsnippy listened and shook their heads. They watched the two tromp by and then heard a different voice come up from behind them.

"Where do the snakes sleep?"

Both Brondanur and Parsnippy nearly jumped out of their skin and turned around. "How did you get behind us, Baldmar?" the beaver demanded, nearly falling back into the water while watching the skinks closely.

"I thought you would come this way. I simply waited."

"You are a devil to find us so fast," the beaver said, grinning and then changing the subject. "Snakes. Why do you want to know that?"

"Because Parsnippy is going to tell them where the skinks are, now that you both saw them go by."

"What?!!! Me!?" he choked, backing away.

"Yes, you," replied Baldmar calmly. "I saw the way you handled them before."

In the darkness, Parsnippy just glared at him.

Brondanur looked over at Parsnippy as if he were a stranger.

"I can see you have more stories to share at the table," he said, looking back at Baldmar. "Yes, I know where they sleep."

"Then take us there now."

After leaving the pond, they walked quietly up the path, where a large outcropping of rocks lay just to their right. Underneath, almost unseen, was an opening made smooth from the comings and goings of what lived within. Baldmar then leaned down and whispered in Parsnippy's ears. Then he pulled his sword out and banged on the stone just above the entrance.

Almost immediately, a diamond-headed serpent thrust its head out and looked at Parsnippy, who was trying to force his legs not to shake.

"YOU! You dare wake us!"

Parsnippy did his best to calm down. "My business is not with you. It's the black one I will speak with."

The snake stared at the intruder closely and suddenly realized it was the same one who had threatened them earlier that day. Furious, it threw its tongue out several times before suddenly withdrawing down the opening. A hiss was heard and the black serpent moved its fearsome head out slowly. "You try my patience," it said in a deep voice.

Parsnippy, wide-eyed now, looked into its eyes and hoped his performance would allow him to survive another minute. "It's not your patience I seek. It's your obedience. You will leave your bed now and follow the trail south until you find two skinks. You will tell them to go no further, for you are king among the serpents. If they resist, then you may eat them both. If they obey, then you will bring them to this one," he pointed to Baldmar, "at my side. Once done, our business is finished."

"And if I choose to eat you now?"

Baldmar, knowing the self-serving nature of serpents, stepped in front of Parsnippy. "You may. He will not resist. However, before you decide, know that an army of lizards, the great dragons of the Northern desert, descend upon this trail as I speak. If you choose to strike now, you, your den and all of your kind will be destroyed by those creatures before the sun sets tomorrow. My brothers will ensure that."

"You lie," it growled.

"Then strike now and be done with it!"

The snake vibrated with fury. It was only aware of the three dragons just south of its den. It paused for a moment and then spat, "Hope we never meet again, for on that day, my fangs will be the last thing you ever see."

"Just deliver the message," Parsnippy said with force. He was about to faint when the snake abruptly turned its head and moved down the trail.

"Brondanur," said Baldmar quietly, "return Parsnippy to his friends now."

An hour later, just as the Ororan expected, he saw the two skinks running up the trail with the snake just behind. They both looked up and nearly collapsed when they saw Baldmar. The snake slithered by the skinks and faced the Ororan. "I have done my part. Now you understand…"

"Enough with your threats. For the moment, we are on the same side. The giant lizards do not belong here and neither does 'The Parsnippy'. If you help us, we help you."

A thoughtful look descended on the serpent's face. "I will look for them. But if you lie…"

Baldmar leaned forward. "Until then, you and your kind will do as I ask." He said it as a statement.

Silence.

"Answer!"

"Yesss," it spat.

"Then leave us now."

After one last stare, it slithered into its den under the rock.

Baldmar looked down at the two skinks and smiled. "Welcome back."

Blue Spear fainted, leaving his brother standing in shock with his mouth agape.

# 37. THE SAURIANS APPROACH

IT WAS ALREADY DARK WHEN FEYORIN, TENARA, JOEN AND THE scouts approached the campsite that the two Ororan warriors had prepared. The only sources of illumination, besides a small fire, were the few tendrils of moonlight that had found a path through the high canopy above. During the walk south, most of the group remained quiet.

Blendefest noticed Feyorin talking to the two remaining Ororans. All at once, they bowed and quickly disappeared into the night. Feyorin then turned and walked over to Tenara, who was sitting beside the fire.

"You're ok?" he asked, sitting down next to her.

"About tomorrow?" she asked.

"Yes."

Tenara stared into Feyorin's eyes. "About why you'll not fight alongside Joen and me?"

"We discussed that," he replied with frustration.

"Yes…we did." She sighed indifferently.

Joen perked up. "I'll be at your side."

Tenara nodded and smiled at Joen. She turned back to Feyorin. "Do you have a plan?"

Frondameer interrupted, "Yes, we would like to know that as well."

Feyorin looked into the darkness. "It is being discussed by the council of Elders."

Tenara shook her head. "I really thought we would have your help in this. Joen and I have come a long way to find our friends. It's just not the rescue I thought it was going to be."

"Miralassen believes you're ready to face this. Do not dismiss the gift that hangs at your side. My queen would not have given it to you unless she saw the courage we have seen ourselves in you. Your friends will depend on that. You must as well. For them and for us, you need to start believing in yourself."

She paused for several seconds and then said quietly, "I cannot believe in something I'm not."

"We will see."

Tenara looked away. "Where's Baldmar?"

Feyorin gazed into the darkness. "That's a question I've been asking myself. He should have been here by now."

"Perhaps you will allow Blendefest and I to search for him?" Frondameer offered.

"I think it better to remain together for the moment."

Frondameer countered with a frustrated look. "We've gained much experience with Shadowguard since then. I'm sure we will be fine."

Feyorin sighed. "I'm sure you would if it were any other time than this. But what you have experienced so far within the walls of this place has been minor compared to what roams its ground by night. I'm sorry, but for now, we must wait."

Tenara looked at the fire and noticed that Joen had made her way over to the food baskets left earlier by the Ororans. Without a care in the world, she watched her rifling through the choices before finding something. "This is really good," she said with her voice muffled by some bread. You gotta try some." She glanced back at Tenara and then dug into the basket for more.

Tenara shook her head in exasperation and muttered, "How can you be so calm?"

Feyorin leaned over. "Because she trusts you!"

Tenara looked at him with irritation and then walked over to Joen.

Within moments, the others joined her by the fire and grabbed some bread for themselves. Just at that moment, Feyorin noticed Baldmar strolling into the firelight. Joen noticed him as well but didn't look up.

"Mmmm… Feyorin, if Baldmar is late, you mind if I eat *his* part?" she asked, winking.

Baldmar heard the remark as he walked up. He looked down, watching Joen still munching away. "Feyorin, it is now obvious to me that the lizards have no chance against this one." Joen giggled and the others grinned while Baldmar reached for some bread himself.

"Problems?" Feyorin asked, looking over. He expected Baldmar to provide his usual terse reply. He had a history of short explanations, many of which were less informative than Feyorin liked. He braced for this one to be the same.

"No."

"Anything else?" He sighed.

His partner replied with a deadpan expression, "Parsnippy convinced the snakes to join us."

Joen almost choked on that remark. Tenara and the scouts' wide eyes glinted against the fire as they all stared at Baldmar in shock.

Feyorin sighed again out loud. He looked over at Tenara and asked casually, "Did you say at one time that you also commanded a snake?"

Tenara nearly lost her food. "W-well, uh," she stuttered, "that was just Butiss. He lives near Rippleshy...I think. Actually I'm not sure." She shook her head. "A long time ago, when he was small, I saved him from a large bird. He doesn't talk too much."

"So talking to snakes is common in Rippleshy," he replied as if it was a fact.

"No!" she blurted back.

"Then Baldmar, would you please explain?"

The Ororan continued chewing his bread for several seconds, keeping them all in suspense. Feyorin shook his head slightly.

Baldmar finished his bread. "Apparently, the snakes think Parsnippy is a wizard. While on his way to join us, he had confronted two of them. When one attempted to strike, the eagle, Nimdoor, appeared and left as quickly with one of them in her talons. Later, she returned and had a short discussion with the other. I believe they think he commands a 'sky demon'."

Feyorin laughed out loud, which was rare. "They believe this?"

Baldmar's face darkened. "Yes, except one: a giant among them."

"Will that one be a problem?"

"Only if it chooses to fight the lizards alone."

Feyorin immediately grasped what was being said. "You made an alliance—very clever! We can use this. And Brondanur?"

"Darmok's message was delivered and Parsnippy is back with his people. I will escort the beaver's family to Orora before the sun arrives tomorrow and return to join you after. One more thing." Baldmar looked directly at Joen. "The skinks are our guests again."

Joen jumped up. "They are?! Did you tie them up?" she demanded.

"No need. It's night here. I suspect they'll keep close to their escorts."

"They continue to work for Keltar?" added Blendefest.

"I think the skinks work for themselves," interrupted Joen.

Baldmar looked back at Feyorin. "As do I. And that may work for us."

"Feyorin," said a heavy voice, interrupting from behind.

Everyone turned and saw the same two Ororans walking back into the fire light.

"It's decided. We must talk."

He and Baldmar followed them out, leaving the others with a puzzled look.

More than a minute had passed when Frondameer broke the silence. "I'm tired of waiting for the Ororans. We need a plan now. I'm not comfortable knowing so little about what we are to face tomorrow."

"I agree," said an unknown voice beyond the fire.

Both scouts swung around with their swords out.

"I'm not your enemy," said Darga with his hands held out. "The Ororans are with you?"

"They are."

"Then you have nothing to fear. Please. Lower your weapons. There are only two of us. We wish only to talk," said one of the Toadans as the second entered the firelight.

Almost immediately, the two visiting Ororans appeared with their bows drawn tight, an arrow pointed at each of the Toadan heads.

"Pleaseee," Darga repeated. His face was drawn tight at the unexpected intrusion.

Feyorin walked up, motioning the two Ororan soldiers to lower their weapons.

"You surprise me," Feyorin said casually.

"And why is that? Have we not agreed to work together?"

"We have, but only because it's in your *interest* as well," he said.

Darga's face showed frustration with Feyorin's response. "Then I suggest we continue to do so, in *both* our interests." He abruptly changed the subject. "Sargon is sending an emissary to meet with Scalar."

Feyorin was caught off guard. "When?"

"Tomorrow morning - early."

Feyorin stiffened. "If it recognizes Scalar…"

"If it does, then we will make sure it does not return to its king. I will see to it personally."

Feyorin stared at Darga quizzically and then turned to face the scouts. "I'm sorry, but I have to ask for your help after all. I need to know where Keltar is, where he camped for the night, and I need to know it now. Please leave immediately." He shifted his attention to the other Ororans. "You two—go with them."

Feyorin nodded curtly at Darga. "Thank you."

The Toadan stared back for a moment and said quietly, "I regret our people did not help you when you crossed the mountain."

Feyorin looked surprised.

Darga continued, "But there was nothing that we could have done. On that day, many of us were also destroyed in retaliation for your escape, killed by the Saurian lizards that changed their alliance to Sargon.

"On that day, we blamed you for our loss. But I've come to know that was a mistake. Only half of us survived to cross the mountain later, after your people had fled. It's the reason I stand here now, offering our help: to live or die to protect what we both have built."

Both Tenara and Joen looked at Feyorin, whose expression was blank. Baldmar nodded ever so slightly.

Feyorin pulled an arrow from his quiver and held it out to Darga. "Together!" he echoed quietly.

The Toadan grabbed the arrow just above Feyorin's hand. "For both our peoples!"

As soon as Feyorin released it, he watched Darga and his companion back away into the night. He then turned to Baldmar. "See to it that the Keltar has some visitors tonight."

His partner dropped into the shadows immediately.

"What do you mean visitors?" Tenara asked.

Feyorin turned to face her and smiled slightly. "We might not sleep well tonight…but neither will they."

Unsure of what that meant, she just nodded and looked over at Joen. "Perhaps asking you to leave Rippleshy was a mistake."

Joen stirred the fire. "You're nervous about tomorrow?"

"You should be as well," Tenara replied with a serious face.

"Don't be. I'm looking forward to kicking some lizard tail."

Tenara's mouth fell open at the bravado. "This is serious, Joen! Anything can happen…"

"Look," she said, interrupting her while throwing her stick hard against the ground, "a lot is going to happen and then we're going home together. Ok? You have a cool sword and I can vanish with my robe. And, I have my dagger tooth. What else do you want?"

Tenara could only stare at her in stunned silence.

*** 

Further north, Keltar and his army were sprawled across the ground at the edge of Shadowguard. While they lay there quietly, the two scouts and Ororan guides carefully watched them for any sign of movement.

Frondameer whispered, "Ok. We found Keltar. Do we return to Feyorin now?" The Ororan nodded and began to stand up just as Baldmar came into view. He spoke quietly to the two Ororans. Then one of them turned to Frondameer. "Come with us," he whispered.

The scouts followed them to a large rock, where they were told to sit and wait. Then, to their astonishment, their guides abruptly backed away into the darkness, leaving both of them alone and confused.

Frondameer whispered, "Is there a point to this?" Baldmar shook his head. "Let's hope they remember to come back." For several minutes, both sat quietly behind the rock, becoming increasingly frustrated and angry. Frondameer was about to suggest they leave when a terrible screech was heard in the woods behind them. Both turned at once to face the danger, swords out and ready for battle. A moment later, a fireball suddenly flew out of the forest and quietly hit the ground behind them, exploding in a shower of sparks a moment later. In a panic, they both started to run when Blendefest felt a hand on his back.

Frondameer whispered loudly, "No. It's them: the Ororans."

"What is the purpose of the Fire Rocks then?" Blendefest replied, frustrated. "Don't they know we're here?"

He started to move away again when Frondameer held him back. "No. Wait. This makes no sense. Something's wrong. We were told to stay here. We're not the target. We can't be!"

Each strained to listen for something they could put their swords against. But all was now quiet. Then it came. A vibration rose up from the ground like a specter in the night, along with a dreadful rumble in the distance that grew stronger by the moment.

*** 

By now, Blendefest had become even more agitated. "What is that evil that approaches, Frond?" The ground now began quivering beneath his feet. Then, all at once, several hideous beasts stampeded around and over them toward the Saurians.

Keltar had seen the flash as well. But the thunder made him look curiously into the darkness. "You," he commanded loudly to one of the soldiers nearby, "see what that is."

The soldier craned his neck toward the sound but did not move.

"Go!" Keltar shouted over the den of noise. "You as well," he said to another nearby.

The Saurian king watched them stand up as the thunderous noise increased. Then, to his astonishment, both soldiers were viciously struck by something larger than he. In a flash, each was catapulted up in the air and into the creek beyond.

Keltar stood up immediately, only to have something tear across his own tail, sending him instantly back to the ground. He jerked his head around to see dozens of similar impacts upon his army, each resulting in one of his soldiers being blasted into the rushing water. Realizing that none could swim, he could only listen helplessly to their gurgling and cries of desperation.

Then, it was over just as fast. Whatever they were, they retraced their steps around his army, leaving only anguished voices behind.

"Gradig?!" the king thundered.

No reply. "Gradig?!" he repeated, booming his name even louder.

"Yes, my king," said his general, limping up slowly to his side.

With no remorse Keltar lashed out. "Have the sentries watch the forest. There will be no more surprises!"

"Sire, give up this quest. We do not belong here. This is not our world."

The king moved within inches of his general's face. "We will continue until we find my brother and those two traitorous friends of his. Or have you lost your courage?"

"As you wish," he answered, ignoring the insult while slowly turning and walking away.

Keltar gazed into Shadowguard with a loathing. Then, to his shock, he saw something very strange above him: a light falling from the sky. Dumbfounded, he watched it fall nearby and explode in a shower of sparks.

Gradig was as surprised as he and stared at the remaining pieces that lay smoldering under his feet. The general just glanced at his king in contempt and walked off.

Keltar looked dumbly at the carnage, where several of his troops had been sleeping just moments ago. The longer he stared, the more his anger rose, until a deep growl pierced the forest.

\*\*\*

Back at Feyorin's camp, Tenara looked suddenly at Feyorin. "What was that?"

"I'm not sure," Feyorin replied with an unseen smile.

Confused, Joen blurted out, "Feyorin, what's going on?"

"A message to the lizard king."

"What did it say?" she asked with eyes wide open.

"Go home," he replied slowly.

"Will he?" interrupted Tenara.

"Unfortunately, no. Keltar has now gambled too much to

withdraw. But in so doing, he has lost the will of his army. And that makes us even."

# 38. PREPARATIONS

TEALICK PUSHED HIS BACK AGAINST THE WALL, TRYING AGAIN TO get comfortable and avoid the constant drip from the ceiling above. Being confined in the darkness had added to everyone's low morale, not to mention the daily threats from the guards that patrolled the door. He looked around and tried to think of something hopeful to say to the others, but nothing came to mind.

There was a sudden splash nearby. He jumped up and squinted into the darkness, looking feverishly for the intruder.

"Tealick?" came a deep voice from the shadows.

"Who's that?"

"Brondanur?"

"Yes. It's time to leave. Get everyone together."

"Finally." Tealick felt a burst of optimism. "You'll lead us out?"

"No. Parsnippy will. Everyone must leave this place now, before the sun arrives."

Brondanur walked into the light of the glow worms and looked at Tealick. "Once you have everyone together, follow him to the entrance and then look for me later when the first rays of sun strike Shadowguard."

"Shadowguard?"

"The name of the Eastern Forest and the home of the giants we talked about," replied Parsnippy.

After making his way back to the entrance, Brondanur carefully scanned for any skink or lizard nearby. Seeing none, he slipped into the pond and made his way to his lodge. After pushing his head through the round hole, he found himself staring up at Baldmar.

The Ororan looked down and asked bluntly, "The ones from Rippleshy, they are ready?" It sounded more like a statement than a question.

Before answering, Brondanur pulled himself up and shut the door. He turned to look at his family, who was now standing in the corner. "How is it that you're up so early?"

"It was my fault," Baldmar apologized. "I thought they would be prepared to leave when I arrived."

"The children were up before me," Brondanur's wife said. "Is there a problem?"

He ignored the question and turned to face Baldmar. "Take them now, but I must remain. Tealick is gathering the others."

"That was not in our agreement. You were to attend to your wife and children."

The kits came in and stood by their mother. Baldmar bowed at them slightly. "You are ready?"

"Are the dragons coming too?" asked one of the kits.

"I hope not," said the other one.

Brondanur shifted his eyes back to the Ororan. "Baldmar,

this is my home and I have a responsibility to the ones who still remain." He turned to his wife. "I will join you soon."

The Ororan grimaced and nodded once. "Then you must assist me in another way. I need you to find Scalar and the other two Saurians. Once done, enter Shadowguard and we will find you."

The beaver's eyes were wide. "That is not a simple task."

"Nevertheless, it must be done and done soon." Baldmar looked at the beaver's family. "Follow me now." He opened the door in the floor and dropped through without a reply, leaving the wife and children to say their goodbyes. Within moments, they were gone as well, leaving Brondanur alone, staring down at the empty void. After a few minutes of thought, he dropped through the hole as well. Time was running out.

The beaver's family followed the Ororan to the headwaters of the pond, where Baldmar carefully scanned the darkness for any threat. Unfortunately, the wind had increased and removed any chance of hearing something close by. Nevertheless, he took the risk and ushered the others to follow him, whereupon they were soon lost in the darkness of Shadowguard.

After Baldmar had left the water, a small blue lizard moved out from the bushes and smiled to himself. Once he was sure the creature would not return, he left at once to warn Scalar.

\*\*\*

Joen woke up when she heard Feyorin talking to some Ororans. She looked around and noticed that Tenara was missing. She quietly called her name, but there was no reply. After walking around the campsite and calling her name a few more times, she approached Feyorin, who was still in conversation. "Where is Tenara?"

"She is not with you?!"

Joen shook her head.

He turned back to the Ororans. "Find her!" To Joen, he ordered, "Go to the fire and wait. Trust us in this."

Within a few moments, one of the Ororans called out in the distance, "There!"

Feyorin saw a soft glow moving toward them that soon coalesced into Tenara's sword. He walked over to her and asked in an infuriated voice, "You left. Explain yourself!"

She stumbled on her words. "I-I heard a sound in the direction of the creek. I didn't see you, so I decided to look myself. You and the scouts have been risking a lot for Joen and me, so I wanted to do my part. I'm sorry."

His voice was still hard. "And what did you find?"

"A Saurian. That's what you call a giant lizard. Right?"

He narrowed his eyes. "You have seen one before?"

"No. But I've listened to you and the scouts describe them."

He paused a moment. "You are sure of this?"

"Yes!" she said adamantly.

Feyorin turned to the other Ororans. "If what she says is true, then find out where it's going. Take whoever you need." He looked down at Tenara and in a softer tone, said, "You are very important to the success of this adventure. My queen would not take lightly if I lost you. Even my kind never ventures within Shadowguard alone. We may have created it, but it cares little for what survives within its borders. Now, let's get back to Joen before she goes missing as well."

Tenara walked into the firelight and noticed the flames throwing strange shadows across the huge trees nearby. The wind howled above her head. Joen didn't bother to look up. "So you planned to fight 'em alone?" she asked, poking at the fire.

"No."

"So why didn't you take me with you? No. Wait." She held up her hand and looked up at her. "You thought it would be too dangerous. Right?"

"I'm sorry, Joen. You were sleeping," Tenara replied softly. She looked at the scouts beside her. "I was awake and worried that something would surprise us. But I kept the fire in sight the entire time."

Joen dropped her eyes to the ground.

A single Ororan walked into the firelight and looked at Feyorin. "She was correct; a Saurian moves north along the creek. We failed to see it." The Ororan looked over to Tenara. "Thank you."

Feyorin looked hard at the Ororan scout before replying, "Contact the team in the south and ensure that they have Brondanur's family. Have them provide escort instead. Then bring Brondanur here."

The Ororan soldier nodded and drifted away.

Frondameer walked over with a serious look. "Feyorin, where is this plan of yours? It's nearly light. I think it is time, is it not?

"It is." Feyorin explained his plan for several minutes while the scouts hammered him with questions. Once done, he looked over to Tenara and Joen. "Are you both ready to travel?"

"We are," replied both at the same time, standing up.

The Ororan stepped over to the fire and quickly extinguished it, leaving only the sound of wind slashing through the high canopy above. He looked up and heard the limbs pounding against each other. It was as if Shadowguard itself was preparing for what was to come.

The scouts flanked Tenara and Joen while Feyorin began walking off. After a few minutes, he nudged Tenara. "Put the sword in its sheath. If we can see it, so will others."

"Sorry. Thank you," she murmured in a listless tone. With the noise of the wind and the absence of light, moving through the darkness became even more difficult. For over an hour, they followed each other in silence. Then they heard the cry of a bird.

"Wait." Feyorin immediately stopped and made a short sound himself. The scouts looked at each other and smiled. "Baldmar."

Within a minute, the tall Ororan joined them and loudly reported over the wind, "Brondanur chose to remain at his home. His family, however, is currently being escorted to Orora. I requested him to join us in Shadowguard once he found the other two Saurians."

"That leaves just one of the lizards to guard the prisoners." Feyorin replied surprised.

"Why one?"

"The other was discovered by Tenara moving north on the trail toward Keltar."

"That could be a problem." Baldmar observed.

"Explain."

"It means that Scalar has no further use for the ones from

Rippleshy, which suggests his alliance with Sargon is underway. If true, then their destruction of the beaver's home may already be happening."

Tenara and Joen blanched at the remark. "No!"

Another animal whistle was heard above the wind. Then, all at once, a large animal sporting three massive horns flew by, nearly goring Feyorin, who dodged it at the last second. "As I said," he continued, looking down at Tenara, "There are times when Shadowguard surprises…" But before he could finish, two other Ororans nearly crashed into him.

"Stop!" Feyorin commanded.

They halted instantly. "Apologies. It got away from us. We knew you were in its path."

Feyorin composed himself. He was becoming weary of surprises.

Blendefest whispered cynically to Frondameer, "This is part of the plan?"

Frondameer elbowed him in the side. They both were frustrated.

Feyorin sighed. "Baldmar, before something else happens, can we assume the ones from Rippleshy are still safe?"

"They are," bellowed a deep voice, running up. "You guys are fast. And I thought beavers could run quickly."

Everyone was stunned when the big mammal galloped up, nearly knocking Joen and Tenara over. Feyorin was getting a headache.

"Sorry," said Brondanur sheepishly. He then noticed Tenara and Joen in the darkness. "Say, how did you two get out of the cave?"

Tenara was the first to reply. "What? We've never been in a cave. No, wait. Well, once with Frondameer and Blendefest. And that was very far away…"

Frondameer interrupted her. "I think he believes you are one of the prisoners of Scalar."

Brondanur, surprised, looked down at the two. "Then you are the two Parsnippy talked about, the ones who left to search for them!" he exclaimed.

"Yes," said Tenara quietly.

"When they first heard of you, they were in shock, my dear. Especially the one called Tealick. Which one of you is Tenara?"

"I am," she replied.

"He asked about you. You have both given him and the others hope."

"He really asked about me?" Tenara asked.

Joen looked up at Tenara grinning and then bumped her in the side.

Tenara shooed her back.

"Brondanur," interrupted Baldmar, "we need to know what's happening."

The beaver, standing a head taller than the Ororan, faced him. "Scalar is missing. The one they call Borgjump remains guarding the prisoners."

"Missing?" Feyorin interrupted. "Then he must be the one meeting Sargon's emissary. Why would he risk himself?" He swung around to one of the Ororans. "Find the Toadan leader quickly and tell them to 'encourage' Scalar NOT to continue south. Give him something else to think about. Whatever it takes—he cannot meet the one coming from the Sorrowful Mountains. Is that understood?"

The warrior nodded and disappeared.

He then looked back at the beaver. "Brondanur, you said there is a way out of this prison-cave that is unknown to the guards?"

He nodded. "It's a wet entrance near the water."

"And you are sure that Scalar and his guards are unaware of it?"

The beaver nodded his head. "They recruited the skinks from the dry lands of the North. Like the dragons, they have no love for the water except to drink."

Feyorin nodded.

"One more thing," added Brondanur. "Other skinks were recruited by Scalar since he arrived, some of which are formidable opponents. Watch for them." He started backing away. "I apologize, but I must return now. Can one of you guide me back to Glen of the Rock? Tealick, Parsnippy and the others need to be led away from it before sunrise."

Feyorin nodded. Another Ororan motioned the beaver to follow him.

Tenara tapped the beaver's arm. "Brondanur." It turned back. "Tell Tealick…hello for me."

"I will."

*** 

Darga was close to the southern end of Shadowguard when the

Ororan warrior arrived. As he ran up, he found himself immediately surrounded by ten Toadan warriors.

Darga took a step toward him. "I'm surprised you found us so easily, Ororan."

The messenger remained silent.

"What is your business here?"

"Scalar makes his way south as I speak. Feyorin requested that I deliver the following message: 'Under no circumstances should a meeting between Scalar and the one from the south take place.'"

"How do you propose we stop it?"

"You have weapons. Put an arrow into his side," he said dryly.

Darga was taken aback at his casual words. "I see. Well, one will not stop a Saurian so easily. You would know that."

"True. But it will confuse them."

Darga stared back.

The messenger continued, "You're clever. I'm sure you will find a way. Tease him, irritate him. Just do not allow him to continue. These are Feyorin's words. The kings of the Northern and Southern clans must continue their lives in ignorance of each other."

Darga was suspicious. He shook his head. "But their meeting was already arranged."

"Arranged by Scalar's minions. My queen swears that Sargon never knew that Scalar had crossed the Anduin Mountain as well."

"You hope."

The Ororan raised his hand. "The council of Aurora suggested that it was a skink that negotiated the meeting. Unfortunately, they have no proof of this: just past experience. What is known is this: another Saurian walking into the land of the Sorrowful Mountain would be immediately captured. Soon after, Sargon would most assuredly find out who his last allegiance was made to and have him killed on the spot."

Darga shook his head. "You have little proof of that. You would have me believe that Scalar would be so stupid as to make first contact?"

The Ororan got ready to speak, but Darga cut him off. "However…." He paused. "We will do what you ask. And then, if… we're successful, he'll likely return to Glen of the Rock with…" a smile fell across Darga's face, "at least one or two arrows in his armor." His face then hardened. "As for Sargon's emissary… we'll allow him to return south."

The Ororan nodded his head once ever so slightly. "I will report this to Feyorin." And with terrific speed, he pulled an arrow from his quiver and jammed it into the ground. "Good hunting!"

As soon as the Ororan left, one of Darga's warriors spoke up. "You would go this far to save *them*?" He pointed north with a smirk.

With a fierce intensity in his eyes, the Toadan leader stared back. "We're saving both ourselves and Bithenar, our home."

***

Not far from where Darga stood, Scalar was pounding his way down the trail in anticipation of the power that would soon be his within Sargon's army. The plan was to promise the southern king an opening to the southern forest and a gift of slaves or food, whichever he wanted. Soon, it would be Keltar's turn to grovel under his eyes.

By now, he had noticed that most of the forest had given way to smaller trees that were adapted to the dryer climate of the south. But water was becoming increasingly scarce. His only sources now were the small remaining rivulets of the Songentrope Creek that trickled south.

He continued forward, smashing over one small tree and then another when he suddenly felt something sting his back. He whipped around violently and noticed an arrow sticking out. He threw his head up, noticed several toads moving their puny bows down, and just laughed.

He felt another hit his leg and bounce off. But this time his smile was replaced with a violence that nearly killed the creature that ran up behind him.

He whipped around. "Parnick!!" he growled, staring at the small self-serving lizard that had first spied for him at Rippleshy. "What do you want?!"

"Sire, something's going on. It's the beavers. I saw 'em all flee to the Eastern Forest."

"Why would they do that? You're making this up!"

"No. It's true. I saw 'em myself!"

He looked up at the toads and wished he had more time to run each of them down and crush them with his claw.

Scalar looked back at Parnick. "Very well. I'll return. But you continue south and tell the other of my kind that we will meet tomorrow."

"Yes. Yes. I will, sire - at once."

The smaller lizard jumped to the right as Scalar pounded his way back north.

One of the toads looked at Darga. "That was too easy…"

"Yes, it was. See to the other one now."

Parnick took off south as fast as he could. But within five minutes, he abruptly stopped when several arrows plunked into the ground around him, creating an instant jail. No matter which way he tried, the wooden lances didn't budge. He looked up to see the bulging eyes of five unknown creatures, one of which was smiling broadly.

***

By now, Brondanur had arrived at the edge of Shadowguard that overlooked his home. As soon as his Ororan escort left, he carefully eyed the entrance to the cave where Tealick and Parsnippy were waiting patiently. By now, the wind had increased, causing a light chop across the surface of the water. He looked up and noticed the first rays of morning sun striking the high clouds. If there was any chance at escape, the guards needed to be asleep or at least unable to hear due to the wind.

He made his way down to the side of the water and moved quickly to the entrance, where he found both Tealick and Parsnippy still waiting.

"I'm late, but it could not be helped." He looked over at Tealick. "Both Tenara and Joen send their regards. They will be here soon."

"We'd almost given up on you!" murmured Tealick. "Tenara? She's really coming?"

"And others as well." He jumped to another subject. "Is everyone behind you now?"

Tealick thought for the first time that he might return home.

"Tealick?"

"Sorry." He shook it off. "Yes."

"Good. What I'm about to ask will be dangerous, but it must be done if we have any chance of escape."

Tealick said nothing.

"I need you, Tealick, to swim to the dam, carefully climb to the top, and watch the dragon lizard. Remain there and signal me if he moves."

Brondanur turned to Parsnippy. "While he does that, you must swim to the head of the pond and tell me what you see. Leave now."

They just stood there, staring, frozen with fear.

Brondanur sat down. "No one but you two can do this."

Tealick and Parsnippy exchanged looks. Then Tealick said lamely, "You ask a lot and we're small."

Brondanur whispered, "Yes, I do, but no more than Tenara and Joen. What happens from here will determine if you get home safely. We're out of time, my friends. If you do not leave before the light strikes this cave, they will see you. Now go."

Tealick and Parsnippy slipped into the water and disappeared. There was no point in further comments.

Brondanur stepped back into the cave, where the others stared up at him with faint hope. "You'll be fine." As soon as he said it, he was ashamed of himself for offering something he couldn't guarantee. Embarrassed, he returned to the entrance and stared at the dam, but there was no sign of Tealick or even if he had made it there. As for Parsnippy, time would tell.

\*\*\*

However, Parsnippy had indeed made it to the headwaters of the pond. He began rising slowly while making sure that his wake was quickly erased by the shallow waves that roiled over the surface. He sighed with relief when he saw nothing moving other than tree limbs bouncing around from the wind. Carefully, he stepped out on the trail, but then another sound came from behind: a long hiss that sent ripples of fear across his back.

He turned around and found himself looking into the eyes of the same black snake that backed down when confronted by Baldmar earlier. But this time, it was coiled to strike. Wishing Nimdoor was nearby, he reached within himself for what courage remained and spoke slowly. "Be careful who you threaten."

"You have no hold on me now, meal," it hissed with dripping contempt. "You are alone."

Parsnippy took several breaths and then stated loudly over the wind, "I echo again the same words spoken to you last night. If you strike now, you will not survive the lizards and never again see another of your young."

"So you sayssss. So IT says!"

"You believe I lie. You think I fear you?"

The snake opened his mouth, where his deadly fangs protruded.

Parsnippy leaned forward. "You sent one of your own kind

325

up the trail, didn't you? He hasn't returned, which makes you wonder, does this meal say the truth or does it lie?"

"Your question means nothing."

Parsnippy realized instantly that he had little to lose at this point and just relaxed. If it meant his death to save his friends, so be it. The stress of the past two days had drained most of his hope away.

He leaned closer. "Then strike now. And once done, you and all your kind will be sacrificed to the dragon lizards mercilessly. My friends will personally ensure that it happens. And if any of you escape, they will make it known to all serpents within Ildon that you alone made the choice for them this day. As for me, my survival is irrelevant. I tire of you now. What will it be: an easy meal or an ally later? Speak!"

"Sssssssssss," is all that came back. Parsnippy stared at the two glowing eyes. "If you lie, I will take the beaver's children."

Parsnippy shuddered. "That's the question, isn't it: if I lie."

The snake stared at him for a long moment and then moved forward, intentionally brushing his face with its head, before slithering up the trail and being lost to the wind.

Parsnippy, shaken to his bones, simply collapsed. He just stared at the pond, wishing he was somewhere else, but time had run out. With what strength he had left, he forced himself to reenter the water and blasted his way back to Brondanur.

The beaver was watching the edge of the pond when Parsnippy, to his shock, erupted from the water. He quickly looked around to see if anyone else had heard the noise. Seeing nothing, he ordered him, "Come with me. Quickly, back to the cave."

Parsnippy was nearly out of breath. "I…saw the snake

again…. he said he would eat your children…if I lied about the dragons…coming here. I'm so sorry."

A smile crept across the beaver's face. "A false threat. Nimdoor watches them all; so do we." He paused. "Right now, I need you to lead the others out. Keep them to the left of the water and as close to the cliff walls as possible. Watch for the trail."

"I see no trail," he said, frowning.

"Look for where the grass is bent. Follow it until you begin climbing."

"But…"

"I'm sorry; I must go to Tealick now. Do as I say and then wait until I return."

The beaver dropped into the water and was gone.

*** 

Keltar and what was left of his army had been slowly marching south. His fierce mood lingered and only vengeance could quench its thirst now. The sudden attack last night had only temporarily shaken his confidence. He glanced at the giant trees of Shadowguard to his left and wondered what other surprises it would bring.

Gradig, on the other hand, had said nothing since last night. His disgust with this pursuit and the cost of so many of his soldiers was growing. Keltar had become irrational. Thoughts of a rebellion began forming in his mind.

After several more minutes, he looked up and spotted another of his kind coming up the trail. He signaled for the others to stop. Then he recognized who it was. "Barkchew!" he growled.

The Saurian lizard looked up in shock. Almost immediately, it bowed after recognizing Gradig. "General, I've come to help bring Scalar back."

Before Gradig could answer, he felt a brutal impact to his side. Keltar angrily pushed past him to face the errant member of his lounge. "You dare come groveling to me. Where is he?"

Barkchew put his head back to the ground. "South, sire, along this creek. I can lead you there."

Gradig thought Keltar would have torn him apart, yet, surprisingly, he replied in a calm voice, "Then lead us."

Barkchew, stunned that his king had spared him, quickly turned around and began retracing his steps. At that same instant, two sets of eyes carefully watched Keltar's army go by. One sought only information and moved deeper into the Eastern Forest. The other, however, remained cloaked in the shadows and was far more dangerous.

# 39. THE BATTLE FOR ANZENAR

BRONDANUR PUSHED QUICKLY THROUGH THE WATER AND WAS now in full view of the upper part of his dam. After arriving at the base, he silently climbed its intricate logs and looked carefully across the top. Only one lizard remained in sight, and it appeared to be sleeping. He looked up at the sun and noticed the light was nearly upon the eastern wall of the valley, extinguishing any possible chance that Parsnippy and the others could stay hidden in the lingering shadows. Time had run out. His only choice now was to order them into the pond. This would cover their movement, but only for a short way before they reached the trail section that would begin the climb out. After that, there was nowhere to hide.

He looked down again and scanned the roof of his home for Tealick, but he was nowhere to be seen. After a minute, however, he noticed him nestled under one of the larger logs near the top of his lodge. He glanced back at the lizard still sprawled on the boulder and noticed it had opened one its eyes. If he called to Tealick, the lizard or one of the skinks might hear.

After thinking for a moment, he carefully backed down to

the water and swam, submerged, until he was directly under the door of his home. After throwing it open and pulling himself up, he moved through his lodge until he arrived at the point where Tealick would be just above, or so he hoped. With special care, he slowly began removing the ceiling until he could see the faintest hints of sunlight. After a few more minutes of work, while ignoring the water that was now falling into his home, he had a small hole.

He pushed his head up. "Tealick," he whispered. But there was no movement. Had he made a mistake?

"Tealick," he whispered louder, but still nothing. He struggled to get his head up further and then looked around. Then he saw a leg. Using his one free hand, he reached forward through the jumble of sticks and touched the foot.

All at once, his sentry yelped. Brondanur jumped down out of the way and watched him fall sideways though the opening and land with a splash next to his foot. Tealick's face, now white as ash, looked up. "Brondanur!" he said loudly with bulbous eyes saturated with fright.

The beaver held a finger to his mouth and then pointed up. Tealick said nothing and watched the beaver push himself up the narrow hole. Brondanur then reached out to rearrange some of the remaining logs, being careful to keep the roof sound. He looked over the top and saw that the lizard had not moved. But this time, it was staring directly at his lodge.

He held his breath and remained motionless while carefully watching its eyes. Then, abruptly, it turned away to look at the skink guards moving slowly down the trail.

He dropped back down. "Tealick, you need to join the others now."

"Did it see us?"

"No."

Tealick looked up through the hole. "You're sure?"

"We would know if I wasn't."

"Yeah, I guess you're right."

"We have little time left. The morning light will soon spread upon the face of the cliff where the others wait."

"Did Parsnippy return?"

"Yes. I want you both to lead the others out of the valley now."

"What about you?" asked Tealick.

"My fate lies in a different direction."

"Whatever it is, don't do it alone, Brondanur."

The beaver leaned down. "My good friend, Tealick, right now, your bravery is needed by the others who fearfully wait for you. Do not worry about me."

"But that would mean leaving you and your family to face the lizards alone. I can help you."

He smiled. "My family is safe. Very soon, a great battle will descend upon this place, leaving little by the time the sun casts its long shadows once again."

"What are you saying?"

Brondanur ignored the question. "Follow me now - Quickly!"

They made their way quietly into the water and remained submerged until they arrived at the natural creek that flowed into the secret cave entrance. Parsnippy and the others had been waiting patiently, still hidden by the remaining shadows of the Eastern Forest.

Brondanur leaned down to Parsnippy. "The sun has already touched the top of the cliff. It will only be minutes before the entire face is exposed so the trail is no longer an option. Take everyone to the place where we met Baldmar last night. Keep them together and underwater the entire way. Once there, come out. You lead. Tealick will be last. Watch for the skinks before coming out."

"But there are too many of us. I can't be sure that one of us will not be seen."

"It cannot be helped. The skink guards will be watching the surface of the lake for any movement. But the wind is on your side."

"And if they see us?" Parsnippy asked nervously.

He ignored the question. "From there, make your way directly to the rock outcropping and begin carefully climbing until you reach the high trees above."

"They will surely see us then!"

"I will distract them."

Tealick spoke up, pointing to the beaver. "He's not going with us, Parsnippy."

"No! Is that true, Brondanur?" Parsnippy felt like he was being stabbed in the heart.

The beaver just stared at him.

"Will I ever see you again?" he croaked.

"I do not know," the beaver said, then smiled.

"Brondanur," said Tealick, "I never had a beaver as a friend before. I was always fearful of them. No more. Thank you for helping us."

The beaver started to reply when a shadow passed over the ground. He looked up and saw the great eagle gliding up the valley from the south.

"Nimdoor," Parsnippy whispered.

The beaver looked back at both of them. "I must go now. Leave no one behind. The cave is dark and treacherous and there are many to watch."

He looked out to ensure he wouldn't be seen, and then slipped into the water, leaving Tealick and Parsnippy alone, once again.

\*\*\*

On the opposite side of the valley, standing near the edge of Shadowguard, a single Ororan warrior stood talking to Feyorin. Joen was standing just behind them, half listening. She looked over at Tenara, who appeared to be preoccupied.

With a deadpan expression, she asked, "You're ready, aren't you?"

Tenara didn't answer immediately. Instead, she found her fingers moving down until she felt the handle of the sword given to her by Miralassen. She thought back about the last words said to her: 'On that day, you will find the courage you need. And it will be in the face of what you fear most.'

"I am," she said with resignation and started to move.

Joen watched her walk over to the valley cliff. She paused a moment and then caught up with her. Both stood silently together, looking down at Glen of the Rock for the first time. Nothing could have prepared them for what they saw.

Before their eyes was a wasted valley, pockmarked by random stumps and brownish mud. Around its perimeter was an artificial wall that ran along each side of the valley from the dam south for several hundred feet. North of it lay a stunning lake as far as the eye could see. And just downstream of the mighty dam, that held it all, was an enormous boulder that reflected the first light of day.

Looking closer, they saw something lying across it.

"Ahhh.... Tenara, do you see that?"

There, sprawled across the top, lay a monster with a head full of spikes and a body bristling with scales. Joen watched, almost hypnotized, as its head shifted toward the dam and then south along the muddy expanse.

"It's a Saurian, like the one I saw last night," Tenara whispered.

"We're to fight that?!" Joen asked pleadingly.

There was no answer.

Joen looked at her apologetically. "I'm sorry I was mad at you. I had no idea."

Tenara voice was without emotion. "How can one look at such a creature and feel we have any chance?"

This time, Joen was silent.

"But, I believe they have a weakness," Tenara added.

"What?!" Joen looked back her incredulously.

"They dismiss us because we're small."

Joen looked at the lizard and back to her friend, wide-eyed.

Frondameer came up from behind. "And soon, before this day is gone, they will know that was a mistake."

Joen looked back at the Scout, astonished.

Blendefest interrupted their conversation. "Look…there," he said, pointing high above the lake. In the distance, they watched a giant eagle gliding down to the surface, causing a contrail of swirling tornadoes behind it. Their eyes followed it as it moved further up the lake and disappeared over Shadowguard.

"Nimdoor," said Feyorin behind him.

Baldmar added, "On the day we crossed the mountain, it chose to watch. Will it choose that path again, or will it fight?"

Feyorin grimaced to himself.

The two from Rippleshy looked back at the lake and spotted some small dots moving out of the water toward the cliff beyond.

"Joen, look, it's them! The ones we've been searching for! Our friends!" she exclaimed, pointing.

Feyorin's sharp eyes saw them as well. "Indeed. Now move your eyes to the dam and notice the water moving against the wind: Brondanur." They all turned to see the ripples go a short distance and then disappear. Feyorin immediately pulled an arrow from his quiver and shot it straight into the water just in front of the beaver.

"You think that wise?" asked an Ororan sentry next to him.

Feyorin turned around. "It was a signal. Escort the beaver here. Take another with you."

The sentry countered, "If the lizard sees him before he leaves the water, he may notice us as well."

"There is little danger in that. We remain in the shadows and he will seek the same."

The Ororan nodded and left.

Feyorin looked back at the valley and saw two skinks moving slowly across the mud at the bottom of the dam. He saw the lizard swing its head around and track them as well, but they were well away from Brondanur.

Then he spotted another ripple moving slowly across the northern surface until it dissipated near the shore. Looking closer, he saw the beaver emerge and begin walking directly into Shadowguard. At that same instant, Barkchew came into view. Feyorin panicked.

The slow-moving lizard smiled viciously. It turned its head back to yell, but no sound came out, for in that moment, a monstrous black snake bolted out of a hidden crevice and locked its fangs into the neck of the dragon. Together, the two rolled down to the water's edge, where Barkchew was pulled under water immediately. Brondanur just stood there, frozen to the ground at the brutal attack. He had seen many things in its life, but such savagery was unheard of. He shuddered.

"Run! Run!" his ears heard.

Brondanur looked across the pond and saw Tealick and Parsnippy waving their arms. Only then did his feet respond. He bolted up the steep embankment of the eastern wall, just as Keltar rounded the corner. The lizard king had also seen the attack and, for a moment, was unsure if another would take place. In less than a day, his confidence had been shaken twice. He growled, "Gradig. Move four soldiers to the front—now!"

The general ran up, looking around. "What happened to Barkchew?"

"He went for a swim. Do as I say!"

Gradig shook his head in confusion and yelled out the order. Within moments, four despondent dragons took the lead with Keltar safely behind, smiling.

***

The two Ororan warriors had now reached the upper part of the valley and were just above the beaver. Both had also been witness to what just happened and immediately grabbed Brondanur and pulled him into Shadowguard.

Keltar noticed the sudden movement and looked up. But the beaver and Ororans remained motionless while they stared back from the cover of darkness. For several seconds the immense lizard continued to stare and then abruptly walked forward. Behind him more of them started pouring into the valley.

Brondanur was quickly ushered over to join Feyorin near the overlook. As he walked up, he spotted the great eagle standing next to the Ororan.

"Nimdoor?" he said out loud, as if it were a question.

She turned away from his face and looked at the far shore. "One still remains, Brondanur, by the entrance to their prison. Did you not see it?"

Brondanur's heart stopped. "That's not possible. Parsnippy and Tealick took them all."

"Nevertheless, one remains."

Tenara and Joen strained their eyes at the same time. Though not as sharp as the Eagle, they too saw the lone figure cowering near the granite opening now fully lit by the morning sun.

Tenara yelled back, "I'll get him!"

"No!" thundered Brondanur. "Keltar will see you! He descends the path as we speak."

Feyorin jerked his head at the beaver. "What?!"

"He speaks the truth," one of the Ororan warriors replied. "The Saurian king has now entered the upper reaches of Glen of the Rock. And there is something else. Barkchew appeared to have been taken by a large snake."

Feyorin looked at Baldmar, who grimaced. "I saw the same. They held to their agreement."

"Did Keltar see it happen?"

"Yes," answered the other Ororan.

"You should not trust the long ones," Nimdoor interrupted.

"We have a common enemy, Nimdoor. An alliance was necessary," replied Feyorin.

"You will find that agreement short lived," she replied in an ominous tone.

"We knew the risk."

Nimdoor looked over to Brondanur. "I came directly from Darmok. It is done."

The beaver looked at the eagle hard. "You're sure?"

"It's coming as I speak, and nothing can stop it."

"What? What is coming?" asked Frondameer. Everyone else looked back to the beaver as if the world was suddenly coming to an end.

Brondanur recited the message out loud: "'*Remember the*

*story of Garanthur. Look for my sign, on the second day, when the shadows are short."*

He then looked down at his home in the valley. "Garanthur was the most famous of all beavers that lived in the northern part of Anzenar. He was the first to have built upon Songentrope Creek, named for the ancient lizards, known as the Songens, and their king, who first arrived in northern desert. Every beaver knows about the grandeur of his dam, which was nestled in the foothills of the Anduin Mountain, and the immense water it held back. But when the Songens arrived, Garanthur soon found that his home had become a place for the lizards to stage attacks on the forest to the south."

Feyorin looked at Baldmar.

"Did Garanthur fight back?" asked Joen

"Yes," he answered sadly. "But not in the way you think. He had no weapons to defend himself or his family, so he denied the lizards what they needed most. He destroyed his own home."

Feyorin blanched. "No! Darmok?"

Everyone glanced at the valley below.

Tenara turned back to face Feyorin and exclaimed, "Then we have no time! I have to get to the one who is left."

"Wait," cried Baldmar, holding his hand out. "Something moves from the south!"

Another lizard was spotted moving north toward the dam.

"It's Scalar!" Feyorin growled.

They watched as it wound its way up the path.

In the valley, Borgjump, still half asleep on the boulder, moved his head when he heard the heavy footsteps approaching. All at once, he stood up with a shocked expression on his face.

"Your meeting is finished? We have an agreement?"

"No, it never started," growled Scalar. "Parnick found me and said..." Suddenly, he spotted the lone prisoner cowering at the base of the cliff.

"YOU FOOL!!! What is that doing out?!!!" he spat.

Borgjump stared across the water, dumbfounded.

"WELL, GO, YOU IDIOT! If there is one, there will be others!" Scalar looked around and saw the skinks scampering up to the cave entrance.

Scalar yelled at the skink guards, "Open that door and count them - NOW!"

"Yes, sire! At once," they yelled back while pulling the heavy barricade away.

Borgjump had bounded off the rock in pursuit of the escaping prisoner.

As soon as Tenara saw what was about to happen, she bolted down the slope. Joen's mouth fell open. She looked back at the others and began running down the valley wall herself.

Brondanur pointed to the other side of the valley. "Feyorin, I must get to Tealick. They may be in danger from the soldiers that follow Keltar." The beaver backed away and raced through the edge of Shadowguard with the two Ororan warriors at his side.

Whatever plans the Ororan council had made now began to unravel. Both Feyorin and Baldmar had been stunned by the turn of events in the last few minutes.

Frondameer moved up to the cliff's edge, shaking his head. "She will not be lost on my watch!" he stated emphatically.

All at once, both he and Blendefest drew their swords and ran forward into the mouth of danger.

"Baldmar," said Feyorin quietly, placing his hand on his sword, "I cannot let them do this alone. I brought them here and I am responsible for them."

At the same time, Nimdoor lowered her head and looked Feyorin in the eye. "Ororan, you will remain here! The future of your people and theirs lie in different directions."

He angrily looked up at the great eagle. "And what is that? To allow a sacrifice that shouldn't be?! This is not her fight!"

"*She* chose this path."

Nimdoor stood up and, in a gust of wind, dived toward the lone prisoner from Rippleshy.

"Feyorin." He felt a hand on his shoulder.

He looked to his side with irritation and saw a highly decorated Ororan. "What!?"

"The Lady sends us to assist."

"By doing what?!" Feyorin was irritated at being caught off guard again. He turned around further. Standing just beyond him were fifty Ororan warriors armed with lethal arrows, tipped with fire rocks.

The captain of the guard added, "We have come at her command."

"Our queen?"

He nodded. "She commands your presence now."

Feyorin looked beyond the warriors and saw Miralassen standing in a shimmering white dress that was sparkling in the morning light.

He bowed.

By now, Tenara had reached the bottom of the valley and was racing across the ground to catch up with Borgjump as he crossed the small stream at the bottom of the dam. But the lizard was faster. Realizing she couldn't catch him, she pulled her sword out and hurled it viciously in his direction, where it bounced off his back and into the water.

Scalar saw Borgjump turn around. "GO!! I'll take this one myself! Get the other one!"

Tenara scooped her weapon out of the water and looked up just as Nimdoor wrapped her claws around the helpless prisoner. Breathing a sigh of relief, she pointed her sword at Scalar. "You will harm no other!" screamed Tenara.

Scalar looked at the insignificant creature and laughed. "You think that little stick will make any difference?"

"We will see!" she howled back.

All at once, she raced to the side of the boulder where Borgjump had lain just moments before. Scalar didn't flinch. He just moved slowly forward, flexing his claws while he watched her climb the rock face. As he walked up to the foot of the boulder, he smiled, expecting her courage to be replaced by fear. When it did not, he began climbing until he heard his name bellowed out.

"SCALAR!"

The voice singed his brain so much that he momentarily lost footing. And, for one eternal second, his feet seemed to be paralyzed. He looked up at the pitiful creature pointing its weapon up at him and then eyed an eagle overhead, carrying one of his slaves toward the other side of the valley. The shock of both made him pause before the voice again crashed into his brain.

"SCALAR!"

He looked to his left and saw his brother coming down the trail with a face of fury unmatched by anything in his memory. He quickly backed off the rock and readied for the attack. To concede now was to submit to a humiliating loss that would permanently end his quest for power. That could not happen. He looked over at Borgjump, who nodded his head.

"YOU!!!!" Scalar growled so loud that the sound echoed throughout the valley.

He then raced across the ground to the foot of the dam and leapt in the air just as Keltar came around its side. In an instant, there was a tremendous impact that blew scales in every direction. For a moment, both were temporarily dazed, but it was not to last. Scalar was the first to move and quickly pulled himself off the ground. Before Keltar could stand up, Scalar lowered his head and drove his spikes into the side of his king, who immediately went down again. Tenara could feel the ground vibrate beneath her feet.

Feyorin was watching it all and motioned to his warriors. "Be ready."

Borgjump, seeing Keltar on the ground, lowered his own head and began galloping across the stream straight at him.

At the same time, Scalar pulled back to watch his brother feel the pain in his side, and then screamed, "This started when you had to chase them across the mountain! The Ororans were insignificant! It wasn't enough for you to fight Sargon with me! No. You had to decide! Just you!"

Before Keltar could reply, Borgjump rammed his head into the side of the king so hard that he found himself falling across the mighty lizard and landing on his back. For a moment, he too lay stunned…but only for a moment. Then he quickly jumped to his feet while nodding for Scalar to attack.

For a second time, Scalar lowered its head and bolted forward. But the powerful tail of his king flew up and plowed into the side of his face, causing him to instantly crash to the ground. Before Keltar could strike again, Borgjump pummeled his head into the king's side, blasting Keltar several feet back.

The lizard king was only dazed for a few seconds, after which, incredibly, he rose to his feet and noticed the four open wounds on his side. He limped over to Scalar while carefully watching Borgjump recover from the impact. "There was never a 'together'!"

Scalar whipped his powerful tail against the back of his king's neck, but the Saurian barely flinched. Instead, Keltar pressed his foot into Scalar's neck. "What was once yours is now mine."

At that instant, there was an explosion off to his right, causing the king to shift his eyes away from his brother. Scalar took advantage of the distraction to roll to his feet, but before he could strike, the king's tail blew his legs out from under him, sending him back to the ground again.

Borgjump, seeing an opportunity, jumped to his feet and was about attack Keltar when several more explosions followed. For a few seconds, Keltar was disoriented. Something was wrong. Someone else was here as well.

He looked down at the head under his foot. "Who are the others who fight for you? Tell me!" Then his eyes wandered up to Tenara, who stood atop the boulder, staring back.

There was no reply.

"You hide behind that?" the king taunted with a wretched smile.

Gradig had finally caught up with Keltar. He shifted his eyes to Scalar and sighed, but it was not from finding him. It was the relief that this ordeal would soon be over and he could finally return to the warm desert of the north and forget about this horrid forest forever. He looked around and saw Borgjump moving leisurely across the ground and then stop. At first, Gradig dismissed it, but then he noticed that his opponent's feet had dug in for an attack.

With no thought to his own king, Gradig shot after him, but before he could make ten steps, he found himself blown back against the side of the dam. Completely disoriented, he saw a rock fall off his chest and felt a searing pain that was almost unbearable. He slowly moved his legs and tried to stand up. He glared back at Borgjump. "You treat your general like this?" he croaked, watching Borgjump search frantically for another projectile to launch with his tail.

The lizard scowled. "General? You mean puppet, don't you?"

Gradig vibrated with the insult. He glanced back at Keltar, who looked indifferent to his predicament, then turned his head back and noticed an immense log lying across the creek. Bearing the pain as best he could, he bent down to pick it up and began stumbling forward.

His opponent blanched at the General's resolve and quickly found another stone. With all of his strength, he shot it back and watched it ricochet off the log, hitting the lizard in an eye. Gradig just blinked several times and continued moving forward.

Borgjump stared back in astonishment. "You have no quarrel with me," he yelled. "It was Scalar who chose to leave."

"And you chose him."

By now, Brondanur had arrived at the bank overlooking the eastern side of the lake and discovered that several lizards had begun crossing the shallow end. He thought their behavior odd until he saw what was happening on the other side. Most of the prisoners were still on the ground and had not starting climbing out. Only Tealick and Parsnippy were up the trail, waving them on. Realizing what was about to happen, he raced down the hill, but before he could reach the water's edge, he lost his footing and crashed into the pond in front of two of Keltar's soldiers. Both of them jumped back in surprise.

The beaver tried to submerge, but before he could move, one of the lizards smashed its tail into the water, just missing his head. From the path, Tealick and Parsnippy watched helplessly while continuing to urge the others up as fast as possible. By now, all attempts at a safe escape had been lost.

Just when Parsnippy reached for another, he was suddenly hit by a gust of wind. He quickly recovered to see Nimdoor dropping something from its claws and then landing nearby.

"What? Who?" Parsnippy stuttered.

"You must keep track of all of them, small one," Nimdoor said.

Tealick looked on in awe for a moment before helping the one dropped to the ground.

"Thank you, Nimdoor. Are you coming with us?"

"No. I must answer to several of my kind for what I have done here today."

"I hope that we can fight together again."

She cocked her head. "Be careful what you hope for."

"You'll remember me, won't you?"

"As well as the serpents that we fought," she said, unfolding her wings.

And in a blast of wind, she pulled herself into the air and, within moments, disappeared into the sun.

"Parsnippy! We have to go!" urged Tealick.

*\*\**

Brondanur saw the lizard move its tail for another strike, but when it didn't come, he looked up to find the lizards being pummeled repeatedly with arrows. The Toadans had arrived. Several were now making their way forward while firing their weapons, despite the fact that most of the arrows bounced off. He looked to the shore and saw Frondameer and Blendefest hacking away at the enemy, but their efforts proved to be too little to stop the lizards, who were determined to cross the water.

Darga yelled, "Tenara's friends, they're moving too slowly!" Brondanur noticed the same, immediately swam to the other side of the lake, and grabbed as many as possible. From there, he hurled them up the hill to where Parsnippy and Tealick were waiting. When he looked back, he saw the first of the dragons coming ashore.

Blendefest realized the same and jumped on the back of the one that came out. But it had anticipated his move. The lizard turned its head and looked up. "You want to ride?!" it barked fiercely. The scout suddenly felt the beast lift his feet. Before he could jump away, it slammed them down, causing the scout to be violently thrown forward into the water.

Frondameer watched in horror when he next saw the tail rise and slam down, crushing his partner with a single blow. With blind rage, he raced across the lake and drove his sword down into its flesh with all his might. But the armor was too thick and caused his weapon to simply glance off. Its enormous head whirled around with a face of contempt and struck the sword away, sending the scout into the water beside Blendefest.

Brondanur's growl was heard across the entire valley as he witnessed the brutal attack. He had started to lunge at the nearest lizard when he saw another close to grabbing Tealick. He spat at the dragon and then snatched the one from Rippleshy and three others before charging up the hill toward safety.

Frondameer helplessly searched for his sword in the water while, at the same time, frantically pushing himself away from the lizard. Then he felt something brush against his leg. In the next instant, a huge snake exploded out of the depths and went straight for the lizard's head. In a flash, it wrapped its body around its prey, forcing both to fall back and disappear beneath the surface. Frondameer jumped back in fright to land under the one remaining dragon lizard. However, it quickly lost interest in the fight after it saw what had happened and ran to the other side of the lake as fast as possible.

Frondameer turned back and saw Blendefest lying face down in the water, only feet away. Fearing the worst, he rushed over and pulled him up to the beach, but there was little life left in his eyes. With his remaining strength, Frondameer carried him back to eastern shore and started up the hill into Shadowguard.

Darga ran over to help and then turned to look at his own kinsmen. By now, they had driven most of the dragons back, but not without a great loss. Several of his warriors and friends had been killed in the skirmish. The ones that survived were carried off to the safety of Shadowguard.

\*\*\*

On the other side of the dam, Tenara stared at Scalar while Keltar's foot continued to press against his neck.

The king looked back at his general. "Gradig, see to it that he's dragged back north for everyone to see his humiliation." He then looked down at Scalar once again. "Know this…" he thundered, "I will TAKE THIS PLACE of YOURs and ALL THOSE THAT HAVE BUILT IT."

"YOU WILL NOT!" shouted a small voice from above. "It does not BELONG to you!"

Keltar looked up at the insolent creature brandishing a weapon.

Tenara continued, "You and your kind are NOT welcome here! Take the one you came for and leave. NOW!"

The king narrowed its eyes and, without warning, slammed the boulder with its tail, causing Tenara to lose her balance and nearly fall to the ground. Shaken at first, she held fast to a crevice and watched him begin to climb up. Realizing what was about to happen, she jumped off instead and started backing away.

But it was too late. Keltar's tail exploded into the ground, trapping her next to the boulder. Seeing no escape, she pulled her sword out and, with all her strength, drove it deep into his tail, causing multiple scales to fly off in every direction. Keltar squealed with pain and bellowed out a roar that shook the valley, causing several to cease fighting for an instant.

Tenara withdrew her sword quickly and raced to the western side of the creek with Keltar just behind. Gradig, standing off to the side, was astonished that his king could have suffered a sting from something so insignificant. However, Scalar and Borgjump relished the distraction and began crawling away.

Tenara glanced to her left and saw Gradig blocking her escape. With nowhere to go, she began climbing the face of the dam. After several steps up the side, she glanced back and saw the monster arrive at the base and begin climbing as well. His face was now a mask of rage as he tore through the logs on his way up.

Keltar noticed Gradig climbing up as well and yelled, "Back. Back!" Keltar thundered, "This one is mine!" Then, something suddenly hit him in the arm. Tenara saw it as well and dropped down below a log for protection.

The king turned his eyes away from his prey to find a flaming rock rolling painfully off his arm. Curious, he looked back to discover several others falling down upon him as well, each turning into a ball of fire after impacting.

"Gradig!"

There was no answer, only the noise of stamping feet below. He looked down and saw his general jumping about as the sparklers danced around his feet. In a fury, he looked around for the source and spotted something within the giant trees that lined the eastern forest. As he continued to stare, a memory crawled back into his mind of something similar he'd seen a long time ago. He shook it off and then turned toward Tenara.

Frondameer, now within the protection of Shadowguard, continued to hold Blendefest to his side, watching for any movement from his friend.

He kneeled down and whispered quietly, "Don't you dare go on a quest without me!" Darga stood beside him, watching. Then there was the tiniest of movements, and the scout's eyes moved. "Go…get…her," Blendefest stuttered back.

Frondameer pulled two arrows from the quiver borrowed from Feyorin. "Darga, you will see to him?"

"He will not be alone," replied the Toadan leader.

Frondameer ran down the side of the hill toward the dam and blasted the king repeatedly with arrows until his quiver was empty. Keltar, however, just plucked them off casually, and then reached for a huge log and threw it violently back, nearly tearing the scout's head off.

Joen, seeing Frondameer sprawled across the ground, had raced down the path to intercept Gradig when she felt a blow to her back that sent her flying across the ground beside the scout. She looked up in a daze and saw Gradig aim its claw at her face. While trying vainly to pull away, something flew past her and straight into the lizard's foot, causing the giant lizard to stumble backwards.

It mumbled, "Yousss betters runssss." Joen looked down and saw a familiar snake attached to the fleshy heel of the dragon.

All she could say was, "Thank you, Butiss!"

Joen scurried out from under the lizard and noticed that Keltar had now reached the top of the dam. By now, most of the Ororans and toads had little left to give. All she could do now was watch and hope that Tenara could get away.

By now, Keltar had completed the climb and was towering above Tenara. Nevertheless, she held her sword high and, with a defiant glare, started to speak. But before any words could be said, she heard a roaring sound that climbed in volume over the den of battle. Everyone in the valley stopped in their tracks. Both Tenara and Keltar looked far up the lake and saw something hideous round the bend.

Joen saw it as well and ran to Frondameer, begging for him to get to his feet.

"Help me! Someone!" she cried. "Please!"

Blendefest, refusing to allow Frondameer to face the battle alone, had left Darga just minutes before. Joen caught sight of him staggering over to her. Together, they lifted the scout and pulled him out of the stream. As they began dragging him over the ground, the thunder grew louder by the second.

Tenara yelled, "RUN!! RUN!!"

Going as fast as possible with their heavy load, Joen and Blendefest grappled their way up the steep slope until they were out of breath and then took a moment to look back. Before their eyes was a giant wave rolling across the surface of the lake, consuming everything it passed. Onward it came, like a malicious monster, grinding its way along the shore and passing just beneath the weary frogs and toads that had the fortune to climb out in time. One unlucky lizard on the side of the lake tried in vain to do the same but quickly disappeared in the mouth of the beast, along with some of the skinks that had done the lizard's bidding.

Standing above, just under the canopy of Shadowguard, stood Red Spear and his brother. Both were hiding behind two Ororan warriors, their mouths agape.

They all watched in horror at the two on the dam. And then, suddenly, they saw Tenara hold her sword up to the lizard.

In a voice that rose above the den of thunder, Tenara looked up at the great lizard and smiled. "I guess your reign just came to an end."

Keltar, the king of the northern lizards, the great Saurian of Gravenbroke, turned its face to see the mouth of the mighty wave ploughing its way across the surface directly at him. He looked back at Gradig and the others for help, but instead saw them running up the hill with no attempt to rescue him. He was abandoned. Then, for some reason, he looked at Shadowguard again and saw another memory standing far above: an Ororan he had chased. "It can't be!" The dragon then growled so loud that his voice was heard above the coming apocalypse.

Within a second, the wave blasted them both off the dam and into the frothy water, where they disappeared instantly. Moments later, the wave smashed into the side of the cliff that once held the prisoners and then ricocheted off to continue its destruction down the valley and on to the Sorrowful Mountain to the south.

## 40. A NEW BEGINNING

For Joen, nothing could have prepared her for this. To see her best friend and sister gone in the blink of an eye was too much, and she fell down and cried. Blendefest and Frondameer, who bore witness to the same scene, turned their heads away, shamed in their failure to protect her.

After several minutes of silence, Feyorin turned away from the devastation to see that less than half of Keltar's army had survived. He knew that those who had escaped into Shadowguard would never return, while the rest would flee north. The desert kingdom of Keltar would now host a much smaller army when they once again returned to Gravenbroke.

Darga walked up. "A price too high."

The Ororan just stared across the valley. "For both of us - thank you." He turned to look at him. "I was mistaken about you as well, and for that, I'm sorry."

The Toadan leader reached into his quiver and pulled out a broken arrow. It was the same one that Feyorin had given to him only days before. He held out both pieces. "When you need us again, ask and we will come."

Feyorin took the pieces in his hand and watched Darga move off to join his remaining warriors and disappear south. He looked over to Frondameer. "You are welcome in my house anytime." He started to move away when he felt a hand on his back.

"Feyorin," said the Ororan captain. "You must step away from the cliff now. Do not forget that you could be seen by the Saurians that escaped the devastation."

Feyorin felt indifferent to the warning when a feminine voice commanded him from behind. "Come with me," Miralassen said in a serious tone. He tuned immediately to see her glimmering in the soft light that was filtering down through the canopy above. He bowed and followed her into Shadowguard.

Joen remained on the ground and stared listlessly at the empty valley. Everything in her life had changed since she left Rippleshy. And without Tenara, she had no wish to return to it and find an emptiness that would remind her about what had happened today. She almost wished the wave had taken her as well.

She heard some footsteps beside her and a hand gently touched her back. She turned around, saw Rilen, and cried, "She's gone."

He hugged her. "My people have allowed me to accompany you some of the way to Rippleshy."

She looked up and wiped away her tears. "Oh, that would be so nice." She looked down to search for the Camelio robe he gave her. "I'm sorry, but I think I lost your gift."

"I made another for Tenara. I want you to have it."

Joen looked away and in a distant voice replied, "I'll just borrow it. I'm sure she'll want it sometime."

Feyorin walked back to the valley cliff and thanked the Oro-ran warriors that had joined the battle. He then walked over to join Joen and Rilen. Baldmar and the scouts came over as well after watching the last of the lizards slide down the valley walls and disappear up the trail.

"Once they are gone," Feyorin interrupted, "we must cross the valley and join Tealick. He will need a guide to lead them back to their village."

He looked at the scouts, perplexed. "However, I am not sure where it's located. Can you lead them, Frondameer? We will attend you part of the way, but then Baldmar and I must return to Orora. My queen has many questions," he paused, "and has demanded to know how we allowed this to happen."

After the last of the lizards rounded the far bend, the six carefully descended into the valley until they came to the edge of the Songentrope Creek. It was almost unrecognizable now. Where crystalline water once ran, there was only mud and debris strewn haphazardly across its bed.

They paused, staring at the logs scattered about the ground, many of which had held Brondanur's home together. In the center, one of them lay stuck in the mud at an angle. Feyorin walked over and noticed that it was a piece of flooring that had a partial rune inscribed on one side. He looked down and read it out loud.

*"There's always a way…"*

Nearby, he noticed the entrance to the cave that once held the captives from Rippleshy. It was totally different now. Instead of an opening just big enough for Tealick and his friends to come and go, it now was three times that size. He wondered to himself about those who were kept there.

"Look, on the hill above! Parsnippy and the others!" exclaimed Frondameer, interrupting his thoughts.

"Do you see the beaver?" asked Baldmar.

"No. I did not," he replied sadly.

Baldmar looked at Feyorin. "His family…"

"Should be safe in Orora."

After several minutes of climbing, they joined Tealick and Parsnippy. Frondameer focused his mind and began pointing the way forward.

Feyorin looked over at Joen. "This is as far as we can go. Baldmar and I must leave you now to return to Orora. Remember that you hold our secret. Help Parsnippy and Tealick lead the others back. We will see you again someday." He moved his eyes to the scouts. "Frondameer and Blendefest. You are my brothers. Keep them safe. I will honor Fladon with what you have done here today, for both our people. Rilen? We need to return now."

"I am disturbed about what happened to Brondanur," Baldmar said sadly.

Tealick walked over. "He ran to the forest when he saw the wave coming."

A huge weight fell off his shoulders. "Then the beaver is on his way to Shadowguard to join his family."

"Rilen?" Feyorin called again.

The young Ororan next to Joen paused. "I guess I can't go all the way with you, but I promise to come and see you one day." He hugged her. "Goodbye!" After catching up with the older

Ororans, he waved again and then disappeared around some rocks.

It took the rest of the day for the group to pass over the top of the mountain, and well into following day before they arrived in the valley east of Rippleshy. The majority of the crowd that followed Joen said little during the trip back. Everyone knew that she had suffered a great loss.

When the sun rose the next morning, Frondameer turned to Joen. "Will you guide them from here? Moss Rock is close, and it's time for us to return. We have much to report to the Colonel."

"I'm not sure I remember the way."

He smiled. "Only because it's still dark. This is the same water you traveled when you first came to meet us. Follow it downstream and you will find Rippleshy."

"You will come and visit sometime?"

"We will see you again. Your adventures are not over, Joen."

"Thanks, but I think they've come to an end," she replied sadly.

Tealick walked up. "All of us owe you and Tenara our lives. Without your courage to leave Rippleshy, none of us would be here now."

Joen half smiled and started down the trail. As they followed the stream around a corner, she heard a noise and, without thinking, brandished her dagger tooth at whatever it was. Everyone held their breath and moved behind her. When she saw it was only a limb that had fallen, she relaxed. She turned back and suddenly realized they had chosen her as their protector.

Tears poured out of her eyes again, but she quickly wiped them away. "Follow me closely."

# CHIP SIMMONS

# 41. RIPPLESHY

LATER THAT EVENING, JOEN ENTERED HER HOME, EXHAUSTED from the trip back. Everyone who had followed thanked her again personally and then returned to their own homes, where she heard screams of joy from parents and friends alike.

The door opened again and Millard Dew came in with Tenara's parents. After a tearful reunion with Joen, they looked around to find their daughter absent. Joen looked at the floor, said, "I'm sorry," and cried.

The next day, Parsnippy came to visit. "You think you'll ever see them again?"

She smiled slightly. "Them? You mean the Ororans? I hope so."

"What do you think your next adventure will be like?"

She looked out the window and said flatly, "My adventures are over, Parsnippy, for I have lost my best friend, my sister and my mentor." Nothing was said for several moments. Then a soft voice from behind her asked, "Don't you think you ought to talk to me about that first?"

Her heart stopped and she slowly turned around. There

stood Tenara in front of her, with multiple scars across her body and a terrible laceration on one side.

Joen screamed, jumping up and down and grinning from ear to ear. And then she noticed the injuries. "You're hurt. How?"

Tenara put her finger to Joen's mouth. "I would say it was a long story, Joen. All I remember is waking up in the cave. The water must have pushed me into its depths before finally dissipating. When I woke, I was upside down and hanging from a rock.

"It was incredibly dark, but then I remembered my sword, which, to my amazement, was still attached to my side. I don't even remember putting it back. After pulling it out, it glowed brightly and I could see to cut myself down. Its light allowed me to discover a stream nearby that flowed quickly into the darkness. The only thing I knew was to ride it, and hope it carried me out."

Parsnippy yelled out loud, "Splishin Falls!"

Tenara started laughing out loud. "How did you know?"

"Brondanur said one night that the cave was deep and traveled far. You must have gone under the mountain while we traveled over its summit!"

Parsnippy ran out, yelling to everyone in Rippleshy about what had just happened. But before he could say a word, Whiskers the catfish started passing around the news that Tenara had returned. Parsnippy stamped his feet, wondering how that busybody knew before him.

At once, Tenara's parents flew into the room and celebrated their reunion of both their daughters.

However, it was another set of eyes that found the information about her survival most useful.

\*\*\*

A few days later in Orora, Miralassen was ushered out of her home to face a visitor.

"You have news?"

It nodded once. "She lives."

"I am relieved. Advise Moss Rock that the Gathering begins now. Where do the eagles stand?"

"With you," replied Nimdoor.

\*\*\*

Several weeks later, Tenara and Joen were relaxing near the edge of their pond, regaling the village elders with their stories when two beavers suddenly surfaced in front of them.

They looked down in shock. "Packard, Mulsey, what's up?"

"A message for you," said Packard. Mulsey was nodding his head furiously.

"What is it?" Tenara asked.

"You must follow us," said Mulsey, nodding even more.

Tenara and Joen looked at each other curiously, stood up, and apologized to the others. "Would you excuse us for a moment?"

The eldest nodded her head and watched with amazement as Joen and Tenara were pulled across the water by the beavers. Within a short time, they found themselves being dragged under and ushered up through a wooden door similar to Brondanur's.

Before them stood Feyorin, who reached down and pulled them both up. Tenara and Joen's eyes became twice their normal size when they spotted Baldmar and Brondanur as well.

Feyorin said simply, "The Lady requests your sword and your presence once again."

# ACKNOWLEDGEMENTS

IN THE FINAL ANALYSIS, A BOOK IS THE COLLECTIVE EFFORT OF many individuals whose contributions and assistance make it what it is. With that thought, I want to express my gratitude to the staff at Deeds Publishing for their guidance and recommendations, especially Ashley Clarke's superb editorial skills and suggestions, which helped turn this book into a finished product.

# ABOUT THE AUTHOR

CHIP SIMMONS IS AN INFOR-mation Technology profes-sional, specifically focused on storage engineering for a vari-ety of major corporations. But his weekends are far from that. Both he and his wife lead a va-riety of outdoor adventures for others, which include hiking and camping along the trails of the Blue Ridge Mountains or kayaking its many rivers. Period-ically, he focuses his telescope on the sky at night and can be found jumping off the trails during the day with just a compass and a map. Since an early age, he has been writing fantastical stories for his family, which eventually led to this first published novel. He is a life-long resident of Greenville, SC.

CPSIA information can be obtained
at www.ICGtesting.com
Printed in the USA
FFOW04n1218201017
41287FF

9 781944 193966